PRAISE FOR
ONE DEGREE:

"Gus Kappler, my friend and Cornell University Medical School classmate, has eloquently captured the importance of the health care triumvirate clinician, epidemiologist, and laboratorian in solving complex medical cases. He effectively outlines why these health professionals also require the assistance of a variety of other persons to unravel medical mysteries, including patients, statisticians, economists, journalists, politicians, and the understanding and input of the general public. In 'One Degree,' Dr. Kappler has written a first-rate medical thriller."

— GEORGE E. HARDY, MD, MPH (RETIRED)
Centers for Disease Control and Prevention (CDC)
Epidemic Intelligence Service Officer, Class of 1966

"An informative, authentic, sizzling read full of medical suspense and intrigue. We are given a snapshot of war's horror that is followed by the surgeon's successful surgical interventions thwarted by an overwhelming infection that leads to death."

— BILL FONTANA
EVP Thai Farmers Bank (Retired)

ONE DEGREE
AN HISTORICAL MEDICAL MYSTERY

GUS KAPPLER, MD

CONTACT INFORMATION

Author's email: guskappler@yahoo.com

Website link: www.guskappler.com

Facebook link: https://www.facebook.com/
vietnamvetgus/?modal=admin_todo_tour

ISBN: 978-1-09831-145-2 (print)
ISBN: 978-1-09831-146-9 (eBook)

WELCOME HOME

to all veterans, and with fondness,

all my brothers and sisters who served with me

at the 85th Evacuation Hospital, Phu Bai, Vietnam,

1970—1971.

In memory of
Seal Special Warfare Operator First Class
RYAN FRANCIS LARKIN
1987 - 2017

"Declare the past, diagnose the present, foretell the future."

    — HIPPOCRATES

"Research is to see what everybody else has seen, and to think what nobody else has thought."

    — ALBERT SZENT-GYORGYI

"After all, the ultimate goal of all research is not objectivity, but truth."

    — HELENE DEUTSCH

CONTENTS

PROLOGUE

American soldiers fighting in Vietnam were routinely ordered to leave the relative safety of their protected firebase. They entered the dense jungle to engage in search and destroy missions seeking out the Viet Cong (VC) and North Vietnam Army (NVA). These forced excursions, sometimes for a month, exposed each grunt to the real risk of severe wounding and death.

Beginning with his plea at the WWI peace talks at Versailles, Ho Chi Minh continued for over fifty years to pursue his wish for a united Indochina. The Viet Cong and NVA were dedicated to Ho's goal. Their predecessors had been at war since World War II when the Americans had supplied and trained them to fight the Japanese. These same men and women in 1954 had defeated their colonial masters, the French. America and its allies were now fighting that same hardened and sophisticated guerrilla foe.

The Viet Cong were experts in fashioning booby traps from unexploded American ordnance. They had studied and understood the impulsive actions of the young Western mind.

A piece of Styrofoam would attract a grunt and be picked up. When given a choice, the less demanding jungle trail would be followed. Both actions resulted in massive injuries from triggering hidden explosives.

Private Richard Burrows became a casualty of Viet Cong expertise.

Following an explosion, he hemorrhaged from extensive white-hot, high-velocity shrapnel wounds to both legs damaging his thighs to his ankles. He was medivaced, resuscitated, and stabilized to prepare for the stress of surgery. His life was saved, and both legs were salvaged at the 85th Evacuation Hospital by the skilled Army trauma surgeon, Declan Burke.

The Private was then leapfrogged for continuing care to several military hospitals before reaching his final destination in the United States. Walter Reed Army Medical Center represented the standard of care not only for the military but also civilian hospitals. After six weeks, Private Richard Burrows' wounds were healed. He walked steadily, realized his strength was back and felt like himself again. Richard was ready to go home to marry his fiancée, Michelle.

Would he?

CHAPTER 1

The malodorous cramped room was dark. He felt claustrophobic. A sleep-deprived Matt Rogowicz was quietly sitting on his wrinkled, sweat-soaked bed at three in the morning. His head was slumped forward in despair and supported by trembling hands that were dampened by his wet brown hair. Matt's elbows dug into thighs that had not been exercised in months. His heart was racing and hammering vigorously against his chest wall. His pale skin was cold from evaporating moisture.

He was terrified.

Getting drunk on Jack and Ginger at the local bar the night before did not bring sleep. This tactic had become routine over the past few months. Even getting laid did not dismiss his mental demons. Matt knew he was suffering Vietnam's delayed stress, today's PTSD[1].

His voice echoed in the confining room, "I can't shake these recurring feelings of fearing death, the guilt of surviving, being forced to murder, the flashbacks." He then lamented, "I'm still lost floating between the morality of my childhood and that of killing."

He had spent six sweltering months engaging the enemy in the dense threatening Vietnam jungle as a rifleman. This was followed by another six months at the 85th Evacuation Hospital as a specialist treating the wounded. For a year, he had witnessed the devastation war rendered on the body, mind, and soul.

---

1   To avoid confusion for the reader, the term PTSD will be used throughout the mystery. However, in reality there is a range of symptomatology from PTS, which is not debilitating, to PTSD, which may be debilitating. See: https://www.brainline.org/article/what-are-differences-between-pts-and-ptsd

His second active duty assignment was at Walter Reed Army Hospital near Washington, DC. There, he suffered the most damaging event of all to his psyche. Being distanced from the menace of Vietnam did not protect him. Matt was a seasoned lab technician at Walter Reed and

had discovered an abnormal white cell in a patient's blood that had never been previously reported. He was convinced it was a significant finding. His superiors did not. Subsequently, that post-op patient suffered an excruciating death. Matt could not shake the guilt of not pressing the issue with the Major in charge of the lab. He would scold his reflection while shaving, "I could have saved that boy's life." Yes, but in the Army, you do not override a superior's decision. Even so, the death tortured him with increasing guilt and depression. Due to the threat of stigmatization by the military culture that ruled his life, he refused to seek professional advice while on active duty.

Matt had been honorably discharged from active duty in February 1972. He was sent back to the U.S. without being counseled on how to reintegrate into a peaceful society, which moreover, treated Vietnam veterans with disdain. He was ashamed of what he had become and had no inclination to return to his hometown. He found himself near New York City, leased a one-room apartment in Queens, NY, and lived on his separation pay. He had no one with whom to share his traumatic wartime experiences and began self-medicating with alcohol to seek relief from his evolving delayed stress.

After a few months he hit the bottom of despair. Matt admitted to himself that he needed help. He joined a veteran self-help group, and with their support, became capable of forgiving himself for the patient's death sufficiently enough to stop drinking. He achieved enough self-confidence to begin managing his lingering delayed stress. He applied to a local college to complete his four-year degree.

It was the last day before leaving to enroll in school. Matt disclosed to his veteran group, "If I could only revisit the circumstances of that patient's death and find out more about the abnormal finding to understand its significance, I would be empowered to shed my remaining demons."

His associates responded, "Go for it."

He retorted, "I don't know how."

They encouraged in unison, "You'll find a way."

CHAPTER 2

14:32 ON HILL 518

Drenched in sweat, the fatigued Private First-Class Richard P. Burrows trudged forward through Vietnam's jungle with Company A, 3rd Brigade of the 101st Airborne Division, based at Firebase Bastogne in I Corps, Vietnam, below the DMZ. The day was August 22, 1971, and for eight months, he had survived the hothouse-like jungle with its relentless clinging leeches engorged with his blood and a deadly, unseen phantom enemy who hunted him in the northernmost geography of South Vietnam. Even during the day, sunlight could be blocked by a thick canopy of foliage.

Nights were terrifying. Would they be infiltrated and overrun? The tripwires designed to trigger the deadly Claymore mines that were placed around their position to kill the stealthy enemy provided some assurance of protection. However, the Americans had to be careful for at night, the VC would turn the Claymore mine around toward the unsuspecting US soldiers. The tripwire was rearranged so that the grunt retrieving the mine would detonate it thus killing himself and a few of his buddies.

The jungle air was sweltering, stale, heavy with moisture, and suffocating. Billowy rolling clouds blanketed the valley's canopy. Threatening humming insects swarmed and darted as if directed by a conductor. Some were just pesky, but others were aggressive.

The jungle's dense vegetation was a kaleidoscope of shapes, sizes, and hues of bluish to more yellow-greens emitted from the tall elephant grass, bamboo, and the broadleaved shorter plants. A misty rain had coated the dense landscape with moisture. The deposited water gathered itself into droplets on the leaves and created sparkles of reflected light. The edges of some plants were razor sharp. A machete was required to advance through this dense jungle environment.

Moisture turned the jungle floor into slippery muddy trails that the grunts carefully navigated. They were not on a picnic. They were being hunted by the Viet Cong. This trail could be booby-trapped with explosives, or there may a camouflaged punji stick pit of spear-like bamboo shafts to fall into. There could be an enemy ambush at any time.

Salty sweat dripped from every pore. Eyesight was blurred. Eyes burned from the torrent of sweat that could not be stemmed by a saturated tie-dyed headband. Everyone carried at least two canteens of water at all times. Leeches were constantly sucking blood from their skin.

The insect bites itched severely. No one could refrain from fiercely scratching these aggravating sites resulting in scattered puss-encrusted, inflamed ulcerations that covered their arms, neck, and torso. They knew the mosquitoes carried malaria. That's why, to prevent becoming infected, they followed orders and took that white pill for prevention every morning. Diarrhea was a frequent side effect.

Fatigues were soaked and adhered to their skin but at times hung from their lanky frames, accentuating the expected fifteen to twenty-pound weight loss. Their shirts were open. Love beads, peace signs, crosses, wedding rings, and other amulets decorated tanned chests, hanging from chains or string around their necks. The grunts' pants were ripped and caked with mud. Even after soaking in the last stream the patrol had passed, they still smelled like shit from recurrent episodes of diarrhea. Their boots and socks were soaked. The soles of the grunts' feet became thickened and inflamed due to a combination of bacterial and fungal infections. It was called immersion (trench) foot and when debilitating, required hospitalization for treatment.

Private Richard Burrows lamented "Can I call this survival?" to no one in particular. "My goddamn hemorrhoids are dropped and hurt like hell. They're bleeding due to constant diarrhea from the malaria pill. My butt cheeks are worn raw. I have these huge draining abscesses on my arms from the freaking insect bites, my feet are puffed up and aching from trench foot, and I reek like an outhouse from crapping myself."

He was eighteen and from Amsterdam, NY, a small city on the Mohawk River, about twenty-five miles west of Albany, the state capitol. He graduated from Fulton Montgomery Community College and had deferred the completion of a four year degree to volunteer for combat in Vietnam. He was an outstanding athlete, adapted well to army life, and had the conviction to honorably serve his country. He'd then return home and marry Michelle, his high school sweetheart.

"Yeah, but at least there are no leeches on this trail," his buddy, Specialist Michael Tucker, shot back. He was twenty and from the Midwest. He tried college, but it was not for him. The Army scooped him up when he did not return for classes in the fall of his second year.

Buck Sergeant Gary Stoller from Mayfield, NY, who was trudging nearby, joined in. He was an outdoorsman, avid deer hunter, and understood stalking and ambushing. Stoller cautioned, "We shouldn't be using this trail cause we've done it too many times already. The fucking VC have scouted us. They know that a newbie lieutenant always takes the easy way. Little prick can't deal with the work of actually using a machete and cutting a trail."

"I've told that SOB to be more careful, but he just blows it off." Corporal Bubba Smith had been in-country for ten months and badly wanted to make it home again to Meco, NY and hunt whitetail deer in New York's Adirondack Mountains.

"Well, we're almost at the LZ. Next stop is the bird out of here." Burrows tried to be encouraging, not knowing that in a few moments, his world would be changed forever.

That morning, the VC had planted a well-camouflaged booby trap made from an unexploded American anti-tank mine just two hundred yards from the LZ. They knew that the exhausted US grunts would let their guard down once they got that close to the LZ, as they anticipated being extracted by the incoming Huey helicopter.

Two of the VC had remained behind, hidden from view, to detonate the device, after which they would stealthily disappear into the dense jungle. When the American patrol approached, they waited until half the men had cleared the kill zone, then triggered the massive explosion. It was a tactic they'd used many times before, making the grunts feel like they were playing Russian roulette every time they went on patrol.

The men dove for cover and hugged the ground, anticipating a barrage of deadly AK-47 automatic rifle fire from the VC, anxious to kill as many Americans as possible. Everyone seemed to be yelling at once.

"What the fuck?" someone shouted.

"Where are they?" yelled Private Bill Papas.

"Stay down!" commanded Stoller.

"Sarge, they must be all around us," another grunt shouted.

Almost immediately, their training kicked in. Even the newbie First Lieutenant recovered from his shock and ordered the men into defensive positions.

"I'll cover Burrows," yelled the medic Corpsman Donn Gates, shielding his severely wounded friend with his body. "Call Dust Off and get him the fuck on the chopper before he bleeds out." He expertly applied a tourniquet to each leg, as high on the thighs as possible. It slowed the life-threatening leakage of metallic-smelling, sticky, warm crimson liquid whose flow disappeared into a maroon stain on Vietnam's boggy reddish-brown jungle floor.

The force of the explosion had blown Burrows six feet into the air. Consciousness was replaced by a dream-like trance. His brain was filled with undulating white light as he landed violently on the slick jungle floor, engulfed by dense vegetation, his mind flirting with reality. For the moment, to his relief, he felt no pain as morphine-like chemicals were released by his brain. This automatic response, programmed over hundreds of thousands of years of evolution, protected him temporarily from the intolerable suffering that would begin to make itself felt during the medivac chopper ride to the battalion aid station.

"Get off me," he said weakly to Cpl. Gates, who lay across him, but Gates didn't move.

Buck Sergeant Stoller soon realized that the VC patrol must have planted the booby trap hours before, and was now long gone.

"Man, I'd like to kill a few of those gooks one day, just to get even, but I never even fucking see them. Saddle up," Stoller ordered the others, "and, get back to the LZ so Dust Off can pick up Burrows."

Richard was aware of being lifted on a poncho and carried to the relative safety of the LZ. A defensive perimeter was deployed.

"I'm going to be all right," he said to Gates when he first heard the *wop-wop-wop* of the 326th Medical Battalion Dust Off chopper's blades. The sound of hope, they called it. It became louder as the Huey approached and descended, spewing blinding dirt and jungle debris in all directions.

"Be careful getting him on," Medic Gates directed as the craft remained hovering, ready to make a quick exit. Burrows was a brother, and his life was in Gates' hands.

Through his mental haze, the wounded Private heard a stray comment from one of the chopper's crewmen on the ride to the aid station. "This guy's legs are really fucked up. Hope he gets to the 85th Evac in time."

Once the chopper lifted off, Richard's first reaction had been to reach down to see if his family jewels and legs were still there, in that order. When he withdrew his hands, they were warm and sticky, coated with dark red blood looking as if he'd dipped them in a bucket of crimson paint. It took him a moment to react.

"Is that blood all mine? My legs are there, right?" asked Burrows. Too many times he'd seen legless buddies with bloody smoking wounds. There were angry-looking charred stumps in place of legs, their manhood often destroyed as well. His hands reported back to his brain that he still had his jewels and two bloodied legs, though the limbs had been deeply perforated by multiple red-hot, high-velocity, irregular projectiles. He exhaled with relief. "Still got my nuts and legs. Can walk, get laid, and have kids."

About twenty minutes away by chopper at Firebase Ripcord, Sergeant Ken Israel, who directed the nearest battalion aid station, shouted, "Booby trap, legs, extensive. Two IVs. Check vitals. Morphine. He's hurting."

Richard was gently unloaded on his stretcher from the rescue Huey (Dust Off). He was placed on sawhorses as a team of corpsmen expertly cut off his destroyed, filthy, jungle fatigues. Two large intravenous needles were inserted into his arms, facilitating the administration of blood and salt solutions to stabilize him before he was transferred to his final destination, the 85th Evacuation Hospital, for definitive care.

Private Burrow's original medivac chopper waited, powered up, on the edge of the helipad to more quickly transfer him to the 85th Evac on the west coast of Vietnam. It was located halfway between Hue and Da Nang on Highway 1 near the hamlet of Phu Bai in I Corps, the northernmost combat area in South Vietnam.

The community consisted of dust-encrusted shacks made of sticks, discarded pieces of metal and irregular wooden boards. Sections of unrolled and flattened beer and soda cans enclosed the walls. They lined both sides of Highway 1. Few men were present. Women in pajamas wore wide-brimmed conical straw hats. There were scattered clusters of bustling children, most with bare bottoms.

Nearby, one could see flooded, rectangular, shimmering, green-shaded rice paddies reaching to the horizon. A few men urged water buffalo to pull the singular bladed plows for cultivation. Others peddled bicycle chains attached to a cup mechanism that lifted water into the paddies for irrigation. Many women were bent over planting rice seedlings. There was a pungent odor of night soil (human feces) that was used as fertilizer.

Richard's travel time from the moment of wounding to the 85th Emergency Department (ED) took less than sixty minutes. That crucial interval was referred to as the Golden Hour, for the survival of the injured was much more likely when delivered to definitive care in less than one hour.

Dust Off co-pilot Bob Nevins celebrated with his pilot, Jerry Rogers. "We'll get him to the 85th ED in forty-five minutes from when we first picked him up at the LZ." They were both veteran pilots and had routinely been engaged by enemy fire. They had survived several crashes. Too many of the 326th Medical Battalion pilots and crew had died flying these same missions. Bob understood the concept of the Golden Hour timeline wherein beating the clock usually avoided the detrimental effects of blood loss shock. Barring any complications, Private Burrows' survival was hopefully more likely than not.

Richard was more alert by the time his ride landed on the 85th Evacuation's square olive drab (OD) perforated steel plate (PSP) helipad.

Its massive red cross within a large white square at its center broadcasted the inherent safety of the hospital. The Dust Off crew could now relax a bit.

On the ride in, Burrows had heard Warrant Officer Bob Nevins notify "Plasma Hotel," the 85th Evac call sign, that he would deliver "one very messed up grunt." Three numbers were often reported with multiple wounded aboard to define his precious cargo, allowing the 85th Evac ED to prepare. The first, KIA; the second, severely wounded; and the third, walking wounded.

As the chopper bounced and settled upon the helipad, Burrows witnessed a swarm of washed-out OD-green fatigues rushing in his direction. He heard hospital Corpsman Duane Wall's consoling voice, "You are going to be fine, you're in the best of hands." All surgeons, corpsmen, and nurses who were not sleeping, otherwise engaged, off the compound, or sick rushed to the hospital.

The 85th Evacuation Hospital supported the 101st Airborne Division soldiers who were based in the surrounding area and to the north of Phu Bai at Camp Eagle. Thousands of men were quartered nearby, and others operated from firebases (Bastogne, Ripcord, Tomahawk, Khe Sahn, and others) scattered on strategic hills throughout I Corps to the north of Hue and west to the border with Laos. The first exit of the Ho Chi Minh Trail entered from Laos, just thirty miles to the west.

All of the 85th Evac's buildings were made of plywood (walls and floors) with corrugated metal roofs. Most were elevated about a foot above ground level on wooden stilts to prevent flooding during the monsoons. Sandbags dotted the metal roofs for stabilization in the wind. There were screened, narrow horizontal windows under the eaves of the elongated roof that allowed ventilation. A rusted metal cot, thin mattress, mosquito netting, and steel locker were the only items supplied. Any other furnishings or decorations were the occupant's responsibility. These additional items were obtained by trading, steeling, bartering, and ordering from stateside or military catalogs.

The ED, operating rooms, and Recovery Room/ICU were placed on concrete slabs to allow hosing the copious amount of blood that seeped from the wounded onto the floors. However, these critical areas did flood during the monsoons. Sandbags did not help much. The ED personnel, surgeons, nurses, and corpsmen at times worked standing in two to three inches of water. The patient wards were elevated.

All of these buildings were protected with six-foot-high corrugated steel revetments filled with sand to absorb the lethal fragments from exploding enemy rockets or mortar. The center of the compound contained the Orderly Room (organizational hub) that was stupidly placed within fifty yards of the concrete ammunition dump. Female nurses, corpsmen, enlisted men, male nurses, and doctors were assigned to separate areas of the compound. Also present were a chapel, armory, motor pool, pathology lab with the blood bank, mess halls, and enlisted and officer clubs.

Outdoor two-or-three-hole latrines and indoor communal showers were supplied.

All of these structures were contained within a defined defensive perimeter containing several layers of concertina wire, flood-lights, and armed watchtowers.

The ED head nurse Marilyn Harasick oversaw the disposition of Private Burrows into the critical bay wherein all hands and supplies were on deck, i.e., anesthesia, corpsmen, doctors, chest tubes, cut down trays, IV tubing, salt solution, etc.

"The patient's airway is guaranteed", anesthesiologist Dr. Stan Rosenberg announced. This comment translated to no airway obstruction, adequate air exchange, and no evidence of significant chest wall trauma or pneumothorax.

Corpsman Duane Wall added, "I'll start a third IV in his left arm. I see good veins," as he slapped the skin to enlarge a vein for a better target for his needle.

Additional blood and salt solution were given. Major Declan Burke, Richard's surgeon, reminded the team, "Let's not overload him. I don't want excess fluid clogging up his lungs and blocking oxygen from moving into his circulation."

Dr. Burke was drafted as an intern in 1965 and granted deferred active duty to complete his surgical training (Berry Plan). He had finished the required five years at the end of June 1970, and after basic training at Fort Sam Houston in San Antonio, Texas, arrived at the 85th Evac in early September of the same year. By then, he had been married for seven years and was the father of a five-year-old daughter and a six-month-old son.

Declan's childhood was comfortable. In Middle Grove, West Virginia, his father was a busy general practitioner and his mom, an elementary school teacher. He was always the tallest in his class. A pleasing smile enhanced his handsome face. A curved one-and-a-half-inch scar existed on his forehead over the right eye running into the eyebrow. It resulted from a competitor's unchecked hockey stick while playing on the local frozen lake. His father had sewn him up. Declan's demeanor was usually reserved and self-deprecating, but he transformed into a fierce opponent on the football field and on the basketball court.

Declan had wanted to be a surgeon since mid-high school. He was studious and achieved excellent grades. Excelling in the pre-med curriculum at Iowa State with a major in chemistry, he was accepted at several top-notch medical schools. He chose Duke University in Durham, North Carolina. Those four years were followed by five years of extensive surgical training at the Medical College of Virginia in Richmond, Virginia under the remarkable transplant pioneering surgeon Doctor David Hume, Chief of Surgery. This residency experience was brutal in its intensity but rewarding in its outcome. He had been transformed into a scholarly and accomplished surgeon.

Now, fresh out of training, he was in an active combat zone in Vietnam with the survival of the wounded his total responsibility. His residency experience had been hands-on, and he was well-equipped for his new role as a wartime trauma surgeon.

As for Private Richard Burrows, multiple x-rays were taken of his chest, abdomen, and extremities and reviewed by the radiologist, Major Robert Hooper, and Declan Burke to help establish the extent of his injuries. With resuscitation completed by restoring circulating blood volume and warming, Richard's blood pressure was stabilized. His body systems were working again. The normalized circulation was evident as his kidneys were producing an adequate urinary output, his temperature was almost normal, and his body was not acidic. His body's cells were close to functioning normally.

Corpsman Mike Clark reported, "His central venous pressure is six centimeters. His blood volume should be good to go," as shown by the saline-filled vertical tubing of the manometer at the side of Burrows' chest which communicated with tubing within a huge vein that entered his heart. This reading indicated that the patient's circulation was stable. He was not overloaded from the frantic efforts of resuscitation.

Dr. Burke comforted and befriended the Private by saying, "We'll do everything possible to save your legs; I feel good about it." The soldier, still in considerable pain, answered, "Thanks Doc, I'll owe you."

Burrows was then brought to the operating room. In OR 1, supervising nurse Lt. Patti Hendrix, who volunteered for Vietnam as had all the very young nurses, held his hand. "You'll soon be asleep and wake up in the Recovery Room. Remember to take the pain shots if you need them." She then warned him, "Don't let the pain get ahead of you."

An extremely competent regular Army nurse anesthetist, Captain Fred Brockschmidt, was waiting for him. He was a big man and instilled confidence. "I've done this over a thousand times. It's not my first rodeo. You'll be fine. Good night." he said. "Phu Bai" Fred then smoothly induced a world-class anesthetic for the duration of his surgery, kept up with fluid and blood replacement, and rendered him awake without a problem. As with flying, in anesthesia, the takeoff and landing are the most challenging.

Private Burrows' skillful surgeon, Major Declan Burke, was able to avoid amputation by expertly repairing the damaged major thigh arteries. Roger King, who had trained with Declan at the Medical College of Virginia, joined him in the OR. They made an accomplished team.

The booby trap had inflicted extensive wounds. Effective treatment required extensive debridement of devitalized muscle. Twenty-eight units of blood were given to replace the amount lost during the procedure.

Mike Clark, who had participated in many similar surgeries, served as the scrub tech during the procedure, expertly anticipating each surgeon's next move and passing the requested instrument at the exact moment either surgeon's hand was extended to receive it.

Mike had been in Vietnam for a long time and had too often witnessed extreme human destruction. The thought of returning to his beloved young wife, Connie, was the force that kept him going. "She is my rock; I'll keep it together for her," he repeated often. They had met when she was fifteen and he sixteen. Within twenty-two months, at seventeen and eighteen, they were married with one year of high school to go. After completing community college, on their second wedding anniversary, he had arrived in Vietnam.

Declan sutured all the deep muscles and tissues as securely as possible.

The fatty and skin-level wounds were left open and covered with antiseptic dressings to avoid the dangers of infection. The Army had dictated, rightly so, that no wounds were to be sutured closed at the primary surgery. These open areas would be healed by direct suture or skin grafting at the next hospital posting, usually the Army Hospital in Tachikawa, Japan, or the facility in Okinawa.

Following Private Burrows' several-day stay in the Recovery Room/ ICU, Major Burke checked on him one morning and declared, "You're good to go, good luck, you'll be walking in a few months."

The RR/ICU was a crucial department of the hospital that challenged doctors, nurses, and corpsmen in their care and support of the most critically wounded while attempting to assure their recovery. The exceptional RR/ICU nurses and corpsmen were the eyes and ears overseeing the patients as the surgeons were engaged in their next trauma surgery. Declan depended on their observations and never doubted their judgment when notified that he should return, stat.

The RR/ICU's cluttered central desk was surrounded by scattered chart racks within this large room of sea-green walls and a dirty white ceiling. The continuously lit recessed lighting created a sense of never-ending daytime. Peace signs were everywhere. Young nurses and corpsmen in fatigues with pens stuffed in their chest pockets, charts in hand, and stethoscopes adorning their necks scurried about performing their duties. However, there was always time to remain at a patient's bedside to offer loving, supportive company.

One could hear the hiss and thump of the respirator as it recycled and filled a patient's lungs with oxygen-rich air delivered through a tube via the mouth into the trachea or a tracheostomy. Clear bottles of salt solution (Ringers Lactate), others colored yellow with vitamins, small bottles of antibiotics, and packets of blood dangled partially empty from IV poles, their tubing leading to a needle secured in the patient's vein.

The patients were bandaged to cover arm and leg amputations, incisions, abdominal and chest wounds, and open wounds that were irrigated with a saline antiseptic solution and redressed several times a day. Occasionally, an alarm would sound when there was an equipment malfunction. The vast majority of patients were transferred within days to hospitals in Saigon, Japan, and Okinawa. A few young men, to everyone's distress, died in this skilled arena despite everyone's heroic efforts.

CHAPTER 3

An ambulance transported the wounded Private Burrows and other casualties from the 85th ICU to the adjacent Phu Bai airport tarmac. Once his stretcher was securely attached on the third level of stacked wounded, the C-130, with a monstrous roar, effortlessly lifted off at an acute angle to avoid enemy fire.

The transport then flew him to Saigon, leaving below the airbase, which was so close to the 85th Evacuation that it abutted the concertina wire protecting the hospital's helipad. The ED routinely shook from the vibration of each C-130's resounding energetic departure. The Lockheed C-130 Hercules is a four-engine turboprop that readily adapted to wartime requirements. It handled unprepared runways, transported troops, medivac patients, and cargo, and could be outfitted as a deadly gunship.

Once at the First Field Hospital in Saigon, his wounds were examined, irrigated with salt solution, and redressed. The next morning, he was medivaced with forty other patients on a massive C-141 to Japan. At Tachikawa Hospital, Richard endured daily cutting away of dead tissue from his raw surgical sites (debridement), followed by irrigation and dressing changes. Eventually, once healthy tissue was present, skin suturing and skin grafting closed the majority of his wounds. After a few weeks in Japan, his surgical sites were healthy and healing without infection. He was then flown on another C-141 to Walter Reed Army Medical Center in Washington, DC on September 12, 1971. Private Richard Burrows had undergone multiple surgeries to save life and limb. Overall, he had received forty-two units of blood. HIV and Hepatitis C were unknown entities in 1971 and testing was not performed on donated blood.

The Walter Reed Army Medical Center campus was spread over one hundred and thirteen acres in the District of Columbia overlooking the picturesque Potomac and Anacostia Rivers and the distant Virginia shoreline. It included the Armed Forces Institute of Pathology (AFIP) and the Walter Reed Army Institute of Nursing. The buildings' red brick exteriors were weathered and crumbling. The grout was deteriorating, the over-crowded internal wards beginning to show the wear and tear of rigorous use.

During his stay on Ward 3, Private Burrows had adjusted to the musty, stale odor that percolated through the poorly air-conditioned Walter Reed Army Medical Center ward, which accommodated twenty-two recovering wounded warriors. He felt embarrassed to be entertained as the paraplegic patients actually raced around the ward while lying prone, only covered by a sheet, on cold metal gurneys. They powered their movement by spinning the front wheels with well-conditioned arms. Partially filled, urine collection bags dangled from the racing frame and danced with each energetic forward thrust. His recently laundered crisp sheets that arrived each Monday had become damp by day's end.

The faded, blistering pea-green walls really needed a new coat of a more pleasing hue. The discolored off-white tile floor was ice cold and stained by years of spilled bodily fluids.

At least he could make it to the latrine and avoid the embarrassment of attempting to balance his wounded butt on a bedpan when nature called.

While enduring the painful physical therapy that now allowed him to make that trip to the toilet, he remembered complaining to the therapist, "Are you trying to kill me?"

He had written home, "The food was nearly tolerable."

It was now mid-December. He believed his Walter Reed Army Medical Center purgatory would soon be a distant, unpleasant memory. He would be in a better place once he got back home to Amsterdam in the majestic green Mohawk River Valley of upstate New York, thirty minutes west of Albany on the NYS Thruway. He enjoyed all the winter sports and predicted to a fellow patient, "Skiing is out of the question this year, but I sure as hell will be able to run a snowmobile."

His envious friend replied, "Good for you."

After three months of hospitalization and physical therapy, Richard began to feel almost normal again. He was ambulating without stumbling too often. His doctors were telling him, "You're doing great, soldier." He was anxious to see his childhood sweetheart, Michelle, who had waited for him. In spite of his deformities and his delayed stress (PTSD), she continued to love him without reservation.

Michelle cried on first seeing him. "How could they do this to you? How could a loving God let this happen?"

They had been high school sweethearts, and marriage was a given. He had been a track star in the 400- and 800-individual and relay events. In fact, his Amsterdam High School relay teams were New York State Champions in 1968 in both distances.

Michelle was an excellent student. She had been inducted into the Honor Society, was the Class of '68 Vice President, and accepted to Syracuse University on scholarship to study political science and economics. She adored Richard. "I love you so much! I'm glad you're home and out of that place."

CHAPTER 4

During his months at Walter Reed, Richard had witnessed enough sickness to know something was wrong. He became alarmed when he began to feel sickly. During rounds that evening, he asked, "Doc, what's going on?" He was frightened and confused. "Come on Doc, I want to get out of here!"

He began to pray more intently to his God. Several days later, he asked a nearby nurse, "What's that red color on my legs?"

"No problem, just from the rough sheets" was her reply.

However, within twenty hours, the skin of his damaged legs felt like a thousand bee stings. The surface of his wounded legs was now red, thick, and weeping.

By thirty hours, that same skin had blackened and crevassed into open spaces oozing feculent yellow-brown-green pus and gangrenous tissue. An unrelenting high fever developed. A nurse restarted an IV in his left arm to administer fluids to prevent dehydration, and to infuse potent antibiotics.

As each hour passed, he sensed his body's accelerated submission to whatever was going wrong. Private Burrows was now rapidly losing his sense of time, place, and person. The taste of food made him nauseous. His body was starving from lack of adequate nutritional intake; he was losing weight rapidly. In an attempt to sustain life, his body was cannibalizing its muscle mass and other proteins to use as energy to keep his body processes functioning and to fight the infection. He felt terrible and pleaded again to his attending physician, "Doc, please help me. Please, I don't want to die."

All the surgical staff conferred. Everyone knew Richard was close to death. An extraordinary lifesaving decision was agreed upon, and emergency bilateral above-the-knee amputations were scheduled for first thing in the morning to eliminate all infected and dead tissue.

At home in Amsterdam, NY, Michelle was excited to answer her phone when Richard called at the prearranged eight o'clock hour. She was alarmed by his message. He wept in an almost inaudible exhalation, "Oh my God, Michelle, after all this, they're taking my legs."

She was justifiably unnerved when hearing Richard's desperation. He was now a shell of the man she had loved for so many years. All his doctor would say to her was, "You better get down here as soon as you can." Michelle immediately left by train for Washington, DC.

His attending surgeon, knowing Richard most probably would die and was feeling defeated, confided to an associate, "Hopefully, this intervention will remove the reservoir of infected tissue that is seeding his bloodstream." The invasion of bacteria into his circulation did indeed lead to sepsis, meaning that deadly bacteria were actually surviving and growing in his blood to be disseminated throughout his body. This septic attack was overwhelming. Richard was suffering from septicemia and very near death. Some on the surgical team wondered, "Should this radical surgery have been done the moment his doctors decided it was necessary?" Perhaps so. Would the timing have made a difference in the outcome? Probably not.

That evening, Richard was sufficiently coherent to remember that the date was December 16, 1971. His birthday was near. He was alone. A nurse passed by and he inquired of her, "I should turn twenty-two next week. Will I?" He desperately pleaded, "Am I gonna die?" She tried to reward him with a reassuring smile.

He predicted to the same nurse, "On my birthday, I will be at the Riley Funeral Home on Division Street in Amsterdam, being readied for burial in a closed casket." The experienced nurse knew what his outcome would be but kept it to herself. He had attended several wakes at home in Amsterdam, NY before deploying to Vietnam. He could picture numerous rows of dark brown folding chairs with fake leather stiff seats neatly arranged in a darkened flower-packed room.

With effort, he imagined Michelle, his parents, and other loved ones weeping, inhaling and engulfed by the offensive sickly-sweet aroma of the well-intentioned flower arrangements.

Many times, he had visited his family's plot at St. Mary's Cemetery on a green grassy hill above the historic Mohawk River Valley. Would he soon receive visitors in that beautiful tranquil setting?

"Will I ever see Michelle and my parents again?" he asked a nervous specialist who was poking his arm for blood to be analyzed. He continued, "What have I done to deserve such an ending?" The young phlebotomist did not answer Richard. He thanked God for having enlisted as a conscientious objector due to his conviction is to not carry a rifle and kill. He would spend his days of service drawing blood stateside and not trudging through a dangerous Vietnam.

Private Burrows lamented that he had studied hard. He did not do drugs and even had volunteered for the Army, deferring his study of civil engineering at Hamilton to serve his country, despite the public's growing negativity toward the war. He prayed daily and had routinely received communion at St. Mary's Roman Catholic Church, just down the block from his home.

A tormented semiconscious Richard screamed in desperation. He pleaded for relief from his pain as his voice echoed through Ward 3 of Walter Reed Army Medical Center in Washington, DC. He finally fell into an oblivion brought on by a darkening, dense cloud of total exhaustion. His primal self, weakly rebelled against the excruciating pain that relentlessly wracked his body. A sickening odor of decay emanated from his wounds as he anguished in knowing that this was the end. Soon, he would disappear into death, through no fault of his own.

The comfort of prayer had deserted him. His last thoughts, as his exhausted debilitated body began to shut down and yield to eternal sleep, were of Michelle and his parents. At 02:00 hours on December 17, 1971, he suffered a cardiac arrest. The alarms sounded, followed by frantic attempts at resuscitation. Richard's depleted, septic body and soul had lost all resilience.

Private First Class Richard P. Burrows' Code Blue was called at 02:40 hours. Those in attendance peered down and stood in silence. Some prayed. Others wept. His attending doctor could not believe what had happened. "What did we miss?" the Major bemoaned to the nearby staff. An exhausted, bereaved Michelle arrived an hour later.

CHAPTER 5

Private Richard Burrows' medical records were explored in-depth at the Morbidity and Mortality Conference, which was attended by all medical, surgical, and senior nursing members of the Walter Reed Army Medical Center's staff. No one could shed light on the origin of his gruesome and fatal postoperative leg infections occurring in a patient with completely healed wounds. It was suggested that if the amputations had been performed sooner, the outcome might have been different. All with experience knew that was most probably not so. After a lengthy discussion, Colonel Charlie Carroll, Chairman of the Surgery Department and the Chief of the M&M Conference, retorted to the attendees, "Whatever the hell it was, I hope it died with the patient."

Unknown to him, tucked away in the Walter Reed hematology lab records, were multiple reports of Private Burrows' blood cells stained and smeared on a slide for microscopic viewing. They covered the time from the day of his Walter Reed admission to the day before his death.

On Burrows' smear from two weeks preceding his death, a lab tech, Specialist Matt Rogowicz, had noticed a variety of infection-fighting white blood cells called macrophages that seemed to be distorted and filled with engorged sacs called vesicles. These white cells' intended activity was to engulf and kill invading bacteria. *How could they be in this abnormal state?* He wondered if they were dangerous to the patient's health.

He had consulted Major Mike Grossman, the attending hematologist at Walter Reed, who was a little put out with Matt's intrusion into his office, and asked, "Sir, what do you make of these white cells? Are they dangerous?"

Matt added, "No other lab techs have reported this abnormality in subsequent smears of Private Burrows' blood."

This oddity was new to the Major. "I don't know what these are," he replied to Matt in a more civil tone.

Dr. Grossman, in turn, consulted the world-renowned experts at the nearby Armed Forces Institute of Pathology (AFIP). After a lengthy discussion, the examining expert hematologists at AFIP admitted never having encountered this white cell presentation and could not render an opinion to explain its origin or significance.

This white cell abnormality had never been reported in the world hematology literature and was unknown to those currently reading blood smears at Walter Reed Army Medical Center.

Dr. Grossman reviewed Private Burrows' clinical record. He concluded that since the patient demonstrated no signs of illness on the day this blood smear was performed, the finding was most likely an aberration due to an altered technique or defective chemicals applied in staining the blood smear slide.

Matt was not at all convinced but an enlisted specialist does not challenge the authority of a field officer. That was the military culture.

Matt knew that the interpretations by other techs of smears leading up to Private Burrows' death did not demonstrate the abnormal macrophage white blood cell. He reviewed those slides. The other techs missed the fact that the abnormal cells Matt described had multiplied in number, enlarged, and disappeared on the day that Richard complained of the rash on his legs. Therefore, this information, oblivious to several lab techs, was not available for Dr. Grossman and the AFIP to review. If the cell changes had been presented to them, they would undoubtedly have begun investigating if a relationship existed between the abnormal macrophages and Richard's fatal illness.

To avoid problems for himself, he decided not to rock the boat and present his findings to Major Grossman. At this point, self-preservation was his primary goal. He would keep his nose clean. But a dreadful thought challenged his conscience, *Will there be additional deaths due to this grossly abnormal macrophage?* Matt would eventually learn that the failure of recognition of the white blood cell abnormality by the medical establishment would prove to have devastating, far-reaching consequences.

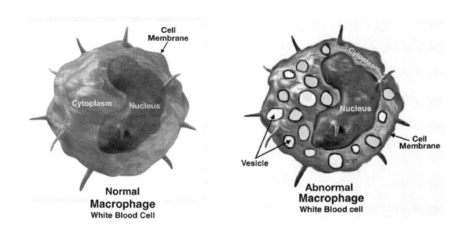

Private First Class Richard P. Burrows' name would eventually be chiseled into the reflective black granite of the Vietnam Veterans Memorial erected in green sloping Constitutional Gardens adjacent to the National Mall in Washington, DC. This edifice will always be referred to as the Wall. Designed by Maya Lin, the unconventional monument design was selected by the Vietnam Veterans Memorial Fund, Inc. over other submissions.

The Wall was dedicated in November 1982. The 58,318 names included those who died in Vietnam and 1571 unaccounted for as missing-in-action. It is L-shaped and composed of multiple black granite panels which progressively increase in height until its two arms converge at the tall right-angle L buried in a hillside so that its top is ground level. The recessed gray lettering appears small and cluttered. A ten-inch-wide border of small bluish gray stones lines its inside base.

The honorable warriors are listed in chronological order. Each name on the Wall is registered with coordinates indicating the correct panel and its line on that panel. The panels are clearly numbered. One must count down the lines of dead young men and women to find the name of the soldier being sought who was killed-in-action (KIA).

Utilizing this system, generations of visitors' eyes, without a second thought, will scan over Private Richard P. Burrows' chiseled name while attempting to find their loved one.

Rubbings will be made. Sentimental items will be left in the gravel at the Wall's base.

CHAPTER 6

Matt Rogowicz had been raised in a middle-class home by caring parents in Milwaukee. A handsome dirty-blond, he was active and presented an inquiring mind. His dad did carpentry and his mother practiced nursing at the local hospital. As a young child, he would spend time with her at work and became interested in the medical field. He grew into a tall and heavy-set teenager who excelled at football and basketball. Being very personable and accessible, he was elected as high school senior class president. Above all, he was religious and adhered to his demanding conscience.

Matt had attended a local community college for two years and captained the basketball team before volunteering for Vietnam. He served as an infantryman with the 101st Airborne in Vietnam for six months before he was finally reassigned to the 12th Evacuation Hospital in Chu Chi to perform the duties of a lab technician for which he had been trained. His second active duty assignment was at Walter Reed Army Medical Center near Washington, DC. There, he was confronted with a choice of whether or not to pursue his conviction about the abnormal white blood cell he had observed. He did not.

Matt continued to feel responsible for the death of the post-op patient, Private Burrows, at Walter Reed. He was concerned others would die due to the occurrence of those abnormal white blood cells that were written off as mistakes in staining technique. These thoughts began to overwhelm his usually clear conscience. He began to feel depressed. He switched from beer to excessive hard liquor. Due to the threat of stigmatization within the military culture, he refused to seek professional advice.

He had been honorably discharged from active duty in February 1972. He was sent back to the U.S. without being counseled in how to reintegrate into a peaceful society which moreover, treated Vietnam veterans with disdain. He would soon become the poster child for PTSD.

Matt was ashamed of what he had become and had no inclination to return to his hometown of Milwaukee. He found himself near New York City, leased a one-room apartment in Queens, NY, and lived on his separation pay.

For a year in Vietnam, he had witnessed the devastation war rendered on the body, mind, and soul. He had no one with whom to share his traumatic wartime experiences and began self-medicating with alcohol to seek relief from his evolving delayed stress (PTSD) symptoms.

After a few months of living in deepening despair, Matt admitted to himself that he needed help. He joined a veterans self-help group and with their support, became capable of forgiving himself sufficiently for the patient's death to stop drinking. He achieved enough self-confidence to begin managing his lingering delayed stress. He applied to a local college to complete his four-year degree.

Matt utilized the GI Bill to complete his degree as an English major at Iona College on Long Island, NY. He then pursued a Master's Degree in Journalism from Columbia University in New York City. He did not wish to be anywhere near medicine. As he told his parents upon returning home from Vietnam, "I've seen enough blood, guts, and suffering for any ten people." He said to his dad, "But I'm moved and haunted by witnessing the devastation of war on body, mind, and soul. I wish to give a true accounting of Vietnam to our nation."

He had photographed and documented his Vietnam infantry and 12th Evac experiences as well as the Walter Reed facilities, activities, and personnel. He also taped as many war stories he could from willing grunts, friends, and patients. Matt focused his Japanese manufactured Minolta SRT 101 to record their faces and wounds. "I wish to publish a historical novel describing and defining a soldier's suffering. Perhaps my work will encourage our politicians not to be so quick to commit our nation to a war of choice and not necessity," he related to his college advisor who encouraged, "Sounds like a great project."

Matt and the Walter Reed medical staff had admitted their helplessness in attempting to prevent Richard Burrows' demise due to this new disease's viciousness and unstoppable progression. These professionals were unaccustomed to failure. The Private's death in December 1971 had engulfed Walter Reed Army Medical Center in a dense cloud of depression and inadequacy. Even after a year, Matt's guilt regularly reminded him of the abnormal white blood cells he described in Private Burrows' blood smear a few days before his death which was dismissed as an anomaly.

In his last semester of his Master's study at Columbia, he was required to create an outline for a historical novel. He began to revisit his Army experience. Private Burrows' death took center stage in his thoughts. That spring of 1972, he began mobilizing his material. He soon realized a shortfall in his information and admitted to his advisor, "What novel? There's not enough research to write a complete work." The historical novel was shelved.

Matt was awarded his Master's Degree in Journalism in May of 1975 on a sunny hot, humid day on the Columbia Campus on the upper west side of Manhattan. He was engaged to a fellow student and planned to marry and raise a family. He needed a job. He wanted to stay in the New York area.

Utilizing Columbia's connections, he secured a position on Long Island at *Newsweek* in its political coverage of Nassau and Suffolk Counties, Long Island, New York. That next year, he married Maggie, who was writing children's books, and within two years, a set of identical twin girls were born to their and both sets of grandparents' delight.

As the years passed, Matt began to tell stories about Vietnam to Maggie, friends, and strangers at cocktail parties. Verbalizing his experiences released stored tension and developed his reputation as a respected veteran. Every day, due to various triggers, his mind returned him to Vietnam for a short time. After ten years, the memories were less offensive and upsetting.

Since high school, Matt had not done well keeping in touch with his childhood best friend, Mike Clark, who had been a corpsman and functioned as an operating room scrub tech at the 85th Evacuation Hospital in Vietnam. Mike was now a certified operating room tech at the University of Wisconsin Hospital and was sought after by the hospital surgeons for the difficult cases due to his Vietnam experience and unflappability.

Mike had dark hair with a sturdy muscled build on a five-foot-ten frame. He was intelligent, observant, and had excellent powers of deduction. The sciences were his favorite subjects in school and becoming a chemical engineer was considered. His complexion was ruddy from all the time he spent outdoors, hunting, and fishing.

He and Matt had grown up a few blocks apart in the Milwaukee suburb of Brookfield and had played football on its high school team. Matt was a blocking back that opened space for Mike as the tailback to run through. They were tight and inseparable until they attended separate two-year community colleges. Following their college graduations in 1969, both had immediately volunteered for the Army to fight in Vietnam. Neither knew where the other went for basic and specialty training. Letters from home informed Matt that Mike was a corpsman in Vietnam. Matt had considered himself lucky to be finally out of the boonies and at the 12th Evac.

Time passed, families grew, and careers evolved. Up until now, they had communicated infrequently until Matt, in August of 1983, considered returning home to Wisconsin and accepted a position as the assistant editor of the Milwaukee Inquirer. By this time, Mike was the Chief of Support Services for cardiothoracic surgery at the University of Wisconsin Hospital and was delighted to have Matt back in his life.

They immediately rekindled their close relationship. Mike became a mentor and advised Matt and his family on housing, banking, lawyers, and schools. In comparing war stories, they realized that both shared a connection to Private Richard Burrows as Mike had scrubbed in on Richard's surgery at the 85th Evac. Matt reviewed in detail the circumstances surrounding Richard

Burrows' vile death at Walter Reed and the dismissed abnormal macrophage observation he had made. Mike was astounded and saddened by this account. He assumed the Private would do well; he certainly was in good shape when he left the 85th Evac.

This event still haunted Matt. "I can't let it go. The circumstances of Burrows' death destroyed me for a while," he confessed to Mike, who asked, "Did you drink to get drunk and forget?"

"Yes," responded an embarrassed Matt.

Mike reluctantly offered, "Don't feel alone; I did the same thing for six months until Connie put her foot down. You must find some answers to free yourself from the guilt."

Matt then decided to pursue the mystery of Private Burrows' death aggressively. He could easily balance the paper's editorial duties with the time commitment necessary to develop this critical investigative project. "I'll discuss this project with my boss Monday morning," Matt said excitedly.

Mike had, in the early '80s, read a retrospective Life Magazine review of Burrows' fiancée, Michelle, and other women grieving loved ones lost to the Vietnam War. He was tremendously impressed by her ability to cope with Richard's death. She had invited anyone with information about Richard's injury and death to contact her. Mike had tracked her down. He had reassured Michelle that he had received the best care possible at the 85th Evacuation Hospital in Vietnam and was fit for transfer to Japan.

CHAPTER 7

After Mike Clark had made the introduction, Matt visited Michelle in Alexandria, Virginia. He had flown in from an editors' conference in New York City. At the airport, her happy, warm greeting eliminated any reservation Matt had in interacting with a dead soldier's love.

Michelle was engaging and energetic. She wore her dark hair to her shoulders, enhancing her youthful, brown-eyed oval face. Her complexion was olive. She was five-foot-six and kept slim by working out at the local gym every other day.

Michelle was very involved in the lives of her three girls. "They're growing up so rapidly I want to be there every minute," she had confided to her husband, Jon. Earlier in her career, she had worked as a legislative assistant to Congressman John Martin Streeby, who represented the 100th congressional district west of Albany in upstate New York.

Michelle admitted to Matt, "In the years just after Richard's death, I had been consumed by my memories of him and the resulting sadness of knowing he was gone."

"Quite naturally," he responded understandingly.

But life went on, and she was now happily married to Jon, a wonderful and considerate husband. They were blessed with and are raising three beautiful, intelligent girls: Katya, 12, Sabrina, 9, and Annika, 7.

She conspiratorially whispered to Matt, "Over the years, I felt compelled to visit Richard's name on the Wall and contemplate what might have been if he had not died."

"I do understand," he softly consoled.

With the passage of time and growing commitments to family and her career, her visits had become less frequent. "But I still feel a strong connection," she admitted.

Michelle had felt compelled to learn more about our nation's Vietnam War dead. She discovered that of the 58,300 plus names honored on the Wall, almost 11,000 died from non-hostile causes such as suicide, murder, heroin overdoses, vehicular motor accidents, drowning, random accidents, friendly fire, etc. She told Matt, "I was horrified that over forty-four thousand on the Wall were twenty-two years old and younger. Richard was one of them," she sadly declared.

Michelle recognized the cruel joke that almost one thousand soldiers were KIA on their first day in Vietnam, and fifteen-hundred died on their last day in-country.

Matt informed Michelle, "Few families know the circumstances of their loved one's death, and the caskets are usually closed."

At times, the arrival of a letter from a son's or daughter's wartime commander or fellow warrior revealed a few details. In-person visits from unit members were rare but especially appreciated.

Michelle told Matt, "Richard's parents never learned the details of his death before they died in an automobile accident." Michelle did not wish to burden them with the gruesome details. A drunk driver crossed the median and killed them instantly just five years after Richard died.

Michelle wished out loud, "If my love had to die, his death should have been as merciful."

All she understood was that after appearing ready to return home and marry her, it only took a week before he succumbed to a dreadful, untreatable tissue-destroying infection.

Matt learned that she had repeatedly wondered, *Where did this killer come from? Was it Walter Reed's operating room? Contamination from other wounded servicemen on the ward? Incompletely sterilized medical supplies? The C-141 flight to Washington? The hospital in Vietnam? The jungle? The enemy?*

Michelle, Matt, and our nation would be astonished when the mystery was solved.

CHAPTER 8

The former Army Corpsman, Mike Clark, made another crucial introduction. In October 1983, Matt, the editor/investigative reporter, flew to St. Louis to interview Mike's Army buddy from basic at Fort Campbell, Kentucky. They also shared specialty training at Fort Sam Houston, San Antonio, Texas. Ryan Larkin was currently pursuing a doctorate in Biomedical Engineering at Washington University in St. Louis. They met in the living room of his small apartment. Refreshments were offered. Both were anxious to start.

Ryan told Matt, "I know nothing of my origins." He was orphaned. His first memory was that of being hungry and cold during the winter on a rough wooden floor in a barren building somewhere in the Midwest. Very young children overran the space. The stench in the air was nauseating. This situation lasted two and a half years. He was blessed with a survivor's mentality and maintained a hopeful polite demeanor.

Around his sixth birthday, he had been chosen and rescued by a loving military couple in their thirties. He enjoyed an openly emotional and sophisticated childhood. His adoptive father was a Naval officer, and his family moved multiple times with him to various postings around the world. Ryan absorbed the personality strengths from those he encountered. He would commit himself to succeed in accomplishing any task he accepted. He was somewhat intense, but not in a repulsive manner. He kept all his ducks in a row. He carefully deciphered the nuances of each environment in which he was thrust. He wished to erase that early childhood feeling of hunger and desperation from his memory. Over the years, his dad repeated to Ryan, "You are most capable of completing any task you put your mind to."

He had grown into a six-foot-two, blond-haired and blue-eyed man, weighed in at about two hundred and ten pounds, and had an angular handsome face and was considerate and engaging. He preferred golf and tennis to football and basketball. Always paying attention to detail, he took pains to dress well but not expensively. He, too, was a patriot and volunteered for military service after two years of community college near Arlington.

After their first meeting at Fort Campbell, Matt and Ryan became instantly close. Their military service had followed similar paths. They performed the same duties in the Army and served as lab techs in Vietnam after six months fighting the VC in the boonies. Stateside, Matt was assigned to Walter Reed and had identified the abnormal vesicle-filled white cell in Private Burrows' blood just before he died. They were astounded to discover that almost simultaneously, within six months, they both had identified that same abnormal macrophage in two separate patients and were told it was a meaningless finding.

Over lunch, Ryan related his story to Matt. Ryan remembered exclaiming in early 1972, "What the hell is this thing?" as he was startled to observe the profound abnormality of a specialized white blood cell, the macrophage, in a wounded patient's blood smear.

Ryan was serving as a laboratory technician at the 85th Evacuation Hospital in Vietnam.

He told Matt, "I had never seen this unique irregular outline, the deep discoloration, the distorted central nucleus, and the mysterious distended vesicles floating within the macrophage." Ryan continued, "I then informed the pathologist of my observation."

Major Douglas Sharp dismissed the finding after he inquired about the patient's status and was told by the attending surgeon that Jameson was doing well following his bilateral above-the-knee amputations and due for evacuation to the Japan military medical facility in the morning. He then advised Specialist Larkin, "Not to worry; the patient's doing fine." Major Sharp had decided, "no harm, no foul." He felt that probably the abnormal white cells were due to a blood smear staining arbitration.

Ryan had replied, "I'm not so sure."

In the following days, the aberrant white cells were not observed again in the blood smears of new patients. Lab tech Larkin's observation disappeared from everyone's consciousness.

More pressing at that moment, there were many specimens to process from the multiple wounded brought to the 85th Evacuation during the recent mass casualty on Christmas Eve due to friendly fire. Somehow, American high explosive artillery was directed, by mistake, at our troops. Following the explosions, nine young soldiers were KIA. Nine others were medivaced to the 85th Evac where three died during surgery, to the anguish of those attempting to save them. They died on the operating room table. Their blood loss exceeded the surgeon's ability to stem the tide and the anesthesiologist's ability to replace the loss. The surgical drapes saturated with blood covered these dying wounded; the cement floor was slick with sticky congealing red-brown blood; the surgeon's gowns and fatigues soaked with blood. If those in the OR were new to this horror, they had not learned to wear flip flops to avoid blood pooling in their combat boots.

Ryan related to Matt that young troops from the 101st Airborne Division crowded the ED area in a weeping huddled group. Most of them were still teenagers. Some were blaming the newbie First Lieutenant. A young First Sergeant repeated the rumor, "That asshole called in artillery on his position."

"Too bad he didn't die too," a friend answered.

The celebratory events planned at the 85th Evacuation for Christmas Eve did not come to pass.

Larkin continued his recollection to Matt, "There's more!"

"Please keep on," coached the eager journalist but, "I need a bathroom break."

"So do I," said Ryan.

After they retook their seats in the living room again, Larkin continued that on his way back to the U.S., he stopped by Tachikawa Army Hospital in Japan to reconnect with a nurse he knew. From her, Ryan learned that the recent 85th Evac patient, Jamison, was showing improvement for several days after his arrival. His wounds were irrigated and cleaned in anticipation of performing skin grafting and closure by suturing wounds that were left open to avoid infection. However, the doctors at Tachikawa were beyond frustrated.

The attending surgeon exclaimed, "What the hell is going on?" A red, raised skin rash appeared on Jamison's thigh amputation sites and progressed quickly into a blistering, sloughing, and necrotizing infection. "Holy shit!" the surgeon uttered to those making rounds with him later that day. The doctors were losing this patient.

A corpsman pleaded, "Somebody think of something to do to stop this." Everything they tried failed to improve Jamison's status, and he died a gruesome septic death.

Matt then paused in his note-taking and said to Ryan, "Now I know Private David Jamison undoubtedly left this world suffering the identical tissue-destroying disease and excruciating death that Private Richard Burrows endured. First at Walter Reed, again at Tachikawa Army Hospital. How are they connected?" he challenged Ryan.

Larkin lamented to Matt that within the most northern Army I Corps combat theater of operations in Vietnam, information rarely moved back up-country to those originally responsible for a patient. Private Jamison's death and the circumstances surrounding his demise in Japan were not reported to the 85th Evacuation Hospital. If Major Sharp, at the 85th Evac, had been informed of what had transpired, perhaps he would have revisited Specialist Ryan Larkin's finding of the abnormal macrophages, which as a lab tech, he had noted in patient Jamison's blood. This shared information could have stimulated investigation into Private Burrows' similar death about four months previously and shed light on the connection between the abnormal macrophage and the usually fatal infectious necrotizing disease. Ryan and Matt had both, as Army lab specialists, described the abnormal macrophages in soldiers who had served in Vietnam. Those in charge declared the findings to be an anomaly, but here were two wounded grunts who had died from a gangrenous infectious disease associated with abnormal macrophages that presented in both patients' blood smears before the onset of symptoms.

Tragically, the medical profession was not alerted. Therefore, doctors were unable to institute precautions and begin research to prevent this vile deadly disease.

Matt remarked to Ryan, "The more I learn about this disease, the more questions I have."

Matt's head was again beginning to pound in the evenings. He even started to drink a little more to relax at night to ease the tension and go to sleep. His wife, Maggie, urged, "Get help, so you don't go down that rabbit hole again." He did, was placed on an antidepressant drug, and stopped drinking. His psychiatrist had served in Vietnam and having dealt with his own PTSD, truly understood Matt's needs.

A month later, Ryan called Matt by landline and related having discovered in recent research the reporting by the CDC of an explosion of similar cases internationally occurring in the late sixties within months of the hideous deaths of Privates Burrows and Jamison.

To follow up on Ryan's information, in January 1983, Matt visited the Centers for Disease Control and Prevention (CDC) in Washington, DC. Matt lamented to the researcher he was interviewing, "A decade of worldwide suffering would not have occurred if our Vietnam findings had been believed and presented in the hematology literature as a warning." Matt learned that the disease occurred in epidemic proportions affecting patients globally during the late sixties, early seventies, and peaking in early 1974. The CDC doctor added, "Currently in 1983, its occurrence is very unusual, almost rare."

In the late sixties and early seventies, patients with skin rashes progressing to necrotizing, infectious and septic gangrenous deaths in military personnel who were either in or had been in Vietnam became a matter of great significance. Cases appeared in Australia, South Korea, and Taiwan. These countries had assisted the Americans by sending their military personnel to fight in Vietnam.

Matt learned that the disease occurred not only in Vietnam active duty military and veterans, foreign office support staff, and contractors but also in innocent travelers to tropical and subtropical countries.

The researcher advised Matt that years ago, he had been appointed director of an investigative group created by direct Richard Nixon Presidential Order to study its epidemiology. "Get to the bottom of this international crisis!" Nixon had implored. The President then pleaded, "Please consider the few facts we do know about this disease and brainstorm for an answer to put an end to it."

The CDC official continued to inform Matt, "Travel within North America, Eastern and Western Europe, Russia, and most of China appeared to be safe." However, those countries did report this dreaded disease in patients who had traveled outside of their country to warmer climates such as sub-Saharan Africa, East and Southeast Asia, Latin America, and South America. He added, "We know specific infectious diseases are prevalent in those warmer climates, primarily due to the insect population. This includes the Anopheles mosquito, which spreads malaria." They agreed; it made sense to assume that at higher elevations, in the same country where the air is colder, the mosquito cannot survive, and malaria should not be transmitted. That would account for the fact that known cases have a subtropical connection.

In an attempt to get ahead of this dreadful disease, the head researcher had directed the CDC to follow a new directive. He declared, "Serial blood smears must become routine in the protocol for patients suspected to be vulnerable to this affliction." If the abnormal white blood cells were confirmed, an in-depth review of the patient's records would possibly reveal some clues.

He continued, "It was routine to find in all patients with this disease that vesicles had developed within the abnormal macrophages a few days before the rash developed." Each day these microscopic vesicles demonstrated an increase in number and size until they appeared to be bulging. Suddenly the threatening vesicles vanished simultaneously with the deadly illness's onset. They probably had discharged a toxin into the patient's bloodstream that caused the lethal infection. Immediately after the onset of the vile disease, the abnormal white blood cells disappeared.

Matt then asked, "Does this have anything to do with a patient's DNA?" The CDC expert responded that in the 1970s, the study of the human genome was in its infancy. But researchers did discover a fortunate segment of the world's population that shared a specific alteration in a grouping of DNA genes on Chromosome 6. In this population, it was unusual to observe the abnormal macrophages.

The appearance of the threatening rash was usually the harbinger of death. But non-fatal cases have occurred after the appearance of rash. In these patients, there occurred for an unknown reason, a minimal number of engorged vesicles within each white blood cell. Therefore, researchers concluded that there was a critical amount of toxin in the bulging vesicles of each abnormal white blood cell that was necessary to produce the dreaded disease. Calculation of the number of vesicles per ten thousand abnormal white blood cells became a predictor of occurrence and severity of illness.

Following this CDC expert's revelations, Matt knew that many questions remained.

He challenged the CDC researcher, "What causes the white blood cell abnormality? How did the vesicles develop? What did they contain? Did the contents of the vesicles cause the disease or instigate a chain reaction leading to disease?"

The CDC official responded, "I have no idea."

Matt wondered if it would be possible through his investigation to document the multiple research efforts over the years into this fatal disease and answer these questions. He would need new allies to bring this issue to fruition.

Would he succeed?

CHAPTER 9

Matt, still at the onset of his quest in 1983, turned his attention to the nationally and internationally published investigative reports of the 1970s and 1980s that addressed this fatal disease. He visited the Library of Congress in Washington, DC, national TV corporation archives, the World Health Organization headquarters at the United Nations, the New York Public Library, and the New York Times microfilm repository.

He was now traveling extensively. Maggie was troubled by his excessive pursuit of information. The children were growing up, and she thought it inappropriate for him to miss their evolving lives. He promised her that he was closing in on all he needed to complete his story and would return to his original routine. His editor realized there might be a possibility of a blockbuster story and placed him on paid sabbatical to allow sufficient time to continue his investigation.

What Matt discovered was that in the seventies across the US medical spectrum, in the printed news, and on national television, there were deluded attempts to explain this new and challenging medical problem. The fanciful false proclamations of a speedy investigation to resolve this disease's transmission to reassure the public were a smoke screen. Our nation's citizens were fearful of contracting this dreaded disease. TV talking heads inflamed emotions by proposing, "Was it spread by breathing the same air, eating contaminated food, having sex, sitting on a public toilet, or being in contact with an infected carrier of the disease?"

Alarmists proclaimed, "The public must avoid contact with those perceived to be infected by this disease."

As a result, in addition to the name calling, egg throwing, and spitting, the returning Vietnam veteran was further shunned and isolated. Schools, businesses, workplaces, movies, restaurants, motels, and other gathering places were becoming off-limits to those who served in Vietnam. A societal disaster was developing. Where would our Vietnam veterans work, eat, toilet, sleep, or attend college? Would not the currently difficult reintegration of the stigmatized Vietnam veteran into US society be made more difficult? An irrational defensive mode gripped the nation's populace.

Matt was invigorated when learning that in the 1960s and 1970s, medical experts, both military and civilian from around the world, had been cooperating with governmental agencies to elucidate this dreaded disease. These researchers agreed with the CDC's hypothesis that the risk for developing the disease endangered all those military personnel who had served in Vietnam. They were susceptible to the disease as a primary patient. The dreadful, deadly disease also occurred in non-military governmental personnel who had resided in Vietnam. Victims included those who visited sub-Saharan Africa and other countries with low altitude tropical and subtropical climates.

He discovered in his reading that the CDC director had also asked his research groups to devise protocols to answer the question. The director had asked, "Could this disease be transmitted from one infected citizen to someone who had never been in Vietnam, i.e., was it contagious?"

This information would be crucial to determine if quarantine were to become mandatory for all, whether military or not, returning from a suspect country to the continental United States.

In the mid-seventies, the CDC, after an in-depth investigation, did finally declare that the disease was not contagious. This finding ended a selfish knee-jerk public need to ostracize Vietnam veterans. The CDC director also had asked, "Are we dealing with a virus, bacterium, chemical, or an unknown protein molecule?" Also considered were questions such as: How does one become infected? Are there insect or animal vectors transmitting the disease, as the mosquito bite in malaria, or the raccoon bite in rabies?

The challenging questions of world authorities, both nationally and internationally, had unleashed a worldwide discussion that continued for over a decade. But Matt knew there was no resolution. He began to doubt there would be one since the occurrence of the disease had currently in the 1980s become unusual and no longer considered a global threat.

CHAPTER 10

It was now early 1984. The political events that had shaped the Vietnam War were still not understood by the majority of American citizens. As a result of this deadly macrophage research, Matt became committed to improving public comprehension of the war. He had to add needed background to his investigative report and delve more deeply into what events shaped the consequences of our nation's involvement in Vietnam. He had second thoughts about pursuing this new avenue of research. It would require increased separation from his family. Although he became anxious and mildly depressed when attempting to rationalize his actions, he had decided to go forward.

In early 1968, there were coordinated countrywide attacks on major South Vietnamese cities during the Tet Offensive by the North Vietnamese Army and the Viet Cong. This brazen accomplishment destroyed all credibility in our government's claim that the United States and South Vietnamese military were prevailing in their effort to preserve the nation of South Vietnam. American forces repelled the enemy, but the fact that they occurred in the first place, with the full knowledge of the Vietnamese population in the cities and countryside, was a game-changer. We were not winning hearts and minds, officially referred to as Vietnamization, as our political leaders had directed. How could we expect to do so when American forces were burning and bombing Vietnamese homes and crops in addition to killing directly (VC) or indirectly (collateral damage), their brothers, sisters, parents, husbands, wives, and children.

He lamented to Maggie, "Vietnamization. Are you kidding me!"

She just mumbled, "Just get done with this Quixotic commitment."

Matt learned about the shameful human losses of Tet 1968. With that in mind, President Lyndon Johnson, with the reluctant approval of his military advisors, decided to change the war's objective, from militarily defeating the northern communists and southern insurgents to the negotiation of a peace that would perhaps protect South Vietnam's sovereignty. In private, our most distinguished national leaders were content with the probability of South Vietnam's failure to survive as a democratic nation and be subjugated by the North.

Our country had assassinated sufficient Vietnamese politicians, believed too many lies from our in-country political appointees who reported the state of affairs in Vietnam, and tolerated too long the intransigence of the South Vietnamese generals to fully engage the enemy. We turned a blind eye toward the Vietnamese governmental representatives dealing in the heroin trade that was decimating our soldiers. We finally admitted that by 1968, over thirty thousand American deaths were an excessive price to pay when realizing no progress toward our stated goal of creating a sovereign independent country of South Vietnam by the use of overwhelming military force.

The U.S., unbeknownst to the South Vietnamese, was about to throw in the towel and leave Vietnam to its corrupt Vietnamese officials and military establishment to proceed on their own.

Matt was angered and saddened when realizing that with the 1968 decision to gradually withdraw, each American death, mutilation, or dismemberment became an unnecessary and pointless personal sacrifice. What a waste! He calculated that there were nearly thirty thousand more American deaths in Vietnam before the war officially ended for the United States in 1975.

Matt was sickened by the slaughterer at Kent State University on May 4, 1970 of four students and the wounding of nine, one resulting in permanent paralysis, by twenty-eight young Ohio State National Guardsmen in thirteen seconds with sixty-seven rounds fired. This travesty galvanized our nation's opposition to the war. Now our children were killing one another!

President Johnson officially washed his hands of this disgrace on March 31, 1968 by announcing to the nation that he would not seek re-election. Matt was excited to receive several psychological reports from 1971, which were uncovered by a Vietnam Marine combat veteran who was now an investigative journalist for Reuters. His superiors vigorously advised him to bury the new information. The veteran rationalized with Matt, "I'll not publish this bombshell information, but I wish this information to become part of the public record. I'll give it to you."

"Thanks," said Matt.

These documents revealed that our fighting men and women were not oblivious to this change in our nation's policy, the protests at home, the Kent State shooting, and the trashing of returning warriors. Many soldiers echoed, "Who wants to be the last to die in Vietnam? Why are we here?"

The Marine journalist had also disclosed that by late 1968, with the US change in Vietnam goals, the fabric of the military, which gave rise to stability in command, was breaking down. Long hair was now in vogue. Troops challenged the commander's orders. If a gung-ho lieutenant became too aggressive in exposing his troops to danger and did not respond to intimidating cues, such as a smoke grenade exploding near him, he risked being fragged with a live grenade or sustaining an M16 round in the back.

Matt implored the reluctant journalist, "Help me out here. Please give me all you have."

As a result, Matt was forwarded documentation by the journalist of the heroin usage by our military and the South Vietnamese government officials' involvement in its distribution.

Not publicly acknowledged in 1984, heroin usage did become an epidemic during the early 1970s in Vietnam and had sparked new enterprises. The soldiers were self-medicating to escape from dealing emotionally with the potential of being wounded or dying in combat.

The soldiers repeated, "Who wanted to be the last to die in this atrocity created by their political leaders who were slowly throwing in the towel?"

Matt was unnerved by the new information supplied to him by the Marine journalist, who then handed Matt a folder with the name "Corporal Pino" stenciled in bold letters.

CHAPTER 11

Corporal Pino ran a tight ship in his early 1972 heroin dealings on the Camp Eagle compound. The devious company clerk, with each visit off base to the massage pallor near the Post Exchange (PX) returned with a half kilo of high-grade smack. The heroin was so potent that even snorting it, like tobacco in colonial times from the hand's snuff-box, could lead to not only the expected high but also the risk of respiratory depression and death. When regurgitated, stomach contents were aspirated into the lungs. The resulting damage caused death by inhibiting life-sustaining oxygen delivery to the body. It was essentially drowning in one's vomit.

The heroin was distributed for sale to the compound personnel through a network of Vietnamese who worked on the base and also trusted American dealers.

Pino had warned his crew, "If you steal from me, you're dead." Private Peter Church had bragged to others, "There's no way he'll catch me." He was successfully skimming from the profits for four months until his bragging to others burst his bubble. A narcotic fogged altercation erupted, sparked by this rogue employee's actions.

Corporal Pino was livid. "You low life bastard. You're dead!"

Consumed by an explosion of inherent evil, heroin, and too much beer, his retribution was a .45-caliber Army issue, semi-auto pistol wound to the culprit's abdomen. The wounded Private Church was rushed to the 85th Evacuation Hospital ED, prepared for surgery, and underwent abdominal exploration with the repair of bleeding vessels and closing of the holes in his perforated intestine. Luckily, his colon was not injured thus, avoiding a colostomy.

Major Declan Burke was pleased with the surgical results. He lamented to Mike Clark, "It's bad enough to be shot by the enemy. Now they're shooting each other."

The miscreant did extremely well post-operatively. The entrepreneurial shooter was arrested and confined to the stockade in Da Nang. Judge Advocate General's Corps Captain, Howard Aison, announced to his clerk, "Charge him with attempted murder. This is the fourth one this month that involved heroin."

While in transit over the Pacific on the C-141 to the United States, the gunshot victim rapidly became septic after developing a rash over his abdomen and died. His wound burst open and evacuated gangrenous viscera that cascaded like a waterfall over the side of his suspended stretcher and bathed the deck of the transport with malodorous human detritus.

When notified of Church's death, Captain Howard Aison instantly revised the heroin entrepreneur's charge. "Now he's charged with second-degree murder."

CHAPTER 12

Matt was anxious to interview the 85th Evac veterans who had been involved firsthand with the disease and were also committed to better understanding this disastrous illness. He especially wanted to pursue Private Church's death.

In June of 1985, Mike Clark introduced Matt to Dr. Declan Burke. The investigator flew to DC and interviewed the surgeon at his George Washington University office.

Matt learned that Declan's tour in Vietnam ended with his discharge from the Army in the spring of 1972 directly from Vietnam. He, his wife Carol, and their two children moved to Fairfax, Virginia, for the surgeon had accepted the appointment as an Attending Physician in general and vascular surgery at the George Washington University Hospital in Washington, DC. There was a struggle initially with reintegrating into civilian life. He was emotionally distraught by war's devastation he witnessed in Vietnam. There was no one nearby who understood except Duane Wall, the director of the GW lab. He had served as a corpsman at the 85th Evacuation Hospital and worked in its ED and operating rooms. Declan was a good guy who served in Vietnam at the same time, and they became close friends.

Duane had taken advantage of his Army experience and pursued the requisite credentialing, ensuring advancement over time to become the director of all GW's labs.

He grew up in Napa Valley. His dad managed the Falcon River Vineyard's Cabernet grape experimentation and production. Duane enjoyed the analysis procedures for soil pH, wine acidity, alcohol content, etc., and shadowed the chefs in Falcon River's four-star restaurant.

The exacting details of vineyard management were exciting to him. He figured he'd study accounting and business at UCLA and begin his career at Falcon River. A life-changing obstacle to his plans was the draft lottery that started in early December of 1969. He was assigned a low number, which guaranteed he was going to Vietnam.

Back home, Declan and Duane utilized each other as sounding boards in dealing with their hidden stress. Seeking professional help was out of the question, for the stigmatization projected would ruin their practice and reputation with the hospital's faculty.

Declan was barely home three months from Vietnam when he began to reflect on his year of surgery in that hell hole. As all inquisitive surgeons, he would intermittently reflect on cases he considered surgical failures. Private Church stood out. Medical journals had accumulated at home during his time in Vietnam. He learned when reviewing and reading that there existed authoritative reports of not only a significant American military but also a worldwide non-military incidence of identical gangrenous deadly outcomes during the late 1960s and early 1970s. They reported a straight-line connection between abnormal macrophages filled with bulging vesicles and this disease.

Matt wished to discuss with Declan the death of the heroin dealer, Private Church, about whom the Marine informed him. He knew from the document he was given that Declan was the doctor of record. As for this Vietnam drug dealer's case, the Aeromedical Evacuation Group 179 did notify the 85th Evacuation Hospital commander, Colonel Sugiyama, and the attending surgeon himself of Private Church's gruesome death in transit. He related that the Air Force was quote, "pissed that such a sickly patient had been certified fit for traveling the long hours to the United States." Declan had become indignant. With the experience of almost a year's exposure to battlefield trauma, he said, "I never doubted that this patient was stable and fit for travel."

Matt replied, "For sure."

Declan had then performed an in-depth review at the 85ᵗʰ Evacuation Hospital of Church's hospital records. The surgeon continued telling Matt, "Usually I did not pay too much attention to a routine blood smear, just the volume of red cells, hematocrit, was sufficient information for me. I was concerned if the blood was capable of carrying sufficient oxygen to guarantee a good surgical outcome. I was on a mission to cover my ass," he added.

Declan continued, "During the review, I did note a remarkable finding, described by a lab tech, on Church's blood smear. There they were, the strange and enlarged macrophages with irregular borders, deep staining, and bulging vesicles." Declan had remembered exclaiming, "What the hell are these?" At that time, he had no information regarding their significance.

He believed that in this case, every aspect of his surgical judgment and patient care was beyond reproach. Declan had rendered his report, highlighting the existence of abnormal white blood cells, up the chain of command to those responsible for overseeing surgical outcomes. He inquired if records of those dying from an overwhelming infection demonstrated similar abnormal white cell findings. He never received a response. Declan decided he had no control in pursuing this issue and moved on to his next wartime surgical challenge. The strange blood smear soon receded from his conscious mind, for there were many more casualties to treat.

Soon, time to pursue solving the mystery of abnormal white blood cells disappeared in the flurry of activity at the 85ᵗʰ Evac that enveloped Declan.

He informed Matt that at the time of Private Church's death, he had no idea of what had transpired with his other Vietnam surgical patient, Private Burrows. He was never informed about his death and the discovery of abnormal white blood cells. He related to Matt that he was troubled when on the local ABC evening news broadcast, he watched a joint conference in late 1972. In it, the Secretaries of State, Health and Human Services, and Defense, along with the United States Surgeon General, claimed that a resolution to this new Vietnam mystery was years away. Washington, as well as Europe, Asia, and other nation-states had run out of options.

Declan told Matt he remembered thinking as he fell asleep that evening years ago that we have to do much better than that. But as expected, over the years, Declan's surgical practice and reputation at George Washington University flourished, and his skills were in high demand.

Declan felt guilty for not following up on this potentially lethal threat. He pledged to Matt, "I will join you in pursuing the association between deformed white blood cells and the patient deaths from the overwhelming infection that we have witnessed."

While flying home to Wisconsin, Matt remembered that in reviewing Church's chart after his death, Dr. Burke had found abnormal white cells. These appeared to be identical to those he had described at Walter Reed Army Medical Center in deceased Private Richard Burrows' August 1971 smear. His superiors did not consider his finding important. Specialist Larkin had also observed these same white cells in Private Jamison 's blood smear in mid-1971 at the 85th Evacuation Hospital in Vietnam. His findings, too, were not considered clinically significant.

Matt said in a quiet voice into his tape recorder, "Here are three patients, Burrows, Jameson, and Church, for whom I now have firsthand information." All three had died of a gangrenous septic disease with these abnormal white blood cells documented in their circulation. He began to experience pangs of guilt, for he, through no fault of his own, had unwittingly been part of enabling this vile fatal disease. He continued, "As a young enlisted man, should I have argued more strongly in proposing the reality of this dismissed fatal finding to my superiors? Had I been subjugated by the military culture?"

Matt dwelled on the fact that sadly there were three identical patient deaths from mid- to late-1971. All three were associated with the same abnormal macrophage, without a connection made among them. Perhaps the same tragic ending could have been prevented for the thirty-one-hundred poor souls who died identically in the intervening years summarized in a CDC review published in February 1978. Am I responsible for those deaths?

He felt a heaviness in his chest, coupled with anxiety. Was this mystery beyond the scope of his ability? Exhaustion from lack of sleep due to the distraction of the task's multiple factors diluted his mental stability. There was an overpowering compulsion to assuage his guilt and a need for several relaxing drinks. Maggie was on his case for his increased alcohol intake. He considered rekindling his smoking habit. The memory of how hard it had been to quit dissuaded him.

CHAPTER 13

A letter from the Blitts regarding a Vietnam hospital reunion was awaiting him when he arrived home to Milwaukee from his visit with Declan Burke. Matt was anxious to attend the first 85th Evac reunion.

In the spring of 1982, Declan, Casey Blitt, the 85th Evac anesthesiologist and his wife Kathy, whom he met in Vietnam, embarked upon completing the arrangements to have the first 85th Evacuation Hospital '70-'71 reunion in San Diego, California. They searched for as many hospital veterans from that period as they could find and arranged for discounted rooms in a nearby motel. The reunion group participated in a program for interactive healing and information sharing. Venues for dinners were reserved, and organized tours of the San Diego Zoo and an aircraft carrier were confirmed. Due to their brotherhood, that September's gathering was a huge success, and the reunion was to become a biannual event.

Twelve years have elapsed since most attendee veterans had been able to interact and reach out to touch their beloved brothers and sisters. Binding emotional relationships persisted. They were somewhat rescued from the dark cloud suffocating them with the reality of war. They embraced and wept. Duane confided to Matt, "I've not felt so comfortable with myself and others since I left Vietnam. I finally feel welcomed home."

There were both male and female nurses, corpsmen, MD and nurse anesthesiologists, internal medicine doctors and trauma surgeons, and a pharmacist. All had been on a first-name basis at the 85th Evacuation, and all were equals. Tree (Dave Anderson) recalled, "Rank was bullshit. We worked well together out of respect, not intimidation. The wounded and sick were the reason we were there."

"Amen to that" was the group's response.

Back in the U.S. were the wives who, terrified of their husband's demise, suffered while keeping it together at home and continued to foster the perception of normality for their children.

"It's comforting to be with women who had the same experience in sharing stress, fears, and emotions. Especially reconnecting with the forever changed husband who returned," shared Fred's wife, Beverly.

Everyone was anxious to share their Vietnam slides. The songs they listened to in Vietnam were played over and over in the background: CCR, Animals, Country Joe, Rolling Stones, Edwin Starr, Sly, Three Dog Night and others. There was a Saturday morning breakfast session wherein formalized slide presentations reminded the veterans of the compound's physical layout, the hospital veterans who were not there, the horrors of modern warfare, and the radical surgery required to address the extent of the injury.

Declan had related during his presentation that, "The repairing of blood vessel injuries by a direct end to end suture or utilizing a portion of vein to bridge an injured gap in the vessel was routine for us in 1971." In WWII, one did not consider surgical repair, and ligation controlled major vessels. That choice resulted in a twenty-five percent amputation rate. In Korea, vascular surgery was in its infancy.

After the scheduled presentations, groups of veterans gathered and continued to bare their souls and share experiences, both from Vietnam and readjusting to home. They accepted that all veterans had become a unique segment of US society. They had served in a combat zone and were forever changed. Few non-veterans would understand.

One of the corpsmen shared with his neighboring veterans, "The realization that I do not demonstrate PTSD and can rationalize and handle my feelings from being exposed to that fucked up war, it's reassuring."

All agreed that they would reach out and recruit as many 85th Evac veterans as possible, continue to keep in touch, and meet biannually.

Kathy responded, "We'll make the arrangements again."

Declan, Duane, Mike, Casey, and the 85th Evac group shared what little they knew of the lethal white blood cell illness and committed to creating a progressive force of fellow veterans and outside experts to advance the understanding of this dreadful mystery illness.

CHAPTER 14

Matt considered, do I have the mental and physical strength to complete my quest? He dismissed his self-doubt and prepared for his next interview. In the Milwaukee Inquirer's archives, he reviewed a very inclusive June 1984 article in the New York Times Magazine featuring Jesse Holt. He was now the Managing Partner of Washington's premier consulting firm, Donoghue, Casano, and Rapello. He discovered that in the early 1970s, a much younger Jesse sought to advance his career. His position was that of a low-level thirty-something member of Minnesota's United States Congressman Wes Doughty's staff. To enhance his brand, he developed a thesis in 1972 to elucidate what was causing the unexplained macrophage white blood cell changes and the resulting infectious deaths.

He had grown up on a small farm in Winston, Minnesota, was a football hero at Winston High School, and graduated summa cum laude from Harvard with a degree in economics. At Stanford, he successfully defended his PhD thesis on the Russian rationale and strategy to continue its worldwide proxy wars with the United States. He excelled at club rugby in college. At 6'4" and 220 pounds of toned muscle, he towered over most of his associates and used his bulk to intimidate by invading his adversary's personal space. Dating beautiful women and getting laid on the first date was routine. He knew how to dress for any occasion and was a charming conversationalist.

"I'm on my way," he'd say as he viewed himself in his bedroom mirror while dressing for the day. He nurtured political aspirations beyond those of the most reasonable aspirant. He charted a roadmap and timeline to become one of the two senators representing Minnesota by age forty-two. Jesse was convinced, along with most in Washington, that Russia, along with China, pursued a proxy war in Vietnam by supporting the North Vietnamese and their allies, the southern Viet Cong guerrilla fighters. He thoroughly digested a 1962 Russian academic paper in the *Journal of Applied Research in Chemical Influence of Human Disease* which described an almost untraceable poison designed by Russian chemists, X-34, that produced severe skin rashes in test subjects, i.e., Siberian gulag prisoners. Within a few days, the affected skin would break down, resulting in purulent gangrenous destruction of tissue. Jesse's hypothesis proposed that the Russian government secretly supplied X-34 to Hanoi in an attempt to further their war effort. Selective dispersal of this poison throughout South Vietnam would attack and disable US and South Vietnamese soldiers, reducing enemy fighting strength.

The basis of his theory rested on the absolute success of the enemy's Ho Chi Minh Trail through Laos and Cambodia along the western border of Vietnam. Hanoi, i.e., North Vietnam, utilized this supply route, actually more like a rough hiking trail through intimidating terrain, to resupply men and material where needed. This Herculean effort successfully sustained the combined North Vietnamese Army and Viet Cong campaign against the Americans and South Vietnamese troops in South Vietnam. To the chagrin and embarrassment of the powerful US military planners, repeated bombing had no effect on the Trail's efficiency. Any resultant damage was quickly repaired by those utilizing this thoroughfare.

With a little imagination, Jesse's theory seized upon the existence of a clandestine communist program that introduced this horrific Russian toxin, X-34, into South Vietnam from Hanoi. This subterfuge utilized carefully selected and trained NVA officers to transport this new weapon. They traveled down the Ho Chi Minh Trail, along the length of South Vietnam, and reached their objective disguised as the men and women who labored to transport rice, ammunition, cannons, and medical supplies by foot, bicycle, cart, and truck which supported the communist war effort.

Jesse's theory continued that the NVA commanders in the field were ethical and professional soldiers who refused to disperse the toxin. The Viet

Cong fighters who were mostly peasants displaced by bombing, US fighting forces, and the spraying of the defoliant, Agent Orange, were eager to even the score.

During the day, the VC roamed the countryside freely, appearing as harmless citizen peasants. They worked on military bases, engaging in activities not performed by our enlisted men. They cooked in mess halls, cut hair in barbershops, and cleaned the troops' living quarters called hooches which were made of plywood with a thin metal roof. The local Vietnamese also stocked the shelves in the PX and interpreted conversations with the Americans. A majority of those employed were VC sympathizers eager to gather information about the personnel and logistics of the military bases and pass it on to the area VC commander. They had ample opportunity to memorize and later document the layout of a base's compound, the number of soldiers, and equipment levels. These enemy sympathizers had almost total access to all aspects of the everyday functioning and planning at our military installations.

Jesse's theory continued that the VC introduced X-34 into food served in the mess halls, thus exposing our troops. He recruited like-minded academic types reputed to be knowledgeable in Russian toxin research. The Senate Armed Services Committee accepted the plausibility of his toxin theory. Jesse informed a group of senators, "This is the real deal."

In the early 1970s, the Department of Defense had been bearing the embarrassment of not preventing the unrelenting number of gangrenous deaths. The Joint Chiefs entertained Jesse's theory, and they quickly introduced measures to investigate its validity. The military developed plans to hinder the delivery of the Russian toxin by increasing the ineffectual B-52 bombing runs over the Ho Chi Minh Trail. They knew this action would not have an impact, however, the US Air Force complied with the order.

Since there were no known samples available, a test to identify the substance in the field was impossible. All the strategies deployed depended on what seemed to be credible inferences proposed by the best and the brightest governmental minions. Opinion papers appeared, and political support was sought. The public interest peeked through surreptitiously leaked committee reports. Russian toxin, X-34, became a household word. The blame game was in high gear. Demonstrators would shout in unison, "Nuke the Soviet Union."

Once the feeding frenzy subsided, not too many Washington insiders were surprised that the quest came to a dead end. No tangible proof substantiated that there existed a Russian toxin.

Jesse became a liability to his boss, the Congressman, and Washington. He fled Washington following his dismissal. After multiple job searches, he was happy to accept a position teaching economics at Fulton-Montgomery Community College, thirty miles west of Albany, just off the New York State Thruway at Exit 27. Ironically, Richard Burrows was buried next to his grandparents five miles from this college in St. Mary's Cemetery, which overlooked New York State's historic and beautiful Mohawk River and Valley.

During his extensive research, Matt was alerted to information on another toxin theory. This one originated in the Korean War. He decided to return to Jesse's story after he tracked down this new lead. He scheduled a return trip to Washington to follow some quality time at home with Maggie and the twins.

"I have to get home and recharge. Maggie is showing signs of stress due to my extended absences. I've missed too many days with the twins."

CHAPTER 15

Back in DC, as Matt sifted through the Library of Congress' documents on the use of toxic chemicals in warfare, he discovered that Senator David Sokolov had headed a congressional subcommittee investigating an accusation of China utilizing a toxin against the Americans during the Korean War, another proxy war. He found valuable information reported in the November 11, 1984 Washington Post, which profiled the rising star of California Senator David Sokolov, a Korean War veteran, whom they praised as a strong presidential contender for the 1988 election. As Matt eagerly read, he entered the realm of American global politics combined with a history lesson on Korea and China.

He learned that the communist Chinese had supplied material and committed ground troops to bolster the North Korean effort against the United States during the Korean War in the early 1950s. This support had quickly repelled the conquering United Nations forces from the Chinese/Korean border. It resulted in the retreat of the 1st Marine Division from the northern Chosin Reservoir back into South Korea.

In July 1953, a negotiated peace treaty declared that South Korea continued to remain sovereign due to the bloody and predominantly American effort. Since then, the UN has maintained a deterrent force of 40,000 troops, fully equipped, to reinforce the Demilitarize Zone (DMZ) intent and participate in joint military exercises with South Korea.

Digging deeper into China's history, Matt learned that after the close of World War II, the Chinese Civil War ended with the Chinese Communist Party, led by Mao Zedong, defeating the Nationalist government of Chiang Kai-shek, who retreated to Taiwan with his followers. The United States supported Chiang resulting in an adversarial relationship between Mao and the U.S. We trained the Taiwanese military in Vietnam, and Mao sided with the Hanoi communists in China's proxy war against United States in Southeast Asia. China was actively contributing economic and military aid to Ho Chi Minh's effort to conquer South Vietnam and unify Indochina. In South Vietnam, there were massive communist troop losses from fighting the Americans. Additional North Vietnamese fighters were conscripted into the NVA and shipped south as reinforcements to sustain troop strength. To replace this civilian loss, China sent 300,000 troops to Hanoi to replace the workforce required to keep the country's infrastructure functioning.

Matt then discovered a review of Army veterans who had served their country as military combatants in Korea and who upon returning home sought and attained national office as Congressmen and Senators. Their group was called the Korean War Veteran Council. They began a movement in 1961 to uncover China's possible involvement in the causation of a disease affecting American troops fighting in Korea that started as a rash and progressed to severe blistering of the skin.

As Matt had previously learned, early in the Korean War, General MacArthur's forces had pushed the North Koreans in retreat up against the Chinese/Korean border at the Yalu River.

China, fearing an invasion, then decisively entered the war. The veterans speculated that, as the massive surge of Chinese Reds was pushing the American and NATO forces back from China's border with North Korea, some of their buddies were sickened due to contact with a weaponized toxic substance. These senators and members of Congress who had served in Korea had firsthand knowledge of a rash developing on exposed skin that progressed into a blistering infection with at times, full thickness, third-degree skin loss. They did not recall any deaths. But they were convinced that enemy artillery delivered a tasteless and odorless toxic chemical that caused skin destruction leading to soldiers' disability.

In a 1962 politically shrewd move and with much fanfare, California's young senator, David Sokolov, had formed a Senate subcommittee that investigated the accusation that China had developed a toxic debilitating chemical agent for use in the Korean War. They allegedly had supplied it to the North Korean Army for dispersing against UN and American forces utilizing the hypersonic explosions of artillery, RPGs, grenades, and booby traps.

The American public predictably became angry and protested. College students reacted by shunning most Asians, and derogatory slogans appeared on placards. Conspiracy theories abounded. Discussions led by talking heads raged on TV networks and public radio.

Eventually, research chemists utilizing sophisticated analytical equipment could not corroborate nor define a responsible substance. All specimens from an extensive search of combat area Korean soil samples, clothing and equipment remnants, and even from confiscated Chinese chemicals smuggled into the U.S. were free of toxin.

The headlines of media across the U.S. proclaimed that Senator Sokolov and his subcommittee exonerated China. They had not used lethal toxins, i.e., chemical warfare, to fight the Americans. Anti-Chinese rhetoric gradually subsided. This publicized coupe would be useful to the senator in future political dealings.

Matt realized at this point that he was flying solo. Yes, there were others with a genuine interest in the deadly Vietnam illness, but they were not turning their lives upside down to investigate the depths of that tragic disease. To assuage his guilt of allowing the delay of the vile disease's diagnosis by not challenging military authority when he first described the abnormal macrophages in Vietnam, he felt compelled to continue his quest. A cloud of increasing strain levitated over his home. Maggie was spending more time at her mother's. He believed that a commitment of just a little more time to his investigation would lead to a definitive answer and solve his domestic problem.

Matt knew he had to better understand China's political, economic, and cultural history to place Senator Sokolov's influence in perspective. Matt's gut feeling led him to incriminate this powerful senator as a prime suspect responsible for the white blood cell catastrophe.

Undaunted, Matt continued his research. He uncovered Mao's Great Leap programs to introduce collective farming from 1958 to 1962 that had failed to forestall the Great Famine in the People's Republic of China. The political influence of the influential communist leaders, Liu Shaoqi and Deng Xiaoping, was on the rise, and they set out to reform the economy and open working foreign markets. China was already importing industrial fertilizer and pesticides from the West.

In China, there existed massive unemployment. Farmers' families forcibly displaced from their land, due to the Great Leap relocation program, were now residing in the cities at subsistence levels. The communist leaders, Liu and Deng, began to entertain and expound a capitalist idea to put these unemployed individuals to work by increasing foreign investment and encouraging international offshore manufacturing in China.

Matt uncovered informative New York Times articles from the mid-1960s. They reported that California's Senator Sokolov was especially thrilled by his subcommittee's conclusion that there was no connection between China, a toxic chemical, and the presumed skin disease reported by American Korean Veterans. Matt investigated the senator's finances and discovered that the political contributions of the wealthy individuals who sat on the various Big Pharma boards financially supported Sokolov's activities. These large companies were planning on expanding pharmaceutical production to mainland China. The cost savings would be phenomenal!

It became evident to Matt that the senator had abided by the wishes of influential Big Pharma board members. With much fanfare, he had publicly warned our nation of a Chinese threat reported by Korean War veterans of the dispersal by weapons of a toxic chemical that sickened our soldiers. He then rode in on his white horse to have the threats investigated and dismissed by his Senate subcommittee. This manipulation eliminated any source of resistance to a proposal by the US Congress to implement offshore manufacturing in China.

Matt had confirmed the subterfuge. Senator Sokolov had created the perception of a public crisis in the Chinese poisoning of our troops fighting in Korea. He was quite sure this politician knew the claim was bogus, established a commission to study the spurious accusations, and benefited financially and politically when no crisis was substantiated. Sources revealed that emissaries from the senator traveled to Beijing and presented Liu and Deng with a guarantee. The companies Sokolov represented would solve the Chinese unemployment problem by engaging thousands of jobless citizens. The Chinese officials involved in the negotiations envisioned creating enviable wealth for China's elite through these cooperative offshore endeavors. The New York Times predicted that Big Pharma's China deal would make China's leaders, Liu and Deng, very wealthy men.

CHAPTER 16

Matt completed his research at the Library of Congress into Senator Sokolov's offshore trading with China and Big Pharma's interest. Knowing that he would be in DC, he had called Declan to arrange further sharing of experiences once he had finished up at the library. Matt wanted to get to know and understand Declan more intimately. There was so much more information for the surgeon to reveal about himself and the fatal infectious disease.

Since Roger King was on call for their practice, Declan quickly cleared his morning schedule. He and Matt shared a few unhealthy doughnuts and coffee. Both were relaxed and comfortable in the other's company.

He said to Matt, "There should be no interruptions."

Matt asked, "When did you team up with Doctor King?"

"Here's the story," Declan replied.

"Please do so," said Matt.

Declan began by returning to 1976. Within five years of establishing his practice, Dr. Burke's general and vascular surgical practice was beginning to flourish. He had become so busy that he wished for more downtime with his family. His wife, Carol, pleaded, "The kids miss their dad. You have to be around more!"

To ease any tension Carol served a fruity Pinot from a Washington State vineyard, a favorite of theirs.

"I miss you too. I'll make some changes," he had promised.

Declan said, "My stress level has increased. I spend less time engaging my patients and I'm in a rush all the time."

Surgery was becoming a job rather than the rewarding profession he had fostered. A change was necessary to maintain harmony. To that end, he and Roger King, who had completed the same training program at the Medical College of Virginia, joined their practices to accommodate coverage, clerical demands, office space, and billing procedures. Their time at the 85th Evacuation Hospital in Vietnam had overlapped, and their abilities, aptitudes, and lifestyle desires matched perfectly. Both were confident in making this union work after all they had in shared experiences. Roger shook Declan's hand, saying, "I know this partnership will work. Our families are the beneficiaries of our joining forces. Let's do this right."

The partners, Declan Burke and Roger King, were both shaken emotionally a few years after returning home from Vietnam. The April 30, 1975 fall of Saigon deeply disturbed them. Both had successfully self-managed their post-traumatic stress, but with this turn of events, their PTSD began to reemerge. They experienced anger, guilt, anxiety, and disgust. The Vietnam wartime horrors they had witnessed and their inability to rescue all the mortally wounded resurfaced. Few people realized the Vietnam experience permanently scarred the surgeons' psyches. Their wives did, though. They would never view the world as they did before that ordeal. One had to have been there to understand completely.

Declan often confided to Roger and the closest of friends, "I left part of myself there. I return to Vietnam daily. I'm changed forever."

Roger hugged him and said, "I'm, at times, back there too."

Their wives had successfully adjusted to the change in their husbands and were supportive. The first months of family reunion after Vietnam were predictably rough. Realignment of familial responsibilities, reintroduction to the children, accepting new disciplinary boundaries, and PTSD challenges were a few of the hurdles to clear.

In the weeks following the fall of Saigon and the predictable defeat of America's misguided multi-billion-dollar military blunder to impose our will on a third-world country, Declan felt physically ill. Few knew of or suspected his anguish. His surgical diagnostic and operating skills were unaffected. He had succeeded in becoming a champion in burying his distress. "With support from my wife, my partner Roger, close friends, and utilizing rehabilitative lessons learned, I'll get through this," he told the psychiatrist from whom he sought counsel. Declan would not self-medicate with alcohol and pot as he had in Vietnam.

"That would be disastrous!" the therapist added.

Declan admitted to Matt in their conversation, "I became haunted by the intrusive memory of the drug dealing patient, Private Church. I had deemed him adequately recovered for airlifting back to the world. Then his situation deteriorated on the C-141 transport aircraft."

With his customary introspection, he asked, "In my self-assured Vietnam persona, had I missed a subtle signal that would have resulted in a better outcome? Had all my years of intensive and, at times, demeaning surgical training let me down?" His only recourse required him to review every detail of this disease. Declan questioned his guest, "Will we ever discover the truth?"

Matt was both shocked and relieved to hear the surgeon's confession. He thought a doctor learned to be immune to such self-doubt. Declan was suffering identically as he was from perceived past failures.

"I have the same feelings about my time in Vietnam," Matt told Declan.

Declan responded, "We all do."

Declan continued his recollection. Over the past decade, he had assimilated every available detail of the macrophage infectious-killer disease by searching his memory, reviewing detailed surgical notes from Vietnam, and thoroughly digesting the relevant world medical literature. Declan uncovered medical journal communications of similar patients with definite Vietnam and military connections. He identified identical case reports from civilian travel to Southeast and East Asia and other tropical and subtropical climates. Almost eighty-five percent of the articles, most published by the mid-1970s, referenced the now-familiar abnormally engorged macrophages in specimen blood smears of affected patients. Declan had researched the George Washington University Medical Library, the Department of Defense, and the CDC. He visited multiple Internet sites with a new tool, Google, to review the Russian X-34 debacle, any references to wartime toxins, Agent Orange, and mysterious illnesses during the Korean and Vietnam Wars.

When pursuing information on the Korean toxin, he became acquainted with Senator Sokolov's China investigation and its opening the door to offshore manufacturing.

"What the hell, China was involved with the NVA and Viet Cong in Vietnam. They would have murdered me without a second thought," he told Matt, who affirmed, "You're so right," before reaching for his second jelly doughnut.

Declan told Matt he thought he hit the jackpot with the volumes of accumulated information on Agent Orange. He noted references to a predictable contaminating by-product, TCDD, a form of dioxin, created during the manufacturing process overseen by the imposing chemical companies Dow Chemical and Monsanto. This contaminant, TCDD, at only a few parts per trillion, caused cancer in laboratory animals; that is one drop in four million gallons of water. The intent of spraying Agent Orange to completely defoliate the Vietnam jungle resulted in improved visualization of the enemy and denying crops for enemy communist consumption. Every soldier in Vietnam suffered exposure to this poison. The liquid sprayed contained dioxin one million times the concentration that caused cancer in laboratory tests. Declan was astounded that Operation Ranch Hand disseminated 20,000,000 gallons of Agent Orange over South Vietnam. C-121 cargo planes and Hueys flew spraying missions. Grunts sprayed from handheld hoses on land and watercraft. At times, clouds of the stuff, dispersed from the aircraft and handheld apparatus, engulfed our military personnel.

"We'd heard a chopper overhead, looked up, and soon a cloud of slimy yellow-green rain completely covered us," a wounded patient once told Declan.

A Vietnam veteran was quoted on local TV saying, "This stuff sucks!"

He read reports of various cancers and other unexpected illnesses in our Vietnam veterans and congenital disabilities in their children. Dioxin was certainly a diabolically dangerous chemical. Most meaningful to Declan, he had uncovered information detailing the development of malignant white blood cell diseases that afflicted Vietnam veterans and others exposed to this toxic chemical. He had also uncovered the fact that the Veterans Administration shamefully denied the apparent causative relationship of Agent Orange's poison, dioxin, and the development of blood cancers. Most onerously, the VA orchestrated a cover-up and denial of disability compensation to Vietnam veterans suffering and dying from these blood cancers. They did so by front-loading the numbers to be statistically analyzed to include soldiers and Marines that had never served in Vietnam and not exposed to Agent Orange. In doing so, the calculated risk of becoming ill when serving in Vietnam would diminish.

Suffused with excitement, Declan said, "If dioxin was capable of inducing malignant changes in white cells, it surely could be the culprit in the findings of the peculiarly enlarged macrophages bulging with engorged vesicles."

"I agree, wholeheartedly," said Matt and added, "This could be the answer to the fatal rash in the gangrenous disease I'm investigating that haunts my soul."

The new friends finished the remainder of the doughnuts. Matt had to fly back to Milwaukee and clear up some procedural matters at the paper. Declan's schedule was intense for the next week.

He told Matt, "I'll get into it as soon as I have some time."

"Great!" replied the journalist as he rushed out the door to catch his Delta flight back home.

Within a few weeks of meeting with Matt, the surgical load moderated and Declan accrued a slice of free time. Roger would not be swamped with post-op patients. Wishing to better understand the actions of dioxin, he scoured the medical literature at George Washington University's medical library. Following that, he thoroughly reviewed the blood disease archives of the Armed Forces Institute of Pathology and national and international cancer journals.

He was especially impressed with Memorial Sloan Kettering Cancer Center's preeminent hematologist and decided to return to a familiar place.

On a bitterly cold January day in 1984, he flew to New York City to interview Dr. Bob Agostinelli, the recognized world expert in white cell alterations due to exposure to stress, chemicals, and viral, bacterial, and fungal attacks. A decade had passed since Declan had flown into JFK and hailed a taxi to midtown Manhattan. JFK was twice as busy, and the taxi fare was three times more than when he was last there. Luckily the weather, although frigid, cooperated without snowing. The horrendous traffic on Bruckner Boulevard did not cause a delay. The dirty dark-gray salty residue of a recent major snowstorm that had blanketed the Northeast a few days earlier partially obscured the side of the roads. The chalky-white evidence of Department of Public Works (DPW) ice-melting salt covered the pavement. His taxi could not line up with the sidewalk in an opening through the snowbank at York and 69th. He slipped, slid, and lunged onto the sidewalk's crunchy white, calcium chloride crystals recently spread to melt the snow and ice. He remembered from his days attending Cornell University Medical College, that since the monstrously heavy garbage trucks plowed the snow, garbage collection was postponed during and delayed after a significant snowstorm. As he walked past the old apartment he had shared with his new wife, Carol, at 425 East 69th between York and First, he observed the stacks of bundled cardboard and somewhat malodorous overstuffed garbage bags covered with snow. In spite of the ripe aroma, he was comforted by a sense of familiarity and reassurance. He cherished the vivid memories of walking these streets and enjoyed fond recollections of classmates.

In June 1965, graduation relieved all of them from the self-imposed pressure of living up to the medical school's expectations. Familiar with the layout of MSKCC, having rotated through a pathology elective there as a medical student, Declan felt comfortable. He once again noticed the lingering aura of the stigma of cancer engulfing him. He quickly found Dr. Bob Agostinelli's office and was warmly received by his secretary.

She inquired, "Good morning, Dr. Burke, would you like some coffee?"

The MSKCC expert consultant had diligently reviewed all the resources Declan had sent him. Bob admitted, "In spite of all the material you sent me and discussions with my colleagues, I can't help. I consulted Dr. Richard Silver, the distinguished Professor of Hematology at Cornell University Medical College and New York. He, too, was stumped."

Bob was not able to enlighten Declan with specific information directly linking Agent Orange's dioxin to the macrophage changes noted in patients suffering from the lethal gangrenous disease. However, he was captivated by the histories of the affected patients. He was interested in their blood smear findings and the rapidity of their demise. They exchanged multiple hypotheses that could be of relevance and pledged, in the future, to share pertinent information.

In spite of not learning of a positive correlation between dioxin and the abnormal macrophages he wished to elucidate, Declan felt his trip was a success. His mind was now spinning with new avenues of investigation to pursue. Dr. Agostinelli's intense interest reinforced the worthiness of his quest to explain the gangrenous disease.

In the late afternoon, he arrived back at JFK with time to spare before his 4:38 p.m. departure on American Airlines, flight number 4252, for the forty-eight-minute trip to Washington National Airport. He called Matt from the airport and recapped his meeting with Dr. Agostinelli at MSKCC. It was most probable that Agent Orange was not responsible for the distortion of the macrophages. He bragged to Matt, "I'll indulge himself with a spicy Bloody Mary and juicy hamburger at the airport's Greenwich Village Bistro."

"They were the best. Is that place still there?" replied Matt.

"I hope so," Declan responded.

It had been a long day, and Declan fell asleep soon after fastening his seat belt. He awoke from a sound sleep as the plane jolted slightly upon landing safely in Washington, DC.

CHAPTER 17

Matt's primary interview with Vietnam veteran and PhD candidate, Ryan Larkin, was in 1983 at Washington University in St. Louis. Since then, they had frequently communicated by email. They exchanged pertinent information. Matt continued to develop his chronological thesis.

Matt learned from Ryan in their first meeting that back in 1973 after his Vietnam tour and before discharge from the Army, Specialist Larkin was ordered to Fort Carson in Colorado Springs, for six months as a supervisory laboratory technician. He presided over the analysis of all types of bodily fluids. During his time in the Army, he had interpreted thousands of blood smears.

In his third month, a junior technician alerted him to a smear which demonstrated strikingly enlarged macrophages bulging with engorged vesicles. As if struck by a bolt of lightning, he said to his junior tech, "I've seen these grossly abnormal macrophage white blood cells before!"

He searched his memory for where, when, and in what circumstance? Which patient was involved?

It was 1972 in Vietnam in an 85th Evacuation Hospital post-surgical trauma patient who, although appeared well when readied for aeromedical evacuation, died within a week of arriving at Tachikawa Army Hospital, Japan. Ryan had inquired if anyone else in Ft. Carson's lab observed these changes. He flinched at the resounding affirmative response.

A few personal but mostly hearsay accounts reported by the lab's men and women who all served in Vietnam declared that the dramatic white blood cell changes delivered the kiss of death for a patient. This response reflected a summation of shared information gathered from many duty stations within the armed services, not only in Vietnam but around the world. Current information confirmed that a number of patients with the fatal disease have been reported stateside. These were in addition to Private Richard P. Burrows' death at Walter Reed Army Hospital.

Ryan tracked down the Fort Carson patient's location on the surgical ward and discovered that he was recovering from an abdominal stab wound incurred in an off-base bar fight. The victim had complained recently of a red rash that appeared enveloping the margins of his well-healed abdominal incision. To Ryan's relief, the skin changes were fading after his aggressive surgeon, Mel Abend who had served in Vietnam placed him on powerful intravenous antibiotics and applied warm soaks to the abdominal wound. By the second day of treatment, the rash area had subsided and was replaced with burnt sienna-colored healthy skin. This kid just dodged a lethal bullet.

Ryan knew that only committed research would defeat this potentially deadly disease.

In the ensuing months, his separation from military service and plans took precedence over all other issues. Just about everyone he knew at Ft. Carson had been in Vietnam. Ryan was especially relieved to have the occasion to interact with other men and women who served at various Vietnam medical facilities. They spoke the same language from sharing identical experiences.

Ryan was grateful that over several orders of Coors when entertaining themselves after duty hours, these veterans began to decompress by volunteering to share their exposure to the horrors of war. Some of the specialists and corpsmen experienced combat before their medical lab posting. Others remembered the traumatic injuries they encountered in the ED, X-Ray, and operating rooms. In baring their souls, discussions overcame boundaries. For some, eliminating stress aided by imbibing alcohol and smoking the ubiquitous pot helped with their rehabilitation and re-entry into a peaceful society.

Abnormal white blood cells, skin rashes, and horrible deaths became relegated to the innermost recesses of Specialist Larkin's brain.

Ryan continued his narrative with Matt by relating that he had earned a degree from North Carolina State in biochemistry before his military service. Having completed his two-year active duty obligation following Vietnam, Ryan's interest in investigative medicine had drawn him to pursue a PhD in biochemical engineering at Washington University in St. Louis.

"My GI Bill came in handy to defer most of the cost," Ryan said, breathing deeply and abruptly standing to pace about his office. The discussion with Matt triggered a moderate degree of PTSD anxiety, self-doubt, and hypervigilance. Ryan knew he must return to the gym, explain his feelings to his girlfriend, and read his favorite comforting Bible passages. Down this road before, through trial and error, he worked out the solutions he would utilize.

Matt counseled, "We have no choice but to titrate our emotions to keep our PTSD under control. I do understand."

Ryan confessed, "I'll not marry for I'm too damaged." He disclosed that he enjoys the company of attractive women. He lived with a few for six months or so but did not wish to accept the emotional responsibility required to be a faithful and supportive husband. He was terrified of having children; he knew he could not guarantee their safety and success. Ryan planned to be married to his work and not expose himself to the mysteries of family. He would drive fast cars and live on the edge for a while.

Matt said, "That attitude reflects unresolved PTSD."

"I know. But it'll never be fully resolved. Why expose a family to the repercussions of my weaknesses that evolved in Vietnam?" he said and added, "I was a loner as a child; I prefer it that way."

"I give you a lot of credit for your choice," Matt responded. "That is a difficult choice."

"Not so much so when I reflect on my alcoholic uncle who destroyed his family." Ryan conceded. "I must not have that first drink. My AA sponsor is a solid Vietnam vet." he offered.

CHAPTER 18

Having caught up with Ryan Larkin, Matt contacted Jesse Holt by phone in his DC office. He explained his colleges' interest in the deadly Vietnam disease and his wish to discuss what happened after the generalized rejection of his Russian hypothesis. He made an appointment to interview both him and his wife, Kim, at Jesse's DC office.

Holt greeted Matt, "Welcome to DC. May I introduce my wife, Kim."

Matt entered the room and greeted her, "My pleasure. I'm anxious to hear what you have to say about all this."

"Thank you for including me," she responded as she gracefully seated herself at the conference table.

Matt took his coat off and accepted the invitation to pour himself a cup of coffee. He knew better, but he scooped two teaspoons of sugar and used half-and-half. He was putting on the pounds associated with traveling to interviews and dining out with his subjects.

With an embarrassed smile, Jesse began his story. As the disenfranchised athletic whiz-kid with the unsubstantiated theory of the Russian toxin sickening our troops in Vietnam, he understood that his reputation must be rehabilitated in the field of economics if he were to advance his career. He needed to refresh his resume after a three-year stint teaching in forced banishment at Fulton-Montgomery Community College, near Amsterdam, NY. He completed a post-doc at SUNY Albany just thirty-five miles east of Amsterdam in New York State's capital city. His field of concentration was the pharmaceutical industry's fiduciary streamlining for maximum profit. After a round of interviews, he accepted an offer at the Washington, DC, consulting firm, Donoghue, Casano, and Rapello, which specialized in marketing Big Pharma. His previous Washington experience benefited him, for he now understood the ground rules of interactions in the DC environment.

Approaching age thirty-two, Jesse decided it was time to settle down. On a business trip to New York, he met Kim during happy hour at Pastis in the City's Meatpacking District. She was an amazingly vivacious and intelligent woman from Amsterdam, NY who worked in the Big Apple as an informational conference organizer.

Kim inserted, "At first, I thought he was an obnoxious ass." She continued, "Once he relaxed and lost his attitude, I realized he was quite nice and a good person with a strong family orientation."

Jesse could not resist, "Yeah, she loved the idea I was a jock. In college, she dated the captains of all the major teams."

Matt then learned that as social chairman of her sorority, she began expanding her network during her time at Cornell University, nestled on the iconic green rolling hills above Cayuga Lake in central New York State. She mastered the skill of engaging in pragmatic networking which enabled her to succeed in the very competitive conferencing industry.

"After dating for two years," she added, "the attraction and respect between us blossomed."

"Never experienced that unity before," Jesse added.

With a short engagement, they married on June 29, 1983 in St. Mary's Roman Catholic Church in Amsterdam, NY. Jesse knew the area well from his years of teaching at nearby FMCC and studying for his post-doc down the road in Albany, NY.

On their wedding day, the sun glowed on the light-yellow exterior of the sturdy church. An off-white trim enclosed large windows with multiple panes, aligned along the exterior walls depicting the Stations of the Cross. The brown-gray tiled roof was pitched at a thirty-degree angle to shed the relentless upstate New York winter snowfall. The welcoming mahogany stained front doors opened to a warm space under the organ's balcony. Well-used carpeting dressed the floors. The church's wooden pews reflected many decades of regular use. There were scars, indentations, and evidence of repeated varnishing. The air held the lingering scent of incense. Tuxedoed groomsmen escorted the guests to seats on either the bride's or groom's side.

The original altar was tastefully ornate but now unused. A second austere alter was closer to the congregation and the priest now faced forward. This reorientation was introduced in the 1960s to have those attending mass to become more involved.

Everything was ready.

Kim related to Matt, "I was distraught as billowing dark clouds invaded the late morning's mostly sunny sky."

Matt gasped, "Oh, oh." He remembered the rain at his wedding.

During the wedding ceremony, the heavens did open with a deluge of densely packed mega-sized raindrops whose violent discordant impacts echoed from the parking lot asphalt, automobile hoods, the church's roof, and the nearby sidewalk. Father Gulley, who was officiating, paused and proclaimed to the gathering, "Not only is this downpour good luck but also the rain will cease by the completion of the ceremony."

"To my delight, the skies did clear as Jesse and I, through a shower of birdseed, raced to our white limousine to begin the rest of their lives together," Kim gushed. Following the rain, a fresh, crisp, and earthy scent wafted through the church.

Her dear childhood friend and the late Private Richard Burrows' high school sweetheart and fiancée, Michelle, eventually married and now lived in Virginia. Michelle and her husband, Jon, along with Michelle's parents and Richard's mom and dad, attended the wedding and sat with the bride's guests in the church and at the reception at the Ramada in Saratoga Springs, NY.

The wedding reception belonged to Kim and Jesse. But actually, Kim's mother enjoyed presenting her biggest party ever.

There were all the amenities the most discerning guest would expect. The *pièce de résistance* near the dance floor was an umbrella-shaded dessert ice cream cart of many flavors from the local Ben and Jerry's, inviting all to design their unique mouthwatering sundae.

Richard, a gentleman of Jesse's father's age, introduced himself as both he and the groom waited in line to construct their delicious desserts.

The stranger said, "This is a wonderful day, my best wishes. You could not have married a more wonderful girl."

Richard explained that he knew Kim well, for as a teenager, she spent many hours at his home in Amsterdam, NY. He then elucidated that his son, Richard Jr., was one of Kim's closest childhood friends but that he had died from wounds suffered in Vietnam. He lamented that his son had recovered from his combat injuries at Walter Reed Army Medical Center in Washington, DC, when a few days from discharge to return home to marry his life's love, Michelle, a vicious course of events took his life in a matter of days. It began as a rash that progressed to his son's gruesome death.

Jesse Holt confessed to Matt, "I was shocked as my mind made the connection. His son represented one of the first patients known to die from the dreaded disease that was known to demonstrate the abnormal macrophage white blood cells."

Matt remained silent.

Kim then added, "Jesse became ashen and lightheaded." His unfilled Sunday dish crashed to the parquet floor. A piercing, high-pitched sound echoed through the Ramada's guest-filled grand ballroom as the empty glass bowl impacted with the floor. A lower-pitched signal emitted as the abandoned Sunday dish bounced several times, wobbled unevenly, and finally fell silent as it settled on the reflective wooden parquet floor.

Jesse added to Matt, "My knees began to buckle beneath me in this déjà vu moment. Several men in line noticed I was about to pass out and guided me to a chair, placing my head between my knees."

Those wedding guests nearby smiled and assumed Jesse was just having too good a time at his wedding reception. Jesse reported that he, the shaken groom, quickly regained his composure and self-consciously retrieved his unbroken ice cream sundae dish from the parquet floor. He added, "I shed the embarrassment and expressed sincere sympathy to Mr. Burrows in dealing with his son's death. My head was spinning as I recalled the wild ride over pursuing an explanation for the root cause of Private Burrows' vile demise by expounding my theory of the Russian toxin."

After finally recovering from his chance meeting of Private Burrows' dad, Jesse rejoined Kim at the bride's table. He found pleasure in his delightful ice cream sundae and enjoyed the remainder of their wedding reception. An after-glow party continued until four in the morning in her parents' imposing penthouse suite in the Ramada. By then, her mom and dad declared exhaustion and sent everyone packing so that they could get a few hours' sleep before sun-up. They knew Kim would be knocking at their door about that time to coordinate guests' names with the gifts and checks she and Jesse had received. Doing so expedited their thank-you note responsibility.

The next morning after breakfast they were driven to the Albany, NY airport for a flight to JFK and a connection to Paris. Jesse and Kim's honeymoon morphed into an extraordinary experience. They loved the city of Paris and its history and knew that in the future, they would return often.

Kim had declared to Jesse, "I love being here with you." Jesse beamed as they strolled through the Arc de Triomphe and down the Champs-Elysees with a stop at Cartier and lunch at Le Gabriel, a dream come true. Their exquisitely quaint room at the Hotel Regina on the Rue de Rivoli, adorned with sloped ceilings and curtained dormer windows, faced the Louvre and presented a view of the distant Eiffel Tower presiding over Paris. They strolled through Notre Dame Cathedral on its island in the Seine, immersed themselves in Monet's art at the Musée de l'Orangerie, and visited opulent Versailles with its thoroughly enjoyable gardens. All too soon, they were back to work in the Washington, DC area. Kim relocated her conference consulting firm there and planned to expand into Jesse's area of expertise, the pharmaceutical industry.

Jesse had informed Kim, "I've rehabilitated my future, and my career path is on track." She had responded, "Our careers are complementary."

Jesse was now a rising star at the consulting firm of Donoghue, Casano, Rapello, and advanced the interests of Big Pharma worldwide. Recently assigned to one of the advisory groups that dealt with companies with subdivisions and partnerships overseas, he worked on projects predominantly in China. That market exploded following the inclusion of a rider, added by Senator Sokolov to a Veterans Administration appropriations bill, now law, which white-knighted Chinese producers as the safe generators of chemicals utilized in offshore pharmaceutical production. Jesse knew full well that the major flaw to all this activity was the fox in the henhouse mentality. Ultimately, quality control became self-regulated by those American offshore companies who participated in the manufacturing. Coincidentally, Jesse's consulting group, in which he was a mid-level participant, wined and dined the same Big Pharma board members to whom Senator David Sokolov was fiscally indebted.

CHAPTER 19

After spending a month at home, to Maggie's delight, and dealing with the Milwaukee Inquirer's internal problems, Matt's directed his energy to determine if influence from Senator Sokolov's political activity reflected a culpable influence in the occurrence of this dreaded disease. He intensified his research utilizing a variety of sources. Extensive research moved forward into federal, state, and county records, local and national newspapers, TV and radio interviews, and military records.

So, it went. He never made it to the gym. He continued to eat too many doughnuts.

After intensive study, he uncovered very pertinent information. California's reigning Senator David Sokolov delighted in his 1980 re-election by an overwhelming margin of thirty percent of his state's voters. They benefited royally. Federal legislation now existed that guaranteed the diverting of adequate water to California for the booming agricultural industry. He announced several years ago a major legislative victory to allow vineyards to ship wine directly to out-of-state distributors and individuals. He influenced the world's largest pharmaceutical company to construct a massive facility on five-hundred expensive acres, with favorable tax consequences, just within Oakland County, where the senator resided on a splendid estate. These accomplishments represented a win-win for the county, California, the drug company, and most importantly, Senator Sokolov.

Matt informed Ryan, Declan, and Jesse via email, "His sphere of influence rapidly diffused throughout national politics at a rapid rate. There were discussions of his running for President."

Jesse responded, "This is something I'll look into."

From the politician's correspondence, Matt learned that Sokolov's wish was to position himself for a run at the White House. The senator knew that in 1964, his influence opened the floodgates for manufacturing commodities in China. Big Pharma companies were especially grateful. Profits soared due to low wages and the absence of requirements to fund the social protections of disability and health insurance. The lack of child labor laws, the vast desperate workforce, and the low shipping costs to the U.S. were all inducements to build facilities in the communist People's Republic.

Matt soon confirmed, through official records, Senator Sokolov's successful scheme to use the power of his oversight subcommittee to indemnify the safety of products of foreign Chinese origin and manufacture. This reprieve resulted when China received exoneration when accused of utilizing toxic chemicals during the Korean War. Contributions to the senator's political war chest and the Asian Immigrant Relief Fund from beholding companies were beyond his expectations. He was an ultra-wealthy success story.

Matt discovered an article in Stanford University's Alumni News that celebrated their biggest donors. It reviewed the senator's life and disclosed that Sokolov's father, a newspaper editor, and mother, a history professor, decided to flee Leningrad and Stalin's oppressive and murderous communist rule. They had weathered The Great Purge between 1936 and 1938 and avoided the fate of close educated friends, i.e., forced labor, kidnapping, and mass executions in the name of cleansing the spirit of the communist party.

The 1940 ice pick assassination of Leon Trotsky was the last straw.

In the fall of 1940, young Alexander David Sokolov immigrated with his parents and two younger sisters to the west coast of America just before Hitler's invasion of Russia in July of 1941.

From early on, David's dreams of success and work ethic were unconquerable. To appear more assimilated, he soon established his name as David Sokolov.

His baseball prowess as a solid hitting, speedy second baseman secured him an athletic scholarship to Stanford University, where he excelled academically, majoring in political science. In addition to a stellar Stanford baseball career, he dominated as a collegiate debater and became active in student politics. After graduation, his involvement with speaking and politics morphed into a career in governmental matters at the state level where he created a political action committee to influence the Democratic Party.

A few years after completing a law degree, again at Stanford, and being engaged by a prestigious law firm, he was encouraged to run for Congress in his California district that included Oakland County. The rest is history. He knew how to play the game, and his successes compounded. He had written and continued to write many of the rules of California and national politics.

From a critical media outlet, Matt recovered that David Sokolov consciously accepted his moral decay and quest for power. Each shady deal reinforced his change of attitude.

Interviews with former allies and friends who decided not to be tainted any longer by his political actions confirmed this metamorphosis. They testified he privately announced that he fully embraced the fact that his idealistic moorings of honesty and commitment for the greater good eroded due to the intoxication of power, fame, and fortune. His involvement in governmental issues evolved to be predicated by what was in it for him. Once a significant donation, commensurate with one's financial attainment, resided in his war chest, he would support a constituent's endeavor to initiate change. Matt had confirmed that Senator David Sokolov subsisted as an overtly greedy self-serving egomaniac. His foundation of power rested on an elite gaggle of very wealthy men and women sitting in a plethora of board rooms of Big Pharma, both national and international. Matt realized that they owned him, and he bent to their will. The most dominating force was Attica Ossining Pharmaceutical Corporation, AOP on the New York Stock Exchange listing.

Matt gained access to Sokolov's political opposition's files and other sources. This new information confirmed his previous discovery that in 1963, the senator, as a congressman, surreptitiously had attached a rider to an appropriations bill for funding the Veterans Administration in its endeavor to offer rural outpatient services. This additional language allowed United States pharmaceutical manufacturers in foreign countries to engage local producers to supply ingredients at a more nominal expense for use in bringing their offshore products to market. The most disturbing concession promulgated by the rider was that quality control was to be the US manufacturers' responsibility. Data developed from the company's manufacturing process and reported to their self-serving boards could quickly bury any threatening information in the records of its proceedings. Sokolov's manipulation was a coupe for Big Pharma. It guaranteed cost savings in manufacturing, a financial windfall for this politician, and a potential disaster for the general public.

CHAPTER 20

Matt again experienced burnout and regression into mild PTSD. He told Maggie, "I'll let go of this rat race for three months and rejuvenate."

"You surely need a break, and summer officially begins in a week. The kids would love to go camping up north. We've got all the equipment."

"You're so right," he said and continued, "I'm angered by my investigative findings. Sokolov and Big Pharma are real sleazy crooks."

Not only did Matt take the summer off, but he utilized the fall to review, edit, and organize what information he had accumulated. By Christmas, he felt rejuvenated.

During the early months of 1985, Matt's investigation continued with a review of his newly organized notes for information pertinent to discovering what was going on with the abnormal macrophage white blood cells. Matt's notes revealed that in the last months of 1973, the US military involvement in Southeast Asia had ended, and our nation terminated boots-on-the-ground in that area of the world. Remarkably, at the same time, the number of rash-initiated septic gangrenous death cases associated with this abnormal white blood cell diminished dramatically worldwide. They agreed that now in 1985, ten years after the fall of Saigon, now referred to as Ho Chi Minh City, the number of reported cases of this disease had become inconsequential to medical science and the general public unless a member of one's family or a beloved acquaintance became sickened.

Matt wondered in a quick phone call to Ryan, "What was the explanation for the reprieve from this gruesome disease?"

The scientist said hopefully, " It's got to be out there; we'll find out."

Their deliberations were about to become reality.

Matt received an emotional invitation from Michelle and Jon to visit them at their home in Arlington, Virginia. She wished to update their background information and report a devastating personal loss that would impact research into the abnormal macrophage white blood cell investigation. In the early winter of 1985, Matt sat down one evening with Michelle and Jon at their welcoming home in Alexandria, Virginia, his second visit. Their three girls were out pursuing their interests and friendships.

Michelle sat slumped and very close to Jon for emotional support. Her eyes dejected, her voice subdued, she concentrated on her wedding rings, twisting them with the fingers of her right hand. She admitted her sadness to both men but did not have to since it was so obvious. She had conditioned herself to avoid bringing memories of her dead fiancée into her conscious thought.

It was almost fifteen years since Richard Burrows' death. Michelle related, "My visits back home to Amsterdam, NY ceased once my parents moved to Fayetteville, North Carolina after Dad retired from General Electric Corporation in Schenectady, NY." He was motivated to make this move by the company's wish to downsize in the Rust Belt. GE completed the transfer of the generator shaft production to a southern state whose economic parasitism did not reflect the obscenity as New York State. Her father had confided to Michelle that the separation package GE offered was too good to pass up.

Michelle continued to remember Richard with fondness. She stated, "As my first soulmate, I guess part of me still loves him."

Matt became a little uncomfortable.

Jon then supported her. "That's understandable. It's the quality I love most about you."

She and Jon had purchased a four-bedroom colonial a few years after the birth of their third daughter, Annika, but continued to reside in Alexandria, VA. Their neighborhood was upscale, its school system well regarded, and there existed easy access to downtown DC.

Jon successfully applied his accumulated knowledge and diligent work ethic to each research project for which he accepted responsibility. His career in computer engineering excelled, developing a reputation in sequencing data and machine testing. He secured employment in several start-ups, arranged recompense in mostly stock, and when both new companies were gobbled up by major companies, he profited. They enjoyed financial security.

About a year ago, in mid-1984, recruited by a newly hatched informational giant, InfoServ, he became a crucial figure in a senior managerial position at their new DC area work facility.

He told Matt, "I have financial stability and the probability of advancement in this company."

Their girls, Katya, 12, Sabrina, 10, and Annika, 7, were beautiful young ladies who excelled academically, in equine sports, and fencing. They were also fluent in French and Spanish.

Michelle related, "Jon will only communicate with the girls in French. All videos are in French. Much of their TV programming is in French. Jon has never spoken a word of English to his children."

Jon finished, "I will not answer them if they speak English to me." In fact, their French teacher remarked, "The girls speak their language as if they lived as citizens of France."

Michelle was also fluent in French. After receiving her graduate degree in informational technology from American University, her career morphed. At the request of the Department of Defense, she began liaising with the French government. She elucidated, "I was tasked after a thorough security check to review and improve their weapon guidance systems to become compatible with that of the United States military."

To maintain their language skills, Michelle and Jon socialized within the extensive French-speaking foreign and domestic inhabitants of Alexandria, Virginia, and the DC region. Most of these friends were politically well informed and aware of the shifting global political environment. Matt learned that a selected few, who were free of time constraints and sufficiently funded, belonged Non-Governmental Organizations (NGO). Jon said, "They volunteered their services to improve the plight of indigent populations both within the U.S. and abroad."

"A noble gift," Matt said and added, "May I have another Pepsi?"

Jon returned, "Want anything stronger?"

"No, thank you, I'm tired and driving."

Jon's upbeat persona quickly dissolved into an anguished pained expression. He said, "Matt, we must now tell you the heartbreaking story of our dearest friends, Claire and Guy Marc." Michelle and Jon, each with reawakened sorrowful memories, both contributed to the evolution of their dear friend's story.

Claire, a young native Virginian from Fredericksburg, attended both the University of Virginia and its medical school, after which she completed residency training and was now an accomplished and respected plastic surgeon. In her early forties, tall with dark wavy hair, and Mediterranean skin, blessed with wide-set brown eyes and prominent cheekbones, she engaged all with a comforting smile. Claire enjoyed athletics, excelled at soccer, and enjoyed the outdoors. She met and married a French national with dual citizenship who divided his time between the Loire Valley and DC. Guy Marc represented a French lobbying firm, which plied their influence to detour as many US dollars into his country's economy as possible. The couple was childless.

They decided not to have children in response to a devastating inheritable disease looming in her genetic makeup. Since the long-term effects of subjecting Claire to continuous hormonal birth control were not as yet understood, she underwent a tubal ligation before their marriage.

Claire engaged with children through New Smile, an NGO. She repaired cleft lips and palates of the impoverished children of Ebolowa, a small city at the center of the cocoa trade in southwestern Cameroon, Africa. To her, volunteerism was satisfying, fulfilling, and heart-warming. If she could not bear children, she would commit to improving the appearance and function of these handicapped children. They would never receive treatment if she did not attend them. Claire traveled to the far reaches of the world to administer her skills. Her list included Vietnam, Cambodia, Haiti, Angola, Nigeria, and now, Cameroon. This trip became her third and last excursion to this country's subtropical low altitude region south of its capital city of Yaoundé.

CHAPTER 21

Michelle and Jon continued relating to Matt a story he surmised would soon become sorrowful and upsetting. Jon resumed the narration. "Michelle, you're too upset. I'll continue."

Claire provided her own transportation and selected first-class on a United Airlines eight-hour direct flight out of Washington National Airport to Yaoundé, Cameroon. Her only requirement was to arrive safely on the predetermined date in early-April 1985 with a current passport and up to date immunization record. Replacement surgical equipment and ancillary support items were deployed by the NGO and arrived well ahead of her visit. To guarantee continuity of care, the NGO made arrangements for another plastic surgeon from the Netherlands as a replacement a few days after her scheduled departure from Cameroon once satisfying her pledged commitment.

Guy Marc had expected to participate in a time-consuming complex negotiation among several European countries. Therefore, Claire decided to extend her stay in Cameroon to accommodate the beloved indigent children. Their congenital deformities appeared not only unsightly but also represented functional impairments. She had committed to a time of the year wherein the monsoon season ended, and the more subtropical climate prevailed.

Upon arrival at the Yaoundé Nsimalen International Airport, the smiling, friendly face of the Frenchman, John Morrell, greeted Claire. They embraced, and she shared, "Thank you for always meeting me. I feel so safe in your presence." Morrell, embarrassed and looking at the ground, said, "How would I not do so for our greatest surgeon."

He was a longtime hospital employee. From serving in the French Foreign Legion, he projected a tough, rugged demeanor. Legally armed and carrying a Sig Sauer nine-millimeter semi-automatic pistol, he drove safely and defensively. His soft heart complemented him as her dear friend. He would deliver her safely to the remote hospital compound, a two-and-a-half-hour drive through the desolate, sparsely inhabited countryside south on roadway N-2.

Claire commented, "This drive seems to take longer each time I come here."

"It seems so," he replied.

They could now see the hospital far off on the downslope of a low mountain.

Claire's arrival prompted a celebratory gathering of the staff, for her reputation of caring, excellence, proficiency, and kindness established a benchmark against which all other New Smile NGO physicians were judged. Already posted, her OR schedule of cases for the following day lifted her spirits.

She accepted the fast pace. She previously told Jon when joining Michelle and him for dinner at their home, "My hard work is rewarded, for around the hospital, there resides so many impoverished children in need of my skills and the three-week stay will pass too quickly. The more I treat, the more functional the entire community will be."

"We understand," they replied in unison.

Her accommodations were Spartan. She was accustomed to the scarcity of stateside amenities. Claire faithfully slept under the provided mosquito netting. She swallowed daily the requisite antimalarial prophylaxis, Falciquin. The Ebolowa region of Cameroon was situated below five-thousand-feet of elevation and designated as subtropical. She applied insect repellant. In this warm environment, the Anopheles mosquito, which transmitted the malarial parasite, flourished. Therefore, as advised by the World Health Organization, antimalarial protection was required to prevent this endemic mosquito-transmitted disease with a potentially deadly outcome.

She did have shower facilities albeit communal.

Air conditioning did not exist. The only respite was achieved by directing a powerful electric fan onto oneself. Claire had complained to them, "It only functioned intermittently due to the hospital's temperamental generators." The consolation prize turned out to be enjoying world-class French cuisine served at each meal by the accomplished Mougins trained Frenchman, Chef Steven. A dieting regime was always necessary once back in the States.

The operating rooms existed in canvas tents measuring ten-by-twelve feet. The staff did eliminate dust from the dirt floor by saturating it with used motor oil mixed with diesel fuel. Rough plywood waist-high benches served as operating room tables. The staff functioned with practiced efficiency. Scrub and circulating nurses knew their tasks. The instruments were up to date and thoroughly cleansed in an old sterilizer. There were adequate supplies of IV fluids, sedatives, local anesthetics, and suture materials. A sterile operative field was imperative in preventing infection. If it occurred, the surgical repairs would not only break down but result in a worsened deformity. Paper disposable drapes donated by Johnson-Johnson did the trick. Pre-op sedation was kept to a minimum to aid in early discharge. Follow up was accomplished in the outpatient clinic.

As in the past, Claire's stint in contributing surgical aid to Cameroon's indigent quickly evaporated. After being separated from Guy Marc she happily returned to Alexandria, her husband, her group practice, and her friends. However, before departing, she had requested her newly arrived plastic surgeon replacement from the Netherlands, whom she respected, to excise a suspicious lesion from the small of her back. The ten-minute procedure under local anesthesia was uneventful. The wound healed without a problem.

Matt remained truly captivated by Claire's good works and saintly persona, as related by Michelle and Jon. He sensed and verbalized to the narrating couple, "There is still a sense of foreboding in your story's aura." Beneath the surface and totally beyond Matt's imagination did hide a devastating story.

CHAPTER 22

With heavy hearts, Michelle and Jon continued their story. Arriving back home to Alexandria in early July 1985, Claire experienced a warm greeting by all those who knew her, loved her, and associated with her practice.

She remarked to Jon, "I feel fulfilled when I return from these trips." She immediately began to diet and exercise to shed the extra eight pounds. "This ordeal gets harder each year," she told her trainer.

He retorted, "I'm afraid so."

As she began a rigorous program to achieve a target weight; her body responded with toning and weight loss. She consumed a dietician approved balanced diet to reach her magic number. However, Claire's scale informed her of continuing weight loss after achieving her goal. She challenged the dietitian, "What's going on?" who responded with, "Perhaps I've overly restricted your caloric intake. Let's increase the numbers."

Claire told her, "I'm worried about this weight loss." Claire, home for just over three weeks, began to feel listless and lost her appetite. She shared with Guy Marc, "I'm worried that I'm getting sick."

The following evening, suddenly, her abdomen, which was usually flat and toned, became distended, and she developed intense throbbing pain in the pit of her stomach. There was an inflamed rash on her low back at the excision site. An urgent trip by ambulance to George Washington University's emergency department for evaluation prompted a very concerned demeanor in the ED physician, Jim Farina.

He announced, "I'm arranging for an emergency surgical consultation. There appears to be a major problem in your abdomen."

Guy Marc whispered in desperation, "Oh no."

Claire's somnolence inhibited her response and humanely dulled her senses, thus, avoiding overt fear and panic. Her current environment surrounded Claire with the frenetic activity of a major city emergency room. It was noisy with nurses, technicians, orderlies, candy stripers, and admissions personnel darting about to accomplish their assigned tasks. The color white prevailed on the ceilings, walls, and floors. White coats were ubiquitous. Shiny reflective metal from bedpans, gurneys, crutches, electric beds and wheelchairs dotted the landscape. The resonating metallic ringing of drapes being opened and closed hopefully guaranteed private examinations. Anxious and impatient relatives, concerned friends, and transients conversed, visited, and snacked. The odors of antiseptic, vomit, stool, potato chips, alcohol pads, Italian subs, coffee, among others, invaded one's nostrils. Screams of pain, fear, and despair echoed. Loud phone conversations offended one's need for quiet.

An abdominal CAT scan in the cold, darkened x-ray room on a hard, motorized table, with both oral and intravenous contrast, demonstrated right upper intra-abdominal fluid just below the liver. There was free air outside the confines of the intestine and gas bubbles in the massively thickened wall of a grossly distended gallbladder.

Michelle and Jon spoke to Matt from memory but did have a copy of Claire's George Washington University Hospital chart to which they referred for accuracy. With disquiet, the ED physician reported the CAT scan results to a stricken Claire and Guy Marc.

He said, "I see the fluid of peritonitis, intra-abdominal free gas possibly from a perforated bowel, and a gangrenous, deformed gallbladder." He reinforced the revelation with, "This is very serious!" Dr. Farina informed Guy Marc that Claire was extremely ill. He advised, "To survive, requires immediate surgery to remove infected organs and tissue. The surgery is high risk, and there will be a prolonged and challenging period of recovery." Dr. Farina added a bit of encouragement. "An extremely qualified surgeon is on his way."

"Thank you," responded the depressed and exhausted Guy Marc.

Michelle continued that by the mid-eighties, Declan Burke, MD was considered an established George Washington University Hospital surgeon with an impeccable reputation. He and Roger King reigned as the favorite surgical consultants of many physicians due to their wide-ranging experience and calmness in desperate situations. Claire's illness required such a physician. Currently on call, Declan assumed the responsibility for the current twelve-hour shift. He arrived in the ED within minutes, for he had just made rounds on his patients at the GWU Hospital.

Declan's shared his first impression with the ED physician. "I'm appalled at Claire's dire situation." Within one hour of her ED admission, she had begun to demonstrate signs of sepsis.

He explained to Guy Marc, "Toxic, cell destructive and deadly bacteria have entered her bloodstream and are multiplying throughout her body's tissues and organs in overwhelming numbers." Exercising compassion, he kept to himself that this situation was eminently lethal!

Her blood pressure was falling, blood oxygen levels dropping, and kidney function was deteriorating. Her temperature was 103 degrees, and she was deeply somnolent. This clinical picture required immediate resuscitation with a salt solution, powerful antibiotics, and presser drugs to elevate her blood pressure and aid kidney function. Special measures were taken, such as the monitoring of her blood pressure intra-arterially. A Foley catheter in her urinary bladder measured urine output, and a Swan-Ganz catheter placed into a large vein that entered the heart monitored her heart's capacity to sustain life. All these steps were necessary to supply up to date information to aid the attending doctors in treating Claire's volatile clinical picture, to determine a plan of action during anesthesia, surgery, and in the ICU during her critical management post-operatively. This previously vibrant, joyful, and talented humanitarian was desperately ill and near death.

Guy Marc and his many friends remained devastated.

One clueless spectator stupidly inquired, "Is she going to die, doctor?"

That was not the question Declan wanted to answer; he knew the answer.

CHAPTER 23

Declan understood that if he did not immediately evacuate the extensive infection from Claire's abdominal cavity, she would have absolutely no chance of survival. He announced to those nearby in the operating suite, "I've seen this before. No matter what I do, our patient will probably die"

The OR, usually a talkative space, remained deadly quiet.

Claire presented an enormous surgical risk and a terrible challenge to the most expert anesthesiologist. To Declan's relief, Casey Blitt, MD, had just a few months ago assumed the chairmanship of the anesthesiology department at the George Washington University. He had acted as the chief of that service at the 85th Evacuation Hospital in Vietnam during Declan's tenure. Casey was defined by the words "world-class and unflappable."

Declan notified the OR of the exploratory surgery the moment he witnessed Claire's condition. The seasoned staff prepared for all surgical eventualities relative to this case.

Casey responded that he would supervise the anesthetic administration. Now stationed at Walter Reed Army Hospital, Col. Fred Brockschmidt, RN, the Army nurse anesthetist who also served at the 85th Evac with Declan now moonlighted at GWU. He would administer the anesthesia freeing Casey to survey and treat the global challenges to Claire's survival. Fred and Casey, working as one, successfully managed the most precarious patient scenarios in Vietnam.

Fred confided to Casey, "This is going to be a bitch of a case!"

Blitt agreed, "For sure!"

The induction of anesthesia evolved from rocky to successful. Casey and Fred prevailed. Now the responsibility of Claire's survival resided on Declan's shoulders to work his magic. They capably maintained Claire's anesthetic at just the right level to eliminate pain and recall but not inadvertently introduce over-medication to depress her heart and lung life-sustaining functions.

Prepped with an antiseptic solution and draped with disposable sterile paper sheets, Claire's grotesquely distended abdomen awaited the surgeon's knife. Upon opening a midline incision into the abdomen, a nauseating, purulent foul order engulfed the OR as feculent gases spewed forth from inside her belly. An avalanche of gangrenous tissue from destroyed internal organs gushed from her. Only portions of intact stomach, small intestine, and colon remained recognizable to Declan Burke's practiced surgical eye.

"Oh shit, she's had it!" was all Declan could say. The OR became impossibly quiet.

Only the back wall of the gallbladder remained adherent in its bed on the undersurface of the liver. This organ appeared to be the epicenter of Claire's challenging illness. An infected gallbladder became gangrenous and in bursting, disseminated life-threatening infection throughout her abdominal cavity. This event resulted in the dissolving of a previously healthy stomach, small and large intestine, pancreas, and spleen. Intestinal gases, noted on the CAT scan as free air, were released from her destroyed bowel. This tissue destruction further added to the excessive infectious inflammatory load Claire's body had to deal with to avoid death.

Declan admitted, "I knew it when I first saw her in the ED."

She did not escape the unescapable. This holiest, talented, and beloved physician died late at night in a GWU University operating room in front of caring and saddened but emotionally insulated witnesses. These OR participants would not remain productive if they internalized the deaths that occurred in their presence.

Guy Marc had presumed a successful surgical outcome was possible having been informed of and taken for granted the skill level of those attending Claire. His devastation deepened as he received the news of his beloved's death delivered to him by a stunned Declan Burke, who had no explanation why her infection advanced so rapidly to become a death sentence. Guy Marc was beyond consoling by his dearest friends. He required sedation with an intramuscular injection of Valium. Michelle and Jon were instructed by a nurse to shepherd him home and administer a barbiturate within a few hours to induce sleep. This devastated, grieving husband did not have family members nearby for support. A cadre of friends drew up a schedule to attend him around the clock. He needed and received assistance in contacting his relatives in France and Claire's in Fredericksburg. Friends made arrangements for burial and the church, writing an obituary, and making legal notifications.

"When will I awake from this horrible nightmare? These things are on the news destroying the lives of others. Not us," he lamented.

Absorbing the cruelty of Michelle and Jon's story, although a seasoned, time-tested journalist, an emotionally distraught Matt teared up.

CHAPTER 24

Richard Burrows' first love, Michelle, and her husband, Jon, had accompanied Claire and Guy Marc to the GWU Hospital in the ambulance. They listened to the prediction of a terrible prognosis and supported Guy Marc during Claire's prolonged surgery. They attempted to comfort him when Declan Burke delivered the unimaginably devastating news of Claire's death in a cold operating room. Many friends were committed to supporting Guy Marc with all aspects of life following her death.

Matt knew he must immediately call Declan and interview him again, this time concerning the most traumatic recent event of Claire's death. He would take a taxi to DC and stay overnight at a hotel close to George Washington University Hospital.

Their telephone discussion was brief. Matt and Declan agreed that Claire's illness and death were identical to those they had chronicled from Vietnam and had plagued the world in the early and mid-1970s.

Dr. Declan Burke lamented, "I would like to confirm that Claire succumbed to the same fatal disease that fifteen years ago had taken the lives of Privates Burrows, Jamison, and Church."

Matt added, "We must uncover all commonalities to discover the cause of this dreadful disease."

Declan retorted, "I'm incensed and distraught by Claire's death." He continued, "I feel compelled to investigate and report why these similar travesties occur in those who have visited subtropical countries."

Matt arrived at GW University Hospital a little after 10:00 a.m. Declan awaited him in the surgery department's spacious conference room. The centrally located polished mahogany table and twelve matching formal chairs anchored the room. The continental breakfast residing on a large credenza on the one short wall welcomed him. The opposite wall boasted a sixty-inch TV screen for presentations and teleconferences. The outside floor to ceiling windows displayed a portion of Georgetown and the Washington Monument and Capitol Building in the distance. An extensive surgical library of multi-colored and variously sized texts adorned the remaining wall. An original ornate Persian carpet, predominately in crimson and tan hues, graced the polished narrow-gauge oak floor beneath the elegant meeting table.

Declan appeared devastated and admitted to Matt the extent of the emotional distress that engulfed him following Claire's death. He also related the experience of an astonishing epiphany.

Matt turned on the tape recorder as Dr. Burke began an accounting of his activity in the first few days following Claire's death. Once back in the surgical lounge and alone, after her demise, Declan had sunk into a deep chair, covered his face, and sobbed tears of guilt. He felt disbelief, defeat, and self-recrimination. In that isolation, he had lamented, "I was so outclassed" in a whisper to no one in particular. "A monumentally overwhelming case," he added and continued, "beyond my surgical experience, or was it?"

Declan then experienced an insightful epiphany. He recalled saying," Oh my God! Vietnam!" He remembered the 45 caliber gunshot wound post-op drug dealer patient who virtually exploded aboard the C-141 over the Pacific Ocean. He pledged, "I must figure this out! What the hell was his name?"

The next day, following a sleep-deprived night and in spite of being rattled by the previous day's traumatic events, he adroitly completed a previously scheduled retroperitoneal abdominal aortic aneurysm replacement. Following surgery, with a moment's downtime, he began to review the intimate details of Claire's George Washington University Hospital medical record. The evening before, he had called the record room and requested it for early that morning.

He sat wearing green scrubs in a darkened cubicle with a Mr. Coffee-rendered cup of his favorite Italian blend doctored with half-and-half and a little too much sugar. He digested every detail derivable from the accumulated information gathered by the hospital staff on patient record number 85-662347, Claire Ferrier, MD.

He told Matt, "Early that morning, I also refreshed my memory concerning the similar tragedies." Declan reviewed the notes from his personal experiences and research notes he'd collected over the years concerning unexplained infectious gangrenous deaths, carefully recorded and cataloged on three-by-five index cards. He reviewed the Agent Orange discussion with Dr. Bob Agostinelli at Memorial Sloan Kettering in New York. All this information became relative to Claire's deadly disease. Its progression appeared to be extraordinarily similar to the case that challenged him years ago in Vietnam, 1972.

He informed Matt, "It's most certainly the same demise suffered by the drug dealer shot with a .45 caliber pistol, Private Church." Declan explained that predisposition to this deadly disease was associated with some or all of these established factors: wounding in Vietnam, time spent in a tropical or subtropical climate, and minimal or significant skin injury or planned surgery. They initially did well post-operatively, only to be consumed by the rapid progression into a septic course and a fatal gangrenous deterioration. Declan related that on the day following Claire's death, he remembered engaging the last pages of her chart. He was flipping through the lab slips, which overlapped like shingles on a roof. He had exclaimed, "What the hell? What's this?"

"Matt, you will not believe it," he said. "There they were taunting me!" he continued in a tense, stricken voice. Precisely as reported over the years in Vietnam and by more recent investigators, there appeared on one of Claire's blood smears the distorted, engorged macrophage white blood cells with bulging vesicles. Declan announced, "The same white cells previously found in other infected patients with a Vietnam connection in the late sixties and early to mid-1970s. There have been no reported cases since 1975. Now here's Claire's identical case presenting in July of 1985."

Matt retorted, "Why the decade long interval between the disease's appearance?"

The emotional surgeon replied, "Beats me; I have no idea."

Matt knew he reported the same abnormal white blood cells in a dying patient's smear at Walter Reed Army Hospital in 1971, but the finding was dismissed as not significant. Private Burrows.

Matt then recalled that Ryan Larkin previously related to him that he had observed the same abnormal macrophage in Private David Jamison's blood at the 95th Evac in Da Nang, Vietnam in 1972. A few months later, Ryan learned of this patient's demise at Tachikawa Army Hospital, Japan. Just before he left the service, Ryan again observed the same abnormal cells at Fort Carson Army Hospital in Colorado in 1972. He checked in on the patient and found that early aggressive treatment by Dr. Mel Abend had averted a catastrophe.

Matt realized, "We have a cluster of patients."

"Yes, we do!" reinforced Declan with a subdued smile as he sipped his sweet coffee.

All four victims of this vile infectious death demonstrated the same grossly abnormal white blood cells. Initially, Privates Burrows, Jamison, and Church died unexpectedly. Now the saintly Claire Ferrier, MD, died under similar circumstances fifteen years later!

Declan Burke then resumed his explanation to Matt. The worldwide incidence of this deadly gangrenous, flesh-eating disease associated with a clinical picture similar to Claire's fatal illness had peaked by 1972 but had become extremely uncommon after 1975 and by the early-eighties, almost rare. Declan continued that Claire's in-depth autopsy did not add anything new. However, a dehisced, intensely inflamed wound appeared on the small of her back, surrounded by darkened burnt-sienna stained skin. It represented the location of the suspicious lesion excised in Africa before returning home.

Matt listened as Declan recalled committing himself to find the George Washington Hospital lab tech who reported the macrophage abnormal finding that connected Claire's death with the Vietnam illness. Declan said, "In a heartbeat, I was on the phone to Duane Wall, the accomplished and respected GW laboratory director."

Without hesitation, Declan invited his longtime friend, Duane, to come to his office to meet Matt. The journalist was thrilled to have the opportunity to engage someone with such extensive laboratory experience.

Duane Wall, a very curious and astute professional, was by now after fifteen years of experience, the GWU Hospital laboratory director. He was a fair administrator who returned to the trenches intermittently to maintain his proficiency and check out any wildly exciting, newly purchased equipment. Declan and Duane were more than close friends; they were brothers. They had served together at the 85th Evacuation Hospital in Vietnam where Duane had been a corpsman associated with the ED and operating rooms. They frequently shared a laugh when Declan reminded his friend of his nickname, Question Man. In Vietnam, a twenty-year-old Duane, anxious to become more proficient, fired a continuous barrage of questions. This habit led to his being ordered, by then Major Burke, when in public to wear a scrub shirt with a question mark embroidered by Vietnamese seamstress on its front.

Director Wall had located the lab tech who identified the abnormal white blood cells in Claire's blood. Searching for additional clues, they reviewed not only all her blood slides but also her entire battery of test results. There was little to analyze, her hospital course being so abbreviated.

Duane knew all too well of the deadly outcomes associated with this abnormal cell. International panic occurred during the relatively short-lived global epidemic of human devastation in the late sixties and early to mid-seventies related to this finding in a patient's blood smear.

Duane challenged Matt and Declan, "How did these abnormal macrophages appear in deceased Claire's blood smear so many years after the original epidemic?"

During their earlier GWU association in the mid-seventies, Duane digested all of Declan's years of macrophage white cell research. He had hit a roadblock, like the rest of the world, in determining what factors initiated the change resulting in the abnormal white blood cells. Did they directly link to the subsequent overwhelming gangrenous insult and its vicious, deadly disease process? Duane and Declan had often brainstormed over a few beers at their favorite pub, the Recovery Room. Their intense conversations usually terminated as two neglected wives signaled enough of this recurring topic.

The upcoming first ever 85th Evacuation Hospital '70-'71 reunion in San Diego that September 1985 excited both couples. This gathering was organized by Declan, Duane, and Kathy and Casey Blitt, who married after meeting in Vietnam. Kathy had served with the Red Cross at the 85th Evac.

Another 85th Evac veteran who excitedly anticipated the September 1985 reunion was Mike Clark who had served as a corpsman. He had assisted Matt and his family in their move to Milwaukee and knew his old friend traveled extensively, pursuing a story about abnormal blood cells. Their conversations centered around sports scores, golf, and hunting, not white cells.

Mike had admitted to Matt that he, like everyone else from the 85th Evac, dealt with episodes of PTSD, which resulted from triggers in their environment, possibly loud noises, the sound of chopper blades, or the smell of canvas and diesel fuel. These transient episodes did not affect his mental stability. He kept physically fit and spent as much time as possible in the woods. He arranged family camping trips with Connie and the boys.

He had emailed the 85th Evac group, "I'm sorry, I did not contact any of those I served with in Vietnam. There's so much to share with my wartime brothers and sisters," and added, "I wonder if you are still dealing with what we experienced over there."

Mike could not know that he, too, would be taunted by the same abnormal white blood cells.

CHAPTER 25

A few months after his consulting with Declan and Duane, Matt revisited Ryan in St. Louis. Much had transpired since their last meeting. The fatality of Claire Ferrier involving the abnormal macrophages was front and center in his concerns.

He asked Ryan, "Does her death represent a new wave of this disease?"

"That's astounding for many reasons," said Ryan. "Let's get started.

But first," he hesitated, "even though I served at the 85th Evac after you all did, the timing is close. I would enjoy attending your September '87 reunion. I've grown close to you, Duane, Declan and Mike, and all the 85th veterans."

"That's a wonderful request. You should attend, for sure." said Matt.

The researcher then began his story.

In July 1984, following the awarding of his Biomedical Engineering PhD, Ryan Larkin remained in St. Louis at Washington University. Due to his groundbreaking research, the University Board awarded him with a generous well-equipped research facility. His PhD thesis and current research pursued techniques to utilize specialized macrophage white blood cells to transport cardiac, antibiotic and chemotherapeutic drugs to the specific organ receptor sites where they would be most effective. He reminded his team of investigators that their mission required the engineering of macrophage white blood cells to not only seek out the correct organ or cancerous growth to treat but also to efficiently transport the drug and deliver it to the correct receptor site. The attachment on that site allowed the drug to pass into that specific cell, therefore, becoming therapeutically effective.

Ryan's group studied and perfected the techniques of other researchers who have reported the capability of growing human cells, normal and abnormal, in customized, nutritional Petri dish solutions, to use in biological studies. His technicians succeeded in isolating, from a healthy bone marrow aspiration, the stem cell origins of the macrophage white blood cell they wished to study. These stem cells were then cultured to produce the macrophages in their specialized Petri dish. With the macrophage white cells' successful growth, there existed an unlimited source of cells to study and engineer.

There were two known subtypes of the macrophage white blood cells. The question was, would one be more effective than another in treating patients? Subtype I proved by far the most efficient in transporting a cardiac drug, a bacteria-destroying antibiotic, and 5-Fluorouracil, a chemotherapeutic agent for colon cancer.

In follow up trials, subtype II demonstrated a weak affinity for the three drugs tested.

Why did subtype II poorly transport all drugs tested while subtype I succeeded? Ryan's group of researchers devoured the relevant medical literature for clues to this puzzle. They uncovered a paper from the CDC in the *Annals of Investigative Medicine* which reported that macrophage subtype II demonstrated in its nuclear DNA a mutated grouping of genes on Chromosome 6.

The new question was now, does the fact that the unaltered Chromosome 6 within the macrophage nucleus in subtype I macrophages have anything to do with the enhanced ability of subtype I to transport therapeutic drugs?

As Ryan continued, Matt was about to learn the additional significance of the Chromosome 6 grouping on the nuclear DNA of subtype I and II infection-fighting macrophage white cells.

Each Friday afternoon, Ryan gathered the twelve members of his research lab. They were undergraduate honor students, research assistants, post-docs, and PhD candidates. Their task was to review their progress for that week and to outline the following week's endeavors.

About two-thirds of the way through a session, during journal club reports, Ryan was consumed by an exciting revelation. This moment resulted from hearing a research journal report of gangrenous deaths that were believed to have been caused by abnormal macrophage white blood cells bulging with vesicles (sacs) that Kathy Gunson, PhD introduced in her journal club review. He studied the photos of the lethal white blood cells that were displayed in the journal report.

Ryan told Matt that he flashed back to Vietnam. He was again looking through his 12th Evac pathology lab's ancient microscope which revealed an identical image of abnormal macrophages bulging with engorged vesicles.

Kathy's report went on to confirmed the altered Chromosome 6 in macrophage subtype II white blood cells and that here were no chromosomal changes in subtype I macrophages. The same journal club report indicated that this alteration in subtype II was thought to be a protective factor against developing the fatal illness that first appeared in Vietnam in the late nineteen-sixties. It had become global for a short time but now rarely reported.

Dr. Gunson informed Ryan that the CDC had also confirmed the presence of the abnormal appearing macrophages in the blood of multiple severely ill, non-military patients who visited Vietnam and other subtropical countries that were afflicted with that fatal gangrenous infection in the late sixties and early to mid-seventies.

Ryan reaffirmed to Matt that he had first observed these white cells in mid-1972, as a lab tech when assigned to the 85th Evac Hospital in Vietnam. They appeared on the blood smear of a patient who eventually died in an Army hospital in Japan. He observed them again in November 1972 at Ft. Carson, Colorado in a patient who developed an intense rash but survived with early intensive antibiotic treatment.

Ryan was well acquainted with the full-blown picture of this awful infection that was rapidly fatal. The vision of deadly demonic abnormal macrophages jeering at him with ridicule through the 10X eyepiece of his microscope had invaded his memory as a young lab tech in Vietnam. His mind flooded with a cluster of thoughts: the engorged white blood cells, filled bulging vesicles, gangrene, death, Vietnam, and the protection offered by the abnormal grouping of DNA genes on Chromosome 6.

Ryan asked his group, "What does it all mean? Will we ever know? How has this monstrous disease resurfaced in poor Claire Ferrier?"

CHAPTER 26

A few weeks after his recording of Ryan's discoveries and new challenges, Matt's newspaper office phone rang. Michelle excitedly alerted him about her recent interaction with Dr. Declan Burke concerning her dear friend, Claire Ferrier and Richard Burrows, her first love.

Michelle began by explaining that Claire's death in September 1985 demoralized the French-speaking community of friends that were central to Michelle and Jon's Washington, DC area social interactions. She continued that soon after her beloved Richard's death in 1972, she investigated the circumstances of his demise. She had traveled to Walter Reed Army Hospital and interviewed Colonel Carroll, who had directed the Grand Rounds that performed an in-depth review of Richard's death. The details were not only detailed in her written notes but also painfully imprinted into her memory.

Listening to Michelle, Matt's anxiety rose as he reflected on the guilt he continued to carry due to his decision to abide by military culture and not push the issue of Private Burrows' abnormal white blood cells. He had observed them in Richard's blood smear at Walter Reed before his death. These cells are now, over a decade later, considered to be the cause of this fatal infectious disease. Someday, he would confess to Michelle his part in her loved one's death, but not today.

Now her dearest friend, Claire, had died under comparable circumstances. Her illness reflected a sequence of events undisputedly mirroring those of Richard's death, separated by over a decade. Michelle continued explaining that she could not dismiss her intuitive feeling that the two tragic losses were somehow related. She was obsessed with feelings of remorse and purpose.

She repeated her query to Matt, "Why were they afflicted with that usually fatal infection? How will I get to the bottom of this?"

Matt learned that having secured Guy Marc's permission, she obtained Claire's hospital records and began an in-depth study. She was perfectly capable of balancing her Washington consulting business responsibilities and the emotionally charged analysis of her dear friend's rapidly fatal illness. She now described to Matt how she had engaged Dr. Burke. About two months after Claire's death, Michelle and Jon had encountered Declan at a George Washington University-sponsored event to raise capital for the addition of two new operating room suites.

Their first encounter at George Washington University Hospital was under the duress of experiencing Claire's death. Chairing the surgery department and being relegated to the status of a war hero for his service as an Army trauma surgeon in Vietnam would inflate most egos. On the contrary, she was impressed by his pleasant demeanor. He had lectured on battlefield trauma, Vietnam's delayed stress, today's Post-Traumatic Stress, and the Veterans Administration's damaging refusal to recognize the reality of various physical and mental disabilities genuinely attributable to a veteran's service in Vietnam. Agent Orange also was a featured topic of discussion for Dr. Burke.

Encouraged by his approachability, Michelle had called Declan Burke's office and arranged an appointment for her and Guy Marc to share their thoughts connecting Richard and Claire. She assured his office that there was no ill intent but only the desire to share the fact that her beloved Richard Burrows had succumbed to the same disgusting fate.

When advised of Michelle's request, Declan could not believe the connection. He was shocked by Michelle's relationship with Richard and was intrigued by Michelle's claim that his demise at Walter Reed Army Hospital shared similar facts with that of Claire's illness. He had successfully operated on Private Burrows at the 85th Evac Hospital in 1972 and discharged him in stable condition for transportation back to the United States.

Declan then alerted Duane that if Michelle's information would confirm the linkage between the grossly abnormal white blood cells and the gangrenous infectious deaths that first appeared during the Vietnam War, "This was a major breakthrough!"

Michelle continued to inform Matt that Dr. Burke cleared his schedule on the following Wednesday afternoon and invited her and Guy Marc to meet him in his office at 1:30 p.m. He suggested to them that Duane Wall, who was familiar with the blood smears both in Vietnam and at George Washington, attend to complement the discussion. As a bonus, Michelle's husband, Jon, recently at his wife's request, created an intricate email account which he administered to invite the registration of individuals familiar with the vile gangrenous deaths. This account would enhance the acquisition of information related to these seemingly related unexpected deaths. Through his associates at InfoServ, he gained access to public national and international databases of email addresses, sought permission, and skillfully incorporated the information into a workable mechanism to blanket all continents of the globe. Slowly, the world began to respond. Jon's computer skills allowed him to ensure accuracy and privacy, to provide needed storage space, and to create an efficient cataloging system for prompt topic retrieval.

Matt listened intently to Michelle on the landline as she continued her dialogue. His heart rate had increased, and he was nervous with anticipation of developing new information reinforcing his journalistic crusade.

Michelle continued with her news. Declan Burke's office resided in a suite of surgical medical offices at George Washington University, just off 23rd St. NW. After exiting the elevator on the sixth floor in the K Wing, Michelle and Guy Marc proceeded down the well-appointed light bluish-gray themed hallway with modern décor to the door of Room 602. Lettering in gold leaf on the glass window announced Department Head.

Upon entering the suite, they noted the waiting room to be empty. There was pleasingly low volume, easy-listening music filling the disinfectant scented air kept at a comfortable temperature. The receptionist stood with a beaming smile and greeted them by name. She then escorted Michelle and Guy Marc down the patient corridor to the same opulent conference room Matt had met in with Dr. Burke. There were a variety of beverages. She announced that Declan would appear shortly.

Michelle commented to Guy Marc, "This room is gorgeous and so well-appointed."

He replied, "For sure," as he offered her a bottle of water.

Within a few minutes, the surgeon entered the room clumsily, balancing a collection of several textbooks, journal articles, and hospital charts haphazardly clutched in his arms. As he was positioning his burden on the conference table's reflective surface, the doctor introduced himself as Declan Burke. He did not use the title doctor for he wished to level the playing field. Declan's understanding of and desire to eliminate the veil of intimidation a doctor could exert upon patients and their families was genuine, and he did not require a title to establish his persona. He then proudly introduced George Washington University's Director of Laboratory Services. With great pride, Declan declared that he and Duane served together in Vietnam.

From the outset, there was no tension in the room; in this venue, all would participate as equals.

For over two hours, Declan, Michelle, Duane, and Guy Marc exchanged a reciprocal flow of information. They were interrupted occasionally by calls that Declan had to field. There were identical abnormal infection-fighting macrophages in the blood smears from the majority of global patents reviewed who had succumbed to this disgusting disease. This review included the cases known to them and those reported in the world's literature that were captured by Jon's computer program. The cell's description with routine staining and the more detailed electron microscopic visualizations were universally consistent. All reports echoed the same enlarged, thick-walled, macrophages stuffed with bulging vesicles that were ever-present at the outset of symptoms but interestingly absent during the active onset phase of the illness. They reviewed written reports from researchers who had attempted to replicate these changes with an imaginative spectrum of chemical, physical, and environmental challenges.

"These researchers all failed," Michelle impressed upon Matt.

The four of them had agreed on the prominent mysteries. What were the common denominators? Were they military service, civilian posting, or touring in Vietnam? What about as Claire and others had done, visiting Cameroon and additional tropical and subtropical climates?

Was there exposure to Agent Orange? There was, but AO usage outside Vietnam was extremely limited.

They asked each other, "What indictable commonalities existed in the tropical and subtropical regions that reported the disease?" The group listed malnutrition, poor education, smoking, alcoholism, high incidence of STDs, unstable central governments, waterborne diseases like cholera, hepatitis A, and giardia, and Anopheles mosquito-borne malaria.

Michelle told Matt that she had suggested, "Is this discussion too generalized?"

"You're right," responded Declan, who habitually drummed his fingers when concentrating. He heard the thumping and stopped.

The group then decided to limit the focus to comparisons between Cameroon and Vietnam since those two geographic areas condemned Claire, Richard, and Privates Jamison and Church. The four of them noted that the World Health Organization strongly suggested geographically specific disease prevention measures for travel to countries outside the U.S. They wondered, were there shared recommended requirements for Cameroon and Vietnam? If so, was the overlap significant?

Michelle paraphrased to Matt that they had confirmed when newly arrived in both suspect countries, everyone was issued mosquito netting to entomb one's sleeping area to prevent being bitten by the Anopheles mosquito, the vector that transmitted the malaria parasite.

This vector, having feasted on blood from an infected animal or human for food, when biting the next victim, regurgitated some of the previously ingested blood infected by the malaria parasite. The contaminated blood was, in effect, injected into the area of the bite, thus introducing malaria to a new victim. Of paramount importance was the recommended daily swallowing of preventive medications to avoid the development of this disease due to inoculation with *P. falciparum* parasite (malaria)-infected blood. The drug eradicated the parasite from its nest within the victim's red blood cells. Claire had taken Falciquin, which was manufactured and distributed by Attica Ossining Pharmaceuticals. They considered whether the malarial medication could be the culprit. Since no incriminating evidence existed, that concept lost favor out of their overwhelming trust of WHO policies.

Michelle remembered that she had wondered out loud, "Did my Richard, who experienced a gruesome death at Walter Reed Army Hospital, take anti-malaria pills while in Vietnam before his wounding?"

"Yes, he did." was Duane's response, "We all had to."

They developed corollary questions: Were similar drugs utilized in each malaria-endemic country's plan for prevention? Were there reports of white blood cell abnormalities as a result of these medications?

From a different direction, they questioned, did any stage in the life cycle of the *Plasmodium falciparum* malaria parasite within the patient have the ability to create the lethal macrophage white blood cell?

Michelle told Matt, "We were mentally drained and physically exhausted following the two-and-a-half-hour session. Declan taped the entirety of the proceedings."

Matt responded, "Great. I'd like to review the meeting."

Declan, a few days later, after summarizing, forwarded the accumulated information not only to Michelle, Guy Marc, and Duane but also to Doctors Agostinelli and Larkin, and Matt.

CHAPTER 27

Matt's brief encounter at Walter Reed Army Hospital in 1972 with the abnormal macrophage had now snowballed into a life-changing experience. The Milwaukee Inquirer placed him on sabbatical with full pay and medical insurance coverage to allow him to pursue a potentially international block-buster of a story. He was excited about having been given access to so many key players in the abnormal macrophage saga. After having received an urgent call from Mike Clark, he would now delve into his childhood friend's experiences and recollections.

It was now mid-October of 1985. Matt sat down on a quiet Sunday afternoon with Mike at The Grunt, the watering hole he owned and operated with his family.

He said to Matt, "Life is great. My family is thriving in Milwaukee. The boys are growing by the day and excelling at middle school academics and sports. Our family business, The Grunt, a cozy bar for food and drink, has a loyal and growing clientele."

His friend answered, "You've earned it." Matt learned that after Vietnam, Mike pursued the steps necessary to become a certified physician's assistant and had first been engaged as a scrub tech in general surgical pro-cedures. This position was a piece of cake for him after having scrubbed for the trauma surgeons at the 85th Evacuation Hospital in Vietnam. He sought further training and had soon morphed into the most requested surgical scrub in the cardiothoracic division.

He told Matt, "As the Chief of Support Services for cardiothoracic surgery at the University of Wisconsin Hospital I am ultimately responsible for the patient's safety. This requires me to insure all the operating instruments, cardiac bypass machines, other ancillary equipment, scheduling, and all support personnel functioned perfectly."

His attentiveness was complete. He understood that there was no such thing as a guarantee in medicine and surgery, and the support personnel's performance could be unpredictable. However, he had engineered and now directed a program that was advocated by the American College of Cardiothoracic Surgeons as a model to emulate for one's hospital cardiothoracic program to succeed. Visitors routinely invaded his department and hounded him and his staff for advice.

Mike advised Matt, "Multiple factors gauge the success of a surgical procedure." He continued, "The most basic factors are did it work and did the patient survive." The enviously low mortality rates at his university hospital were hard-won by analyzing all outcomes and stressing excellence. For open-heart surgery, wherein mechanical bypass was necessitated, and more specifically, aortic valve replacement, the outcomes were world-class. A patient entering his hospital for this procedure could assume that an excellent functional result and survival were all but guaranteed. All staff participating in these operations felt empowered to be successful.

As with any institution that did not cherry-pick and accepted all cases, regardless of surgical risk, there were patient deaths in the operating room, cardiac intensive care units, and even a few at home post-operatively.

Mike shouted, "Matt, I aged ten years after what I'll next share with you!"

In early September 1985, Summer Anderson presented to the University of Wisconsin Hospital as a vivacious, intelligent, pretty seventeen-year-old senior from Fox Point High School just outside Milwaukee. The leaking of her aortic valve had progressed in severity to curtail her ability to swim distance races. She was ranked eleventh nationally in the eighteen and under grouping by the Amateur Athletic Union (AAU) in the 100-meter breaststroke event. She was scholarship-bound for sunny UCLA to join their nationally ranked women's swim team.

In Summer's case, blood was ejected by the large ventricular chamber of the left heart into the aorta. The trap doors of her aortic valve that kept blood traveling forward into the body never closed completely. For her entire life, blood would leak back into the left ventricular chamber's muscular space. That required an extra volume of blood to be thrust forward with each contraction. For the longest time, the amount of blood lost to her circulation which leaked back into her left ventricular heart chamber was not enough to produce symptoms of heart strain.

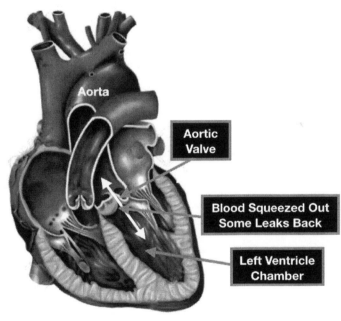

Summer's Heart

The extra burden of blood was accommodated. But to do so, the left large ventricular chamber dilated somewhat and contracted more vigorously to push blood forward into the aorta for distribution to her body.

She had kept herself in tip-top shape. Her doctors prescribed diuretics and other drugs to support her heart's function and health. She was capable of competing at a high level, having placed fourth in the state's 1984 high school 100-meter breaststroke competition. Once Summer entered late-adolescence, the less-than-perfect aortic trap doors began to allow more blood to flow backward into the left ventricular chamber of the heart. Repeat ultrasound studies of her heart confirmed the worsening of the aortic valve's structure and increased backflow.

As a result, her left ventricular chamber heart muscles were stretched to their maximum and began to become inefficient. More and more blood accumulated in the stressed left ventricle; pressures increased in the lung's circulation; there was less effective oxygen exchange for carbon dioxide; and her exercise tolerance diminished significantly.

As her symptoms worsened, she had lamented, "Is there anything else short of surgery that would help me feel normal? I want to reach my goal of swimming at the Olympic level."

In early 1985, she did not compete during the team's travel season. By the following April, she could only negotiate one flight of stairs before shortness of breath from lack of adequate oxygen in her circulation ended her ascent. She had to stop to catch her breath and occasionally in the middle of the night, was forced to sit up straight to relieve her air hunger. The latest heart ultrasound in mid-May demonstrated extensive backward flow into an enlarged left ventricle chamber with dangerously high pressure. She now required aortic valve replacement of her ineffective valve to prevent imminent heart failure.

Summer's high school graduation propelled 420 young adults into the future. A rare few were destined to become household names. The vast majority would be satisfied living as middle-class Americans. She had attended the senior prom with Tony Turel, a heavily recruited star athlete, the football team's All-Conference Center, straight-A student, and friend since grade school. He was not a boyfriend but someone who treated her as an equal and with whom she felt respected and safe. She knew her evening would be perfect.

That same feeling of safety and presumed best outcome levitated Summer and her family on September 16, 1985 as she was admitted to the University of Wisconsin Hospital for a routine aortic valve replacement to be performed by a most respected surgeon. Her mother had told Mike, "I know in my heart that all this will work out just fine."

CHAPTER 28

Mike Clark continued Summer's story with additional background information. Matt listened on attentively.

In late 1984, when she should have been participating with the travel swim team, Summer began to gain weight. The discipline of rising early to hit the gym before classes and swim sprints after school was not a part of her current lifestyle, and she was astonished by the shameful changes reflected in her bedroom mirror. She had gained puffy pounds and lost the slim sexy contour of her body. This reflection was not the image she wished for herself.

Summer complained to her mother, "I can't stand myself. I've got to do something to look good again."

Due to her weak heart, engaging in intense exercise to shed the pounds was not an option. Summer restricted her dietary caloric intake as much as she could tolerate, to no avail.

In fifth-period study hall, she noticed that several of her friends had lost weight without appearing to have made significant sacrifices. She had heard whispers of a pill that miraculously transformed teenagers into Vanity Fair models. Initially, Summer received denials when inquiring of the newly reshaped girlfriends whether or not they used something to obtain their present appearance. After several futile attempts to extract what she wanted to know from her small group, she cornered Susan near her locker at the far end of the hallway.

She pressured, "Ok, what's the deal?"

Her entrapped prey bowed her head in surrender. "Yes, there is a pill, but it's unavailable in the United States. If you have a prescription, you can order it from Canada." the informant said.

"Do I get a prescription from my doctor?" Summer questioned.

"No" was Susan's hesitant response.

"Then, where?" A long pause ensued.

"We have access to forgeries" was the reply. Susan agreed to make the arrangements for Summer to obtain a bogus prescription for the miracle drug.

Wishing to be well-informed, she read the magic bullet's name on the fraudulent document and discovered only the commercial designation, T-Loss, not the generic name. The signature of the prescriber was illegible. The prescribing office was somewhere in New Mexico.

Not to be deterred in her quest to regain her svelte appearance, she, as did her friends, addressed the envelope containing the contraband script and with a money order for one hundred and twenty-seven US dollars, to a distributor in Canada called the Montreal National Pharmacy Consortium. After several anxious weeks, a small cardboard box addressed to Summer arrived at her home on McKay Road. Her parents knew she traded pins and swimming memorabilia with young people around the world, so a small package from Canada was not unusual.

Her mother said, "By now, you must have a huge collection."

Summer hid her anxiety and smiled, "I sure do."

Using the T-Loss allowed Summer to shed all her unwanted pounds.

On the day before surgery, as was his preoperative routine, Mike Clark reviewed Summer's present illness, past medical history, physical exam, and latest laboratory results. Aside from death, the most dreaded adverse outcome in the world of surgery is an infection at the surgical site or around an implanted device such as a titanium total knee, a Dacron graft, or a metallic heart valve. Foreign bodies like these were not biodegradable. Bacteria indelibly adhered to their surfaces. If an implanted device's site of placement into the body became infected, the device must be removed for an infection to resolve. This occurrence was a tragedy for the patient and a windfall for the salivating malpractice attorneys.

During his review of her chart, Mike noted the reporting of a recently healed area on her posterior right shoulder that was mildly inflamed and surrounded by an inch in diameter burnt-sienna-colored rash. It was an accidental wound suffered as she helped her dad thin out the thick vegetation bordering their home's backyard.

As Mike carefully re-examined the routine laboratory findings, he was startled by a cryptic reference to a few enlarged, somewhat distorted vesicle-filled macrophage white blood cells.

His primitive brain's fight-or-flight response was almost uncontrollable. He remembered saying, "I'm in my Vietnam combat mode again!"

Mike had begun sweating and felt cold and clammy; his heart raced, time slowed, hearing dampened. He became hyper-alert, felt nauseous, and experienced his heart pounding. This episode mimicked the mental state which overwhelmed him on guard duty at the 85th Evacuation perimeter in Vietnam when sensing the imminent threat of the Viet Cong. Yes, fight or flight.

Mike had exclaimed, "Oh my God!" after reading Summer's lab work.

He, Declan Burke, Duane Wall, and Ryan Larkin had just a few weeks ago discussed the definitive implication of these evil and deadly abnormal macrophage white cells in early September 1985 at their 85th Evacuation Reunion in San Diego. Up until this fortuitous exchange of vital information, Mike would have had no idea that the abnormal macrophages referenced in passing in Summer's lab report were of any significance. Even though the abnormal white cells' distortion appeared to be moderate, he was alarmed that there was a significant threat to the success of Summer's aortic valve replacement and a statistically significant risk of death.

He remembered announcing to his assistant, "I have to tell Dave about this!"

He immediately notified the attending surgeon of his findings. Dr. Dave Schlageter was unaware of the impending disastrous result if he had proceeded to operate the next morning. His respect for and trust in Mike's judgment and opinions were well established and always rewarded. He would say, "Mike's the real deal."

The attending surgeon canceled Summer's surgery.

As a result, the patient and family would have to be informed, the OR canceled, and the surgical team's efforts applied to another case. Having gone through the mental gymnastics of preparing oneself to surrender control and place your wellbeing in the hands of strangers, Summer was at first angry and extremely disappointed. Once she and her family understood that a potentially lethal outcome could result from proceeding, the appeasement of their exasperation was complete.

"Thank you for being so careful and saving my life." the young swimmer said to Dr. Schlageter, who promptly introduced Mike Clark and credited him with making the critical observation.

"This is the guy you should be thanking," the surgeon responded.

Mike realized the most pressing question now was how did these abnormal white blood cells come to be present in Summer's blood. He quickly ordered multiple vials of blood to be drawn for analysis. Permission was received to do a biopsy of Summer's back lesion for histologic examination, culture for bacteria and fungi, and chemical analysis. However, much debate has ensued concerning the safety of such an approach, as there was a fear that even a minor surgical intervention may very well trigger a disastrous outcome. Therefore, a unanimous decision was reached not to challenge the status quo, to treat the wound with soaks and antibiotics, and to dismiss the notion of performing a surgical biopsy.

The only new factor in Summer's routine was the ingestion of the weight control drug, T-Loss. She admitted to Mike and her parents that she ordered the drug from Canada, as instructed by her friends. There were no reports of adverse side effects from the obscure T-Loss but, just to be safe,

Summer was instructed to discard her supply of the drug. The chance of it being the causative factor seemed remote but, safety was paramount.

The hospital possessed a light source microscope to visualize and examine Summer's abnormal macrophage white blood cells utilizing a variety of stains to define as many details of the cell's definitive structure as possible. The hospital did not have access to an electron microscope. Mike determined that these were definitely the same abnormal macrophage white blood cells that were noted in Vietnam War patients.

Mike hesitated, took a deep breath and a sip of water and continued his emotional story to a transfixed Matt.

Following this discovery, Mike then called Ryan Larkin at Washington University in St. Louis. He said, "We almost lost this girl." He added that in Summer's blood samples, "We now have the actual abnormal macrophages that have been causing the infectious gangrenous deaths first observed in Vietnam." Mike continued, "I'll arrange to transfer Summer's blood to your laboratory."

Ryan responded, "We'll grow these little bastards in a specialized nutrient solution and have an unlimited number of abnormal macrophages to utilize for further study." He celebrated this break for their investigation.

In spite of following all required procedures outlined by Ryan for shipment, to the disappointment of all concerned, Summer's precious specimens did not respond to culturing techniques. Repeat blood samples from Summer demonstrated only a rare diabolical cell, not a sufficient number for Petri dish culturing. There would be no source of these cells to investigate.

Mike told Matt, "Ryan and I were acutely disappointed."

Matt replied, "I do understand."

Following Mike's disclosures to Matt, the communications among Matt, Mike, Ryan, Duane, Michelle, and Declan became intense. They concluded that yes, Summer's abnormal white blood cells were identical to Claire's lethal macrophages noted on her initial emergency room sample.

Moreover, the cells appeared to be a match to those in other patients, especially those from Vietnam, who suffered this deadly disease.

A month following the derailed surgery, an examination of Summer's repeat blood panel was absent the abnormal infection-fighting macrophages. There existed only a perfectly normal blood smear slide specimen. The risk and timing of proceeding with her aortic valve replacement was now the pressing issue. To be thoroughly safe, all agreed upon the decision to postpone the surgery for two more months to allow periodic screening of her blood's status.

UCLA granted Summer deferred admission for medical reasons. She would take courses at the local community college near her home to keep her academic juices flowing.

Having divulged her distress at her body's unbecoming conformation, the hospital nutritionist guided her along a pathway in regaining her sleek image. Summer, at discharge, was instructed only to take the medicines prescribed by her cardiologist.

"Nothing else!" said the dietician, "especially that weight control drug, T-Loss."

"I promise" was the response. "I know I dodged a bullet." She abided strictly to that proclamation. She flushed her remaining pills.

Coincidentally, the continued ingestion of T-Loss lead to an incapacitating nausea and vomiting in her weight-conscious classmates. The medication was voluntarily discontinued.

Because of a flood of negative publicity, the bogus prescriptions became unavailable, and the Canadian supplier went underground.

Of great significance, there were no pills to analyze for chemical content.

Did a potentially lethal culprit evade detection?

CHAPTER 29

Senator David Sokolov projected influence over all the prestigious political institutions of Washington, DC. His dishonesty, greed, underhanded dealings, extraordinarily important contacts, especially in Big Pharma, and being the declared spokesperson for the Democratic Party all propelled him into national and international prominence.

"I've arrived," he boasted to his massive bedroom mirror, surrounded by the extravagance of his Orange County, California palatial home.

"I plan to run for President in 1988," he told his closest advisors. He had been entirely satisfied with being the most powerful senator. However, his handlers in the pharmaceutical industry wanted more. They influenced the current President and had pressured him into appointing Senator Sokolov as the Secretary of Health and Human Services. That position was a windfall for their prized industry. Guidelines were surreptitiously revised to allow shortcuts in drug manufacturing. They diluted the required warnings about addictive potential when advertising the newly developed opioid painkillers to physicians and the public. They knew full well the heroin-like addictive qualities of this class of drugs and ignored the potential for disaster when marketing these products. This repugnant omission of a potential addiction warning was considered full disclosure by the yardstick endorsed with the senator's oversight as the Department's Secretary. The greedy nearsightedness portended an epidemic of opioid overdoses and deaths in the ensuing years that would become the dominant public health crisis in the twenty-first century.

With the national stampede to manufacture more inexpensively by utilizing offshore facilities, currently China and India, the senator knew any inclination to institute oversight regulation was swallowed up by having to deal with the overwhelming number of companies involved and inadequate recordkeeping. Computer expertise and the Internet were still in their infancies. The human resources and dollar expenditure required to accomplish this oversight would become unacceptable. The senator's divisive manipulations would proceed unchecked for the near future.

Big Pharma had allied with giants in other industries to create and sustain a consortium of players that, in the real sense of the word, ruled the world economically and politically.

This ruling class wished to control the most powerful man in the world, the President of the United States. The group's obvious choice for the Democratic Party's presidential candidate was Senator David Sokolov. He was delighted.

"This is my destiny!" he declared to his wife and their most intimate friends at an exclusive dinner party they had hosted at their movie star home near Oakland, California. All present dutifully applauded his pronouncement.

The Democratic Party's machinery was fully engaged. A national platform confirmed, competitive nominee challenges squashed, a National Convention programmed in a politically supportive city, voting districts realigned, Vice Presidential candidates screened, battle plans for campaigning and fundraising designed and executed effectively. The US national political map of Blue and Red states was defined. Democratic representation was primarily along the coasts. The Republican influence was inland. Six states were up for grabs and would require added effort.

Nationally, the Democrats were on a roll as their party's current President scored a sixty-two percent approval rating after eight years in office. Their programs were not only increasing employment but also fostering improved spending power for the average American. Senior citizens were happy with their more than adequate retirement savings and comprehensive Medicare medical coverage.

As Secretary of Health and Human Services, Senator David Sokolov's face and voice were seen and heard regularly in all the visual and print media. He endorsed programs that fed and provided health care for those in need. He engaged international leaders to support measures promoting the prevention of malnutrition and infectious diseases in developing countries.

World leaders from Europe to Asia to Africa endorsed Senator Sokolov as an influential leader with whom they shared universal principles and objectives. The universal speculation was that this tsunami of support would undoubtedly sweep the senator into his first four-year term as the forty-second President of the United States of America.

CHAPTER 30

During a sirloin steak dinner at DC's noisy Old Ebbitt Grill, Jesse toasted Kim and himself with his sweet Jack Daniels Manhattan. He said, "Kim, you have cornered the market on educational conferences for continuing medical education programs that are funded by the folks who run the drug companies."

"I'm thrilled about that," she responded, and added after taking a sip of her Jack and Ginger, "After relocating here, I worked hard, and it paid off."

He continued, "I'm now on a first-name basis with those who are striving to propel Senator Sokolov into the White House."

Jesse was a master at persuading, from those who knew better, the divulging of privileged information. He was a favorite visitor at the Senator's Department of Health and Human Services office and meticulously recorded his fact finding in a cataloged file. He heard the whispers concerning pharmaceutical industry drug contamination in offshore manufacturing. These stories recently reported results of the improved capabilities in the chemical analyses that were now filtering into the public domain. With this increasing awareness, if adverse reactions resulted following a drug's application, the Food and Drug Administration then screened for purity, the accuracy of the composition, and dangerous chemical by-products. An inclusive battery of patient blood values was analyzed to determine any correlation between that drug and reported harmful patient effects.

Around this time, bookstores were displaying Vietnam War historical novels, *Dispatches* by Michael Herr, *Rumor of War* by Philip Caputo, *Short-Timer* by Gustav Hasford, and *The Quiet American* by Graham Greene. Jesse internalized the books' information and what he read in old news accounts. He became affected by a mild but real case of survivor's guilt. After all, this guy did have a conscience. Having been rated 4F by his local draft board for a knee injury incurred playing rugby, he was relieved to have avoided Vietnam. Jesse wondered, *would he have fought as unconditionally as the vast majority of those who did serve in that war?* These men signed a blank check to the United States of America committing to offer their lives in defense of their country.

As a result of these feelings, Jesse began to become involved in veteran affairs by supporting agencies who sought to alleviate, prevent, and treat post-traumatic stress disorder, homelessness, drug and alcohol addiction, domestic abuse, and suicide. He became enraged when informed of the Veterans Administration's intransigence in awarding legitimate disability benefits to those who served.

He complained to Kim, "How could America discard so easily those who served to protect Her?" He was especially ashamed by how a kill-the-messenger attitude of anti-war activists had insulted, taunted, and denigrated the Vietnam War heroes. He reflected upon how he had hypothesized the Russia toxin theory as a cause for the gangrenous Vietnam deaths. That position had derailed and almost destroyed his intended career path.

He probed Kim, "Was it possible that the inciting factor in the grotesque Vietnam deaths may have been a contaminant in a manufactured product used during the war?" Jesse added, "Just as dioxin's presence is a predictable, deplorable by-product in Agent Orange production." He continued that this toxin's cancer and mutation-causing impact on our Vietnam soldiers, their progeny, and the Vietnamese people continues to be substantiated. But these facts are ferociously denied and covered up by Dow Chemical executives who issued fabricated research papers defending their claims denying a cause and effect association. He remembered, to our nation's shame, the Veterans Administration had diluted statistics to prevent an honest accounting by including veterans who never served in Vietnam in their analysis of dioxin's scourge. In growing numbers, Vietnam veterans were actively and vociferously demanding recompense through the payment of disability. Their claims were still ignored and denied by the VA, but to a lesser extent since inroads by political action were slowly resulting in positive change.

Jesse's wife, Kim, and Michelle, Private Burrows' first love, grew up as neighbors in Amsterdam, NY. They faithfully kept in touch. Michelle related to Kim the extent of her group's findings into the abnormal lethal macrophages. She referenced Matt, Declan, Ryan, and Duane's contributions. Kim shared this information with Jesse.

Jesse began to research the medical literature in the George Washington University medical library for information on the hideous Vietnam era fatalities. His firm, Donoghue, Casano, Rapello, was a generous supporter of the University, and with a simple phone call, its members utilized, without hesitation, all GW facilities. He found references to the prominent researchers in this area of interest: Ryan Larkin, PhD, of Washington University in St. Louis, the CDC, and Bob Agostinelli, MD, of MSKCC in New York City.

He read the riveting case reports by Declan Burke, MD, Chairman of the Department of Surgery at GWUH detailing the horrific deaths of his Vietnam patients, and more recently, plastic surgeon, Claire Ferrier, MD, at GW University. Jesse was intrigued by the repetitive mention of circulating abnormal macrophages bulging from overstuffed vesicles.

One evening he shared the realization with Kim. "This usually protective macrophage white blood cell, under normal circumstances, is intimately involved in fighting infection and quick-starting the healing process. Somehow re-engineered, it became the culprit in a devastating deadly disease." The topic had become their dinner conversation. She knew his commitment was growing.

Kim replied, "Are you ready for dessert?"

While cross-referencing the topic of the macrophage, he discovered a current paper published in the *Surgical Complications Review*. It reported the postponement of a surgery for aortic valve replacement due to the discovery of the abnormal macrophages in a pre-op patient's blood. A major disaster was averted and probably a life saved by the quick-thinking Chief of Support Services for cardiothoracic surgery at the University of Wisconsin Hospital, Mike Clark.

He said to his secretary, "I have to talk to this guy." And followed up with, "I'm beat, it's late, I better get home to Kim and the kids before I'm disowned."

The next morning, Jesse's office phone rang on his private line. He said, "This should be interesting," for only a handful of his closest contacts had the number.

"Good morning," issued a commanding voice. "This is Marine Brigadier General Hank Leak."

"Yes, sir," was Jesse's immediate response. *How'd he get this number?* Jesse mused

"We want you to be an integral part of the committee to elect Senator Sokolov President of the United States," the general commanded and continued, "Your literary abilities have come to our attention, and we urge you to participate in developing the content of the senator's speeches."

General Leak abruptly hung up and Jesse said, "Holy shit, what an opportunity, a White House appointment for sure."

He did comply very quickly with a return phone call, and thanking the general for the opportunity, he guaranteed an exceptional performance. His first call was to Kim, who was lovingly excited for him but foresaw his having even fewer waking hours at home for her and their two children. The kids were now pre-teens and required more direct parental contact. To become a more effective mom, she had relinquished her full-time position in favor of becoming a self-employed conference planning consultant. Her reputation was one of the finest in her field as a pharmaceutical conference coordinator, and she had secured the commitment of a few of her best clients to continue to utilize her services. Jesse's second call was to the firm's ecstatic managing partner whose anticipation of an influential connection into White House decision making erased any anticipated loss of production due to his diverted attention.

Jesse enjoyed adding relationships within his new political assignment. He loved to compose meaningful prose and was thrilled to anticipate his words spoken on the national and international stage. His duty was fulfilled by responding to a requested attendance at campaign headquarters on K Street at a moment's notice to create a politically inspiring flow of words.

Jesse continued to increase his dedication to Vietnam veterans. He read *The Best and the Brightest* by David Halberstam and reviewed the Washington Post's exposé of the *Pentagon Papers* that were released by Daniel Ellsberg. He became disheartened that our elected and appointed leadership would disregard the apparent fact that our invasion of and attempted nation-building in Vietnam was pointless and doomed to failure. Political reputations and legacies had become more precious than the lives and futures of our youth who found themselves being slaughtered and maimed in Southeast Asia. The major irony was that many US companies were now vying for influence to negotiate trade and manufacturing agreements with this recent enemy who had slaughtered our youth.

Let bygones be bygones, maybe, but not so soon! Money does talk.

Jesse was distraught when he dwelled on these realizations. He asked Kim, "What was it all for?"

CHAPTER 31

After being advised of Jesse Holt's involvement by Michelle, Matt tracked him down and made arrangements for an interview in his Washington, DC, office. They bonded on the landline while sharing their enthusiasm to expose and elucidate the vile macrophage disease, and selected a future date for the meeting.

Matt said, "I'll be there at 3:00 p.m. We'll talk, and I'll treat you to dinner. You choose the place, I'm not familiar with DC dining."

Jesse responded, "You're on."

Jesse was anxious to update Matt on his evolution into a veteran advocate over the recent months. A few weeks ago, he had secured Mike Clark's number from the hospital operator and called him in his office at the University of Wisconsin Hospital. He introduced himself, reviewed his connection with Michelle, and declared his interest and involvement in the abnormal macrophage blood cell mystery. After briefly reviewing what he had researched about the disease, he complimented the Vietnam veteran on saving Summer's life and proposed a meeting.

Mike's impression was that Jesse was genuinely interested in discovering the truth. He accepted an invitation to visit DC and confer with the investigators of this macrophage white cell disease. Mike's trip, if he could free himself to travel, would be at Jesse's consulting company's expense, for he had access to discretionary funds. Jesse offered a round-trip, first-class ticket on an airline of his choosing and lodging at a four-star hotel.

"An offer I can't refuse," Mike told Jesse," and added, "I want answers too!"

During their telephone exchange and after defining the areas of expertise of those individuals involved in this mystery, Mike suggested that Jesse contact and include Vietnam veterans Ryan Larkin, Declan Burke, and Duane Wall in addition to Michelle and Guy Marc. He recently had shared information with the three veterans at the 85th Evacuation Hospital's September 1985 reunion, relative to the known Vietnam fatal abnormal white cell patients and Claire Ferrier's identical death. With this new revelation about the abnormal white blood cells, Mike had avoided a similar fate for Summer. He would inform the others of Jesse's interest, exchange contact information, and help him coordinate details for the DC meeting.

Jesse's company's offices resided in Foggy Bottom, an easily accessible DC location. He would arrange a date and time suitable for all involved.

Within a few weeks, a plan had evolved. Declan Burke and Duane Wall, who lived and worked in the DC area, were easy to coordinate. Mike agreed to be there for the mid-November meeting. He'd have sufficient time to rearrange schedules and delegate his responsibilities. Ryan offered to coordinate his more flexible schedule with the others involved. Michelle and Guy Marc were appreciative of Jesse's invitation. They agreed.

Michelle then said, "What a great opportunity to consolidate information and share theories."

The conference room at Donoghue, Casano, Rapello was reserved all day on an agreed-upon date in November 1986 with the IT staff on call, a continental breakfast arranged, a delicious lunch to be presented by the famous Martin's Tavern and all sorts of beverages available for consumption during the meeting. Looking east, the view overlooking DC from the twenty-first floor was magnificent. It encompassed the White House, the Mall, the Washington Monument, the Lincoln Memorial, the Potomac River, and much more.

CHAPTER 32

An excited Ryan had called Matt, "I've got great news for you!"

Matt had interviewed the researcher twice before and was again in his cramped Washington University's St. Louis office.

Ryan exclaimed, "We did it!" He was pleased on a bright sunny day in May 1986 to report that his lab had reached its goal. It successfully transported a potent chemotherapeutic agent attached to a subtype I macrophage into the multiple metastatic breast cancer sites nested deep within the liver of a forty-eight-year-old mother of three. He knew the cancer-fighting chemical was delivered. His technicians had attached radioactive and fluorescent markers on the surface of the subtype I delivery macrophages. An ionizing radiation detection device showed the patient's liver lighting up like a Christmas tree. A liver biopsy viewed with a fluorescent microscope confirmed the therapeutic macrophage subtype I white blood cell's presence. Therefore, the cancer-fighting drug was proven to be located deep within the metastatic tumor deposits.

"We're on our way there!" he had exclaimed to those gathered around. The patient's treatment was scheduled every week for a month. Serial abdominal CAT scans revealed the change in tumor size, if any. To the team's delight and most certainly to the patient who was running out of treatment options, the tumors were shrinking.

He continued to relate his story to Matt that a senior technician, who was responsible for the cell and tissue growth cultures, approached Ryan with an excited expression. The tech shook him and said, "You've got to see this."

Almost breaking into a run, he had led his boss to a bench set up with several microscope stations. The 10X magnification field showed a dense carpet of macrophages. But upon further examination at a higher power with 50X magnification, he noted that these macrophage white blood cells demonstrated thickened irregular cell membranes and were distended and contained numerous engorged vesicles. A prospective bone marrow donor for transplantation supplied the stem cells from which this batch of abnormal macrophages had been grown in a culture media Petri dish. The recipient was a leukemia patient scheduled for recolonization of the bone marrow after his cancerous blood cell producing stem cells proved to be eradicated by high-dose chemotherapy and radiation.

Ryan's senior technician shouted, "Here they are, the cells that sign a patient's death warrant." He added, "The cells that have defeated us all these years."

Ryan could not contain himself as he addressed his lab, "This is a great opportunity to examine the culprits, analyze their chemical and structural composition, search for a causative factor, and perhaps put an end to this evil disease." It was evident that the stem cells from the marrow of this prospective donor would not be transplanted into the leukemia recipient.

The responsible physician, a hematologist, was notified.

Ryan dispatched his tech to obtain the donor's name and particulars. At that time, blood samples from the original blood draw were still available. The individual was invited, at no expense to him, to come in for an interview and the drawing of additional blood samples. To repeat the very painful bone marrow biopsy and aspiration was out of the question.

To his delight, Ryan's senior assistant discovered ten milliliters of the donor's marrow frozen and stored in the hematology department. Ryan announced to his group, "We now have something to work with."

The donor was very understanding of the researchers' sense of urgency and made himself available to Ryan and his staff at his first possible opportunity. He said, "My brother served in Vietnam; I have to do this." This donor was asymptomatic.

A review of his business travels was completed. He had very recently spent time as a civil engineer advising several sub-Saharan African countries in the most efficient usage of their often meager water supply by recommending the installation of more efficient dams, pumps, and irrigation ditches. He had received the required immunizations, utilized a mosquito net, and faithfully swallowed, as directed by the World Health Organization, his antimalarial pill not only in-country but for eight weeks after that. He was still taking it and had only a week's supply remaining; he recalled that the name of the pill was the Attica Ossining Pharmaceutical drug, Falciquin.

When reviewing the donor's new blood smear, a few suspicious macrophage white blood cells appeared to be present. However, the lab techs reading the blood smears, concerned about missing a diagnosis, did at times over-read the changes indicating the dreaded culprit. They checked with Ryan who responded, "No, the donor did not demonstrate signs of illness."

For his protection, the donor was instructed to advise all medical personnel he encountered of the risk of a devastating infection if he underwent surgery. The donor accepted instructions to return in three months for follow-up. No one knew how long he would be at risk since there was no understanding of why his bone marrow's stem cells were prone to creating the mysteriously appearing abnormal macrophage white blood cells now referred to as the Killer Macrophage.

There was now a new acronym, KM. No one in Ryan's lab came forward to admit culpability in naming the potentially vicious abnormal macrophage as KM. His chief technician whispered to his friend, "I don't think it'll be a big deal if Ryan discovers it was me."

There were no permanent secrets, and his boss thought KM was the right choice.

Feverishly notetaking with his tape recorder running, Matt could not believe his luck.

He told Ryan, "All this great information and more to come." He added, "I can't believe the progress."

Ryan did present the fundamental question to his group. He challenged, "Was there an inherent, flawed genetic predisposition to develop KM, or was there an agent such as a virus, bacterium, antibody, or chemical that induced a cascade of events that resulted in the KM production?"

They reviewed the world literature seeking to discover a genetic influence in this disease. In one hundred and sixteen cases accumulated by the World Health Organization, wherein generational history did exist, there was no indication of a familial genetic connection.

However, Ryan knew from work reported by the CDC that demonstrating a *mutated grouping* of DNA genes in Chromosome 6 in humans with macrophages of *subtypes II did protect them* from the development of the KM disease. This finding was most notable when these survivors were living in an environment wherein others with subtype I macrophages were dying from this evil KM affliction.

Patients living in KM disease-prone areas with macrophage blood cells of subtype I, which *did not* demonstrate the mutated grouping of DNA genes on Chromosome 6, showed susceptibility to the disease.

Ryan revealed to Matt, connecting the dots, "My previous research showed that the same mutated grouping prohibited the macrophages of subtype II from transporting therapies into cancerous target areas successfully. The subtype I macrophage white cells without the mutated grouping did effectively transport drug therapy." He continued, "I've reached my original research goal. It's time to go in another direction and pursue each subtype's role in the KM disease."

To begin achieving this goal, he directed technicians to extract roughly one hundred KM cells of subtype I from the bone marrow donor's abnormal macrophage white cell tissue culture media. After washing the cell surfaces and fracturing them with ultrasonic vibrations into a microscopic slush, a portion underwent analysis by advanced technology that weighed each molecule present in the slush and derived its elemental composition. This process defined all the molecules that composed the Killer Macrophages. The fluorescent screens and graph paper readouts revealed multiple spikes. Each one was representative of a known, sometimes unknown, substance. The results of this study showed that the majority of molecules were fundamental building blocks, at established proportions, expected to be generally present in white cells. However, there were ten outliers, i.e., unexpected molecules.

Six of the outliers from the KM slush analysis were dismissed as insignificant once an advanced study of standardized macrophage white blood cell cultures, used as controls, identified those same molecules. Ryan commented to Matt, "These molecules exist in all human white blood cells; therefore, they are not significant to our research. That left four outlier chemicals to be defined.

Ryan asked, "Where within the KM white blood cells do these four new found strangers reside?"

The next steps would involve performing intricate ultra-micro sampling of the KM cell's internal structures.

The boss then asked his techs, "Do we possess a technique to aspirate the contents of the vesicles?" and, "Are our current techniques sufficiently sophisticated to perform these isolations?".

"No!" was the answer to both questions, as reported by his experienced technicians.

Ryan shared with Matt, "We knew that cutting-edge analytical instrumentation was essential for success."

Most importantly, adequate magnification of the macrophages was required for accuracy in the extraction of the specimens from within the cell. This could be accomplished with the refinement of the electron level microscopic technology for use on living cells. One could then see the most minute structures of the KM white blood cells and accurately direct the aspiration pipette. Specialized technicians with extensive electron microscopic experience were assigned to make it happen. It required only three weeks.

Ryan's brief oral response to this success was, "Good job." His demeanor expressed grateful relief.

To aspirate the targeted material without cross-contamination required new instruments, ultramicroscopic pipets. The P. Voges Glass Company in Hamburg, Germany, was tasked with this requirement. A month after mailing specifications to the Voges designers, a UPS package labeled fragile was signed for by Ryan's Chief of Integrated Research.

Ryan announced, "That was fast. Now we're ready to go." He posed the question to the weekly lab group meeting, "Where to start?"

After an emotional group discussion, the decision was made to zero in on two targets. They would be the cell's content (cytoplasm) near the mitochondria which were next to the KM cell nucleus and the material within the vesicles.

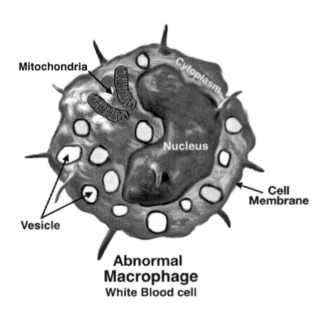

Abnormal
Macrophage
White Blood cell

"It is imperative to accomplish this technical goal," announced the Chief of Integrated Studies. He was responsible for creating three cross-trained teams of researchers. They were given strict parameters of operation and tasked to solve as many procedural questions as possible, with ultimate accuracy, in the shortest possible time frame.

"Let's get this done!" Ryan had directed.

The teams were not to compete but to share all accomplishments and lessons learned. The unity of the group's efforts was inspiringly productive as each strived to excel beyond previous personal performances. Within three months, the most exquisitely designed revolutionary techniques were developed to deliver the extreme accuracy necessary to sample the contents in targeted regions of the KM cells, i.e., the cell content near the nucleus and the material within the vesicles.

As practice runs were repeated, individual technical dexterity improved. When compared with what was just yesterday considered state of the art, the group was astounded to have gained such extraordinary visualization within a human cell and the advanced ability to aspirate its contents selectively.

Ryan praised his team, "Your pursuit of our accomplishments is nothing short of a miracle."

Researchers realized that they must rule out the existence of a DNA distortion in the KM cell's nucleus that was causing this disease. Therefore, the contents were extracted from the KM white blood cell nucleus and sent to the Geiger DNAnalytics lab in northern Massachusetts for genomic interpretation and sequencing. To avoid damaging the specimen, they strictly adhered to preservation methods and shipping requirements demanded by that facility.

Each research group's expressed commitment was summed up by a bright PhD candidate's proclamation: "We will leave no stone unturned to achieve perfection. Let's proceed with this extremely delicate experiment."

Utilizing the ground-breaking technology, the contents of the KM cell cytoplasm (cell's body material) in the area of the energy-producing mitochondrial power plants were sampled, as was the material within the vesicles of the KM cell. To successfully extract sufficient amounts of material for analysis from the contents inside the vesicles required an additional level of precision because of their small size.

All retrieved specimens from both areas were analyzed by advanced technology that weighed each molecule and defined its elemental composition. If there appeared to be any vagueness in the identity of molecules discovered in each of the two areas of testing, the protocol required repeating the analysis until all results were unfailingly reproducible.

The *same* ten molecules identified in the KM slush experiment were defined. Again, six existed in healthy macrophage white blood cells and were excluded. As before, four outlier molecules remained. They were *identical* to those found in the KM slush experiment.

These four chemical compounds were not identified in the ultrasonically created slush of *healthy* macrophage cells. Therefore, their presence in the KM cells was significant.

Three of the four appeared to be protein compounds, i.e., molecules whose structures were composed of carbon, oxygen, hydrogen, and nitrogen atoms, which are bound together by electronic charges. The remaining one appeared to demonstrate a basic six-carbon atom ring structure called the benzene ring.

Two of the protein compounds were the result of a known larger protein splitting in two. The investigators dismissed their significance. "Now we are down to two distinct compounds," Ryan told Matt.

"Are they the same two you found before? If so, where are they located within the KM cell?" prodded the euphoric journalist.

To increase the suspense, Ryan did not respond. But he said, "Let's call these two molecules that are not in a normal macrophage, compound A and compound B. The A is a protein and the B is a six-carbon ringed molecule. Compound B is near the mitochondria. Compound A is in the vesicles." Ryan speculated, "What is the relationship, if any, between these two compounds? Does one exist due to the action of the other?"

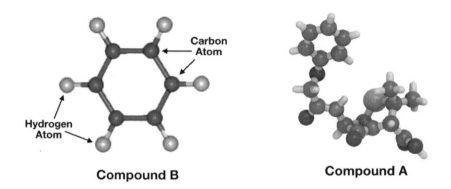

Compound B

Carbon
Atom

Hydrogen
Atom

Compound A

"We have come a long way!" he announced to Matt. He added, "But now we'll engage J. David Warren at New York's Metropolitan Medical College to determine the composition and structures of both compounds A and B."

CHAPTER 33

All human cells contain mitochondria. They are necessary for the all cells to survive and are considered the power plants of life. Oxygen is utilized by them to create a chemical fuel that supports metabolism. It's called ATP.

Ryan's lab analysis also revealed that compound A resided in moderate amounts near the location of the cell's mitochondria, the energy-producing small structures within a cell that support life.

With additional micropipette sampling, it was determined that the concentration of *compound A* was highest within the vesicles near the outer surface of the KM cell.

The KM cell mitochondria were saturated with the mysterious molecule, *compound B.*

Ryan theorized, "Perhaps under the influence of compound B, the mitochondria synthesized compound A which was then released into the macrophage's cytoplasm." He expanded his theory with, "Then A was collected, concentrated, and stored within the vesicles awaiting delivery to the outside of the KM cell. Once in the bloodstream it would establish its influence throughout the victim's body and cause the fatal disease." Ryan emphasized, "Compounds A and B did not belong within any human cell, much less that of a human macrophage infection-fighting white blood cell. Moreover, these contaminants have never before been identified within a normal or abnormal cell or in nature."

Both A and B were unique substances. However, until analyzed in Dr. Warren's lab, there would be no confirmation of our findings. With their elemental structures defined, there would be the capability to create both compounds for experimentation to begin the process of identifying their origins.

Now the work begins was Ryan's final thought.

Ryan implored his group, "Experimentally defining he relationship between compounds B and A is essential to revealing the causation of the fatal KM disease. Of equal import is the determination of compound B's origin."

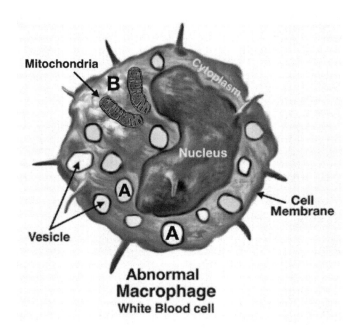

Abnormal
Macrophage
White Blood cell

CHAPTER 34

Michelle disclosed to Matt by landline that shortly after her informative Washington, DC, meeting with Dr. Declan Burke, Duane Wall, and Guy Marc Ferrier, she had received Declan's concisely formatted review of their discussion. It reiterated that the threat of malaria was a common denominator in the history of the fatal gangrenous disease. She urged her husband, Jon, to disseminate the meeting's findings via his email-blanketing program throughout the world.

She confided in Matt, "I hope this new information helps prevent another Claire."

Within seconds, Jon's email rocketed into a vapor that enveloped all the globe's continents. Of course, many recipients would be sleeping, and their response delayed. Jon's intake cataloging program filed responses in separate categories referencing the deadly disease by dates of diagnosis, country, prevailing climate, the use of the word malaria, month of the year, peak incidence years, mortality rates, and specific laboratory findings. The world was now effectively put on notice by Jon's computer blast.

Returning emails at first trickled in. In half a day, his innovative computer program was processing a steady stream of valuable information. At five days, Jon duplicated the email process to all electronic addresses that had failed to respond. There followed another wave of input, not as intense, but sufficient to increase stored information by an additional twenty-two percent.

Jon remarked to Michelle, "This program works well. I should publish its mechanics."

He noted three thousand four hundred and sixty-seven emails processed. Three hundred and four were nonsensical submissions, some by
twisted minds. The remaining three thousand one hundred and three were
legitimate when screened by Jon's program parameters. The bottom line of
this sophisticated endeavor revealed that the KM white cell disease was almost
universally fatal, and the vast majority of cases presented around fifteen years
ago. Laboratories documented abnormal appearing macrophages were in
ninety-two percent of the patients. Ninety-four percent of the patients spent
time in a tropical or subtropical environment, and in ninety-three percent,
the threat of contracting malaria in their geographic location was high. They
all utilized the preventive measures of mosquito netting and antimalarial
prophylaxis with oral medication.

Michelle noted to Matt, "Jon's findings reinforce the consensus of the
malaria connection we reached during the DC meeting in Dr. Declan Burke's
office." She immediately emailed this validating information to Declan, Duane
Wall, Matt, and Guy Marc.

Declan, in turn, forwarded Michelle's email, with his supportive opinion, to Ryan Larkin, Jesse Holt, and Mike Clark, for they were committed to
defining the details of this disease and would be attending the November 1985
meeting in Jesse's Washington office. By this time, each of the crusader's
thoughts and findings were immediately shared in group emails.

Matt's investigation became less stressful with all the information he
required to move forward being literally at his fingertips on the computer. He
now spent many fewer hours in airports. His time at home ballooned. The
symptoms of PTSD subsided. Maggie and the fourteen-year-old twins were
over the moon. "I now have time to begin an outline of my exposé," he shared
with his wife.

Declan became delirious with excitement when Ryan's email response
informed him that he had isolated two unique molecules from the KM white
blood cells: compounds A and B.

Ryan exclaimed, "They are the key to unraveling the KM mystery. I feel good about this."

Declan fired an urgent email to everyone heralding Ryan's work and informed them that the details would soon arrive. Declan then addressed the group with several key questions. Was there a direct linkage between the malaria parasite and the deadly disease? Was there an indirect linkage? What did compound B have to do with all of this? If compound A is the decisive instrument in causing the illness, where and how did it do its damage? Where did it come from?

Ryan informed Matt that he accepted the realization that he was the one who must pursue the answers to Declan's challenging queries. He announced to all, "This project's resources must grow. I need additional funding. I'm in for the duration."

One of Ryan's first thoughts after discovering compounds A and B was that of young heart surgery patient, Summer Anderson, who almost became a KM victim. He reminded his chief tech, "We could not culture KM cells from her blood. J. David Warren had analyzed Summer's blood and reported it contained only compound B. Interesting! Why not compound A?"

Ryan informed the group, "We'll have some answers soon from J. David's lab as to the validity of my lab's findings."

It took a few days. Dr. Warren repeated the Ryan lab's analysis of aspirated samples near the mitochondria and from within the vesicles of the KM white blood cells grown from stem cells retrieved from the bone marrow donor.

J. David excitedly called Ryan to tell him, "My analysis mirrors yours exactly. I found two distinct molecular compounds, A and B, that should not be present in normal macrophages."

He applied x-ray imaging, highly specialized techniques to determine the weight and molecular structure, and performed computer-generated modeling of compounds A and B. Not only did J. David successfully confirm the composition and architecture of both A and B compounds but he also developed a process to synthesize each compound for further experimentation.

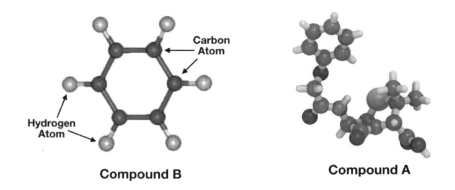

Compound B   **Compound A**

All agreed that *compound B*, found concentrated near the macrophage white blood cell nucleus, was located most probably within the mitochondria. As theorized previously, it consisted of a six-carbon atom benzene ring. A variety of atoms or groups of atoms that attached to the carbon atoms defined its influence within the targeted white cell.

Compound A was a protein molecule derived from amino acids, or small proteins, created from the body's building blocks of carbon, hydrogen, oxygen, and nitrogen atoms. They are combined by sharing electrons to create a large complex molecule, in this case compound A, a destructive enzyme antibody. Compound A represented a distortion of the normally appearing enzyme, which is generally released by healthy macrophages in minimal amounts. The unaltered enzyme antibody's healthy function was to protect the body by stimulating white cell production, tuning up the immune system, and attacking bacteria at sites of injury by inducing inflammation.

J. David wondered, *how was this enzyme's defined activity distorted to create a modified destructive enzyme antibody leading to gangrenous tissue, necrosis, and death?* He possessed the capability of synthesizing both A and B in his lab. This fact would guarantee an inexhaustible supply of these compounds to utilize in unlimited experimentation by Ryan's research group.

Each chemical's effect on healthy human tissue could now undergo testing. J. David was thrilled to have relayed his successes to Ryan. He was ecstatic and disseminated the exciting news to the group of committed investigators, Jesse Holt; GW surgeon, Declan Burke; Cardiothoracic Surgery Supervisor, Mike Clark; GW laboratory director, Duane Wall; Claire's husband, Guy Marc; and the deceased Private Burrows' fiancée, Michelle. All agreed that the scheduled meeting that November 1985 in Washington was premature, for Ryan required at least four months to institute his new line of investigation. They would share emails on a biweekly basis.

CHAPTER 35

Matt now felt it necessary to talk directly to Ryan and was rewarded with his enthusiasm and insight. His short flight from Milwaukee to St. Louis was by now routine. He knew where to stay and the restaurants to frequent. The Milwaukee Inquirer was excited about his accelerated progress with his investigation. Maggie had adjusted to his routine. She was grateful that even though his PTSD was initially exacerbated, he now had better control and had begun to share his feelings of guilt and depression with her. They were in the best place ever in admitting mutual emotions and concerns.

Ryan informed Matt that he reviewed Declan's email of proposed vital questions:

1) Was there a direct linkage between the malaria parasite, *Plasmodium falciparum*, and the deadly KM disease?

2) Was there an indirect linkage?

3) Where did compound B originate? Was it involved with the macrophage changes?

4) Did B, since it probably was within the mitochondria, initiate the production of compound A?

5) Recognizing its high vesicle concentration, if compound A is the decisive factor in causing the KM illness, where and how did it work?

Ryan had queried his staff meeting with, "Did compounds A or B originate from the malaria parasite in any of its life stages?"

If so, the patients demonstrating KM white blood cells must be actively infected with malaria and show the parasitic invasion of their red blood cells. These findings are easy to observe on a routine blood smear. Jon's global query proved that the malarial parasite did not appear in any of the diseased patient smears reviewed. Therefore, Ryan announced to Matt, "A direct effect of the malarial parasite in causing the KM disease does not exist."

Next, he addressed the indirect linkage. He proposed to Matt, "Was there an increased risk of developing lethal KM cells from being in an environment that exposed one to the threat of malaria infection?" He answered himself, "Definitely yes!"

Surely there seemed to be a connection, considering that most all those affected with KM white blood cells had resided in or traveled to malaria-prone countries with tropical and subtropical climates. As established by Ryan's concentration studies, which were confirmed by Dr. Warren of Metropolitan University Medical College, compound B primarily resided in the affected KM cell cytoplasm near the nucleus where the mitochondria resided. Ryan reminded Matt, "Compound B acted upon a site close to the macrophage nucleus and was most probably within the mitochondria." He then repeated his previously stated theory that compound B may incite the disease by influencing the mitochondria to produce compound A which was collected by the vesicles. The threatening compound A would then be released into the body's bloodstream circulation and distributed to all parts of the body.

He continued to theorize in more detail that the vesicles engorged with compound A attached to the KM cell's membrane wall and disrupted it with eroding chemicals thus releasing compound A from the KM cell. It was then transported from the fluid surrounding the cell through a capillary's thin wall to enter the body's circulation and eventually exert its deleterious effect downrange. Ryan exclaimed, "Where this occurs is a mystery."

To Matt, he emphasized the pressing questions were, "Is there an environmental reservoir of compound B that initiates the production of A within the cell? How did B achieve residence within the victim?" The Anopheles mosquito bite inoculates victims with the malaria parasite. Ryan asked, "Did this vector transmit compound B from one victim to another?"

Corollary inquiries existed. Could compound B's introduction result from injections for routine immunization, established treatments, oral ingestion, sexual contact, etc.? In his frustration, Ryan challenged, "Was B naturally occurring, or was it created by human technology?" Could one assume that compound A, which may be created by the action of compound B, cause the distorted and thickened macrophage membrane, cell enlargement, and bulging of the vesicles noted in the KM white blood cells? Perhaps of most significant importance, Ryan asked Matt, "Where are the tissue target cells and receptor sites where the destructive enzyme antibody, compound A, attaches to induce tissue destruction after its lethal journey through the bloodstream?

Matt returned home, utterly overwhelmed and confused.

CHAPTER 36

Ryan and Jesse Holt had hit it off during their exchange of email messages while negotiating visits, investigative avenues of research, and determining the relative importance of new information. They were about the same age and shared many of the same interests, especially the shooting sports and hunting. Both had spent countless days in the woods, fields, and waters of Minnesota for Jesse, and of Maryland for Ryan. They bonded and soon were sharing hunting experiences.

Both had established hunting connections to offer the other. Jesse offered goose and pheasant hunting in New York State, and Ryan had access to duck and deer hunting in Missouri. They also were quite accomplished skeet, trap, and sporting clay shooters and shared visits to the other's area gun clubs. They were friendly competitors, but as is the moral code at most shooting venues, they offered helpful criticism to affect the other's improvement. Each used their field guns for the shooting sports, the weapons with which they hunted. A shooter could severely deplete his bank account if they wished to purchase specialized weapons with which to compete.

Jesse told Kim that shooters believed "You can't have too many guns."

Their latest adventure was to engage brothers Frank and Matt Chavez at New Mexico Trophy Outfitters for an extraordinary elk hunt near Moro, New Mexico, about two hours north of Albuquerque off Route 518. The beautiful Sangre de Cristo Mountains were a constant backdrop. Frank and Matt, accomplished outdoorsmen, had grown up in the Moro area and had hunted every square inch of its hills, mountains, and plateaus. They were weapons experts. Frank was detailed to protect the New Mexico governor, Tony Anaya, and Matt directed a SWAT unit protecting the US facility at Las

Alamos, NM. Their parents and another brother still lived in the area. Their father processed the harvested animals and provided taxidermy services for full mounts, European mounts, or just antlers. Their mother cooked the most delicious Southwestern meals. When in Moro, the hunters became family.

Several years ago, Jesse had successfully hunted with these outfitters. He reassured Ryan, "Frank and Matt have known the local ranchers for years." He shared that they had purchased state-issued elk permits from ranch owners whose land sustained trophy animals the brothers had spotted when scouting by glassing or whose image appeared on a trail camera. After being spotted by Frank and Matt, the guides plotted the location and travel routes. The elk permits from those ranch locations were prized. All hunters fantasized about harvesting a six point elk with a massive wide spread.

Jesse and Ryan had flown individually into Albuquerque. They joined three other hunters, Bob Weisgerber, Jim Stark, and J. D. Arnold from New York State at the Ramada for an overnight stay. Jesse was surprised to learn that he had previously encountered one of the New York hunters, Bob, at his wedding reception in Saratoga Springs, New York. He was a childhood friend of his wife, Kim, and also of Private Richard Burrows. This realization triggered a mild episode of panic and urgency that he did not share with Bob. He decided to disclose the connection to Ryan when they were back in the room.

The hunt for all the men involved was successful and safe. All harvested remarkable animals. Jesse and Ryan were overwhelmed with excitement and satisfaction as they packed their frozen meat into coolers, gathered clothes and equipment, arranged for their trophies to be mounted, and boarded Frank's truck for the trip back to the Albuquerque Airport. They would recommend Frank and Matt Chavez without reservation to all who inquired about planning a single elk hunt. Ryan queried, "Frank, may we commit for the opening week again next year? "You're on" was the response.

CHAPTER 37

In an email, Ryan revealed to Matt how he put the squeeze on Jesse. He said to Matt, "We had had such a great time in New Mexico that I was sure Jesse was in a giving mood." Ryan continued, "I needed a significant financial infusion of cash to continue my research."

He informed Matt that grant writing was an art form, and he and his group were very accomplished in this activity. There were billions of research dollars floating around in the corridors of hundreds of governmental agencies, private foundations, and individual benefactors. The problem arose if one requested support for a project that was not popular, in the news, or trendy. KM white blood cell deaths were now, in 1986, an unusual occurrence, and their most notorious impact was over a decade ago. Ryan knew of Jesse's involvement with Senator David Sokolov's presidential election committee as a speechwriter and political consultant.

Ryan informed Matt, "I was encouraged. Perhaps Jesse's positive attitude toward veterans and genuine interest in solving the KM white blood cell travesty would induce him to solicit the senator's favor in securing the all-important research funding." He recalled Jesse's emotionally charged reaction when, in Albuquerque, engaging a hunter he had previously met at his wedding reception in Saratoga Springs, New York. This fellow had grown up with one of the early KM victims from Amsterdam, NY, Private Richard Burrows.

Early one Sunday evening, not long after the New Mexico trip, Ryan called Jesse at home in Alexandria, Virginia. Ryan proceeded to summarize the progress in understanding the gangrenous disease and, most importantly, J. David Warren's definition and replication of the two molecular compounds, A and B, which were key to the causation of the deadly illness. Ryan continued that extensive testing will be required to define each chemical's influence on the macrophage white blood cells and how that influence changes a normal white cell into a KM cell.

He told Matt, "I pleaded, 'Jesse, we are so close. We just need sufficient funding to prove those crucial relationships between both compounds and the KM disease.'"

Jesse was well versed and sympathized with the tainted morality, political quagmire, atrocity, long-term effects, and universal suffering from the Vietnam War. He was keen to eliminate the threat of the KM white blood cells, perhaps another obscene legacy of Vietnam. The macrophages were still, over a decade later, a menace since their origin was not scientifically defined. Therefore, it was foolhardy to disregard this disease as a threat to society. It did not matter to Jesse if only a few suspected cases occurred annually. He considered the KM cells, in their perfect storm scenario, as being the epicenter of a potentially wide-ranging national or even international public health crisis resulting in thousands of deaths.

Jesse had said to Ryan, "Not only could the United States but also the world be at risk."

Ryan then described to Matt how Jesse approached and solved the financial deficit.

Having been brought into the inner circle because of his unique and exceptional political insight and speech writing skills, Jesse had direct access to Senator Sokolov. He understood that the persons concerned with the success of this politician's campaign were amenable to strategies to bolster the senator's approval ratings.

At a staff meeting of Sokolov's stratagem advisors, Jesse proposed the eradication of a potentially deadly disease that not only had killed our Vietnam soldiers and veterans but also recently killed Americans and may eminently attack our country. He had suggested that a plea could be sold, by Sokolov's staff, to the public that eradicating this threatening disease was imperative, or Americans will die. The threat will be dealt with by the champion of the people, Senator David Sokolov. The politician's inner circle of advisors salivated at the potential for political gain.

Without hesitation, the senator began to exercise his power to fast-track a financial procurement agenda for Ryan through the legislative process. As an astute politician, he knew how to advertise a threat to the public and then appear to eliminate that threat, therefore, achieving instant approval from that same voting public. The candidate reflected that he would reap a ton of votes riding in on his white horse.

With national and international fanfare, the NY Times, the Washington Post, CBS, NBC, and all conceivable media lovingly endorsed Sokolov's decision to spearhead the allocation of massive funding for research into the KM white blood cell, now considered a global threat. The bill to allocate funding passed in Congress and the Senate with little opposition.

This accomplishment heralded far and wide, producing an eight-and-a-half percent boost in the senator's polling numbers by the day after the current lame-duck Big Pharma beholding US President signed the one-and-a-half-million-dollar appropriations bill into law.

With Sokolov's masterful allocation of these funds, Ryan would have free reign in devising, directing, and bringing to fruition the research necessary to eliminate the potential KM white blood cell scourge.

Ryan excitedly disclosed to Matt the bonus of Attica Ossining, the most preeminent Big Pharma international conglomerate and Senator Sokolov's most powerful puppeteer, recognizing this potential mega-windfall of positive publicity. A matching bequest from AOP materialized at Washington University in St. Louis for discretionary use in Dr. Ryan Larkin's research. This most generous humanitarian gift to eradicate a dreaded disease was heralded robustly, to Attica Ossining's greedy self-satisfaction, in the national and international media. The senator and the self-serving drug company radiated the intoxication of being in control of their destiny.

The senator rejoiced to Attica Ossining board members, "We, as a united front, are now the most powerful, influential, and obvious shoo-in for capturing the 1988 White House Presidency and its rich rewards." The same officials celebrated among themselves that they would be represented in the most powerful corridors of the United States government by a beholding President.

Ryan continued to inform Matt, "Jesse and I realized that there was a symbiotic, i.e., self-serving relationship between Big Pharma and Senator Sokolov. But we rationalized that this arrangement met the usually accepted standard of political interaction and influence peddling. We were thrilled that with the generous funding, it will hopefully enhance humanity's future and well-being."

Jesse Holt, the public relations expert, and Ryan Larkin, the committed researcher, had no realization that Attica Ossining thoroughly owned the senator. He was their puppet. This situation heralded excessive influence by the drug industry upon national and global political decisions.

CHAPTER 38

As a result of his recent discussion with Ryan, Matt was excited to uncover the Attica Ossining Pharmaceutical connection with Senator Sokolov. He researched the company's history, which turned out to be a fascinating story.

In a rural setting just north of New York City, the brothers David and Jacob Atticowski founded Attica Pharmaceuticals in 1918. They were Russian Jews who had fled Moscow to escape religious persecution resulting from the increasingly widespread acceptance of the perceived threat of Jewish Bolshevism. This idea arose from the belief that the combined socio-political activities of Jews, Germans, and Bolsheviks were the origins of the incessant fervor for revolution in Russia.

The brothers were born into the modest circumstances of a family whose household head was a clerk and accountant in a mid-level Moscow bookkeeping enterprise that employed twelve men. Anna, their domineering mother, worked as a chemist in a factory that created scented soaps for distribution regionally and into Western Europe. The boys often accompanied their mother to work and became fascinated with the innumerable aromas derived by basic chemistry from an inexhaustible global supply of flowers, herbs, and plants.

David had said to Jacob, "I love watching Mother work. The scents she isolates are so pleasing."

"I do, too," replied his younger brother and added, "I want to learn how to figure out the ingredients that create the aromas."

Only a few years apart in age, they both excelled academically, and predictably, pursued careers in the field of chemistry. David, the oldest, concentrated on organic compounds, and Jacob, a few years younger, became an expert in analytical methods. They wished to examine accepted herbal remedies and identify, extract, and reproduce the active compounds that could advance modern medicine.

They were devotees of Shropshire Wellington, MD, an English botanist, geologist, and chemist who had observed the efficacy of the foxglove plant when administered to patients with dropsy, i.e., congestive heart failure. In 1785, he reported the isolation of the plant's medicinal compound, digitalis. This drug was still fundamental to the treatment of heart disease in the twentieth century.

Jacob had said, "Would it not be extraordinary to discover such a great contribution to medical science?"

David's response was, "Anything is possible."

For example, he divulged that the chewing and swallowing of the outer layer of the bark of the cinchona tree was a treatment for malaria since the early sixteen-hundreds. Eventually, in 1820, quinine was isolated from the cinchona bark and defined as the responsible compound.

In Russia, by late 1916, there began to appear the threat of revolution, the decline in general prosperity, and decreased freedom of expression. Also, liquidity of cash declined, and anti-Semitism grew. This frightening deluge of factors fostered David and Jacob's decision to abandon their birthright. They were encouraged by their parents. Their odyssey would take almost two years.

They traveled separately by train into Western Europe. David journeyed to Warsaw and on to Berlin. Jacob made his way southwest to Vienna into Austria-Hungary. They would meet again in several months' time at the De Lutece Hotel near Notre Dame in Paris and contact Willy Schmidt.

"Don't worry," David reassured Jacob. "I trust Willy to keep us safe and complete our arrangements to flee persecution in Russia." This fellow, a

German citizen, as a child, had lived in Moscow with his family. His father was a visiting professor of art history at Moscow University. The young man had attended primary school with David and Jacob. He then apprenticed in the Paris studios of van Gogh, Gauguin, and Seurat and now resided in that city as a respected artist of the Post-Impressionist era. Willy abhorred anti-Semitism and acted as a facilitator in accommodating the immigration of Jews to safer environs. He had accumulated great wealth as the demand for his artwork escalated. He was more than happy to prepare the brothers with proper documentation, cash, and travel arrangements. Willy arranged for a trustworthy contact in Marseilles who, with an established network, would guarantee the Atticowski brothers' safe passage to New York City.

"We can't thank you enough, Willy," said David.

Jacob added, "May God bless you."

Despite being a hugely successful artist, Willy was reserved and humble. He hugged both old friends, knowing he would never see them again. He said, "God bless and be with you," then abruptly departed.

They languished in Marseilles for three months, awaiting the creation of forged documents and the arrival of a sympathetic ship captain who, for a fee commensurate with the risk involved, would accept the brothers for passage. The voyage across the Atlantic within the confines of the *SS Normandie* was a test of their enterprising spirit. Their time at sea increased due to the necessity of circumnavigating a monstrous storm.

They found themselves near the bow and four levels below deck. Here the ship pitched, rocked, and swayed more so than other areas of the vessel. Seasickness, vertigo, and nausea became constant companions. David and Jacob shared with four young Italian male passengers a sweaty, cramped, dark, and cluttered sleeping quarter. It was foul-smelling from years of transporting numerous unwashed men in a crowded space designed to accommodate two. With only one bunk bed, dice rolled each evening to determine which two would sleep with some comfort. For makeshift beds, they were able to scrounge a few extra mattresses to cover the cabin's cold, damp, mildew-covered, vibrating steel deck. The Italians had traveled with a generous quantity of their hometown Chianti and did freely share their libation with the Atticowski brothers.

David decided, "I'll drink enough to numb this sickening experience."

The ship's food was barely adequate in amount and flavor. Their Italian traveling mates offered cheese, meats, and slightly stale bread; the brothers welcomed these gifts.

The communal bathroom with its low ceiling at the far end of the passageway was cramped and cold. Its toilet and sink barely functioned. There was no shower. This facility quickly became inadequate to service the horde of men attempting to relieve themselves of vomit, urine, and stool when nature randomly called. Seasickness was a recurring problem, and more often than not, the nauseous passengers erupted with indiscriminately aimed bile-tinged hurl of their latest stomach contents that splashed off the nearest wall. The repellent air integrated the combined olfactory presence of sweat, vomit, urine, defecation, sea spray, and diesel fumes.

Seeking relief from these trying circumstances, those capable, in hopes of breathing fresh air, headed for any deck space that was not already overwhelmed with distraught passengers.

"Thank God this voyage only took twelve days," Jacob choked to David, breathing in deeply the refreshing damp, slightly wood smoke-scented New York Harbor air. They excitedly observed the distant Ellis Island.

There was an overwhelming number and variety of ships and other watercraft cluttering the vast expanse of grayish steel-blue, white-capped water of the harbor. It was so vast that it almost disappeared into the far off horizon. New York City, from this distance, appeared to be a child's miniature playset of model wood and brick structures of varied sizes and shapes. The bright blue sky was sullied by puffy curls of undulating black-tinged smoke that reached upward and eventually dissipated.

There was a cacophony of noise from a multitude of steamships' whistles. Waves aggressively splashed against their ship's hull. Floating seagulls squawked in protest when dispossessed by a vessel's authoritative progress. These sounds and the cheers and celebratory hoots and hollers of their fellow shipmates welcomed a new chapter in the lives of the brothers Atticowski.

As their ship glided below her, they were delighted by the beckoning of France's gift to the United States, Eiffel's elegant Statue of Liberty on its own small New York Harbor island. The golden flame of her torch stretched into the cloudless blue sky.

"This is our new home," David declared.

"I can't believe we are here," Jacob answered.

Just beyond Lady Liberty, they spotted Ellis Island. The brothers understood they would undergo screening as they passed through the prominent three-story French Renaissance Revival designed red brick building with limestone trim. There was sufficient dock space to accommodate their large ship's mooring. Other unimpressive outbuildings dotted the landscape.

After disembarking and tagging their luggage, they entered the main building. The recording of the ship that transported them, the date of embarkation, one's name, occupation, and the amount of cash on hand were required. The United States only wanted to admit those who could support themselves and possessed sufficient start-up money to do so. They ascended the scuffed marble steps as directed, up a staircase to the second floor to undergo a medical examination. As they ascended, experienced eyes observed the new arrivals for signs of disease, be it weakness, infirmity, shortness of breath, or signs of mental illness. There followed a thorough physical examination with a chalk designation written on one's jacket if additional evaluation were deemed necessary.

David received a large X in a circle chalked to his coat's left breast pocket to indicate further evaluation of his heart. To their relief, re-examination by a more experienced physician determined his heart demonstrated no significant abnormality.

"That could have been a disaster!" David, now relaxed, sighed to Jacob.

Next, they underwent an eye examination for trachoma, an infectious eye disease that could cause blindness. If detected, entrance into the United States was instantly denied.

Following the medical examination procedures, the brothers underwent one additional bit of processing. The clerk's auditory acuity was not sufficient to clearly hear and thus accurately transcribe the Atticowski name. He took the liberty to shorten it to Attica, their new last name.

They reclaimed their meager luggage and were transported by barge across the remaining stretch of the harbor to their new home. As their transportation approached the lower tip of Manhattan Island, the miniature buildings seen from afar became an intimidating, undulating smoky confluence of structures, large and small, of wood and brick.

Jacob announced, "After all this time, we're a breath away from making it to our new life." David wept silently.

The size, congestion, and confusion of negotiating New York's streets in bustling lower Manhattan were daunting. The avenues were crowded with darting people, slow overburdened pull-carts, elite horse-drawn carriages, hawkers selling their wares, and mounted horses. These activities were challenging obstacles to the most sophisticated new arrival. Adaptation and acclimatization to their stressful surroundings were made less burdensome by having engaged, before setting sail from Europe, a sponsor in this new land. Willy, their Paris contact with years of trial and error in these dealings, had established a first-rate stable of advisors with specialized expertise to aid the wide variety of new arrivals.

At three in the afternoon on April 13, 1917, David and Jacob introduced themselves to a gentleman dressed elegantly and wearing a shiny top hat. They were on the steps of the Alexander Hamilton Customs House at 1 Bowling Green, on the southern tip of Manhattan. He was their prearranged sponsor who, after arriving in New York, had established a successful small company that manufactured paint, both commercial and residential. He kindly offered them free workspace in his waterfront factory and access to his suppliers. Adjacent to the eight-hundred-square-foot workspace, they would utilize a comfortable bedroom with an attached indoor bathroom, a luxury for those times.

Jacob announced, "What an improvement from what we put up with on the ship."

David could not believe their luck.

CHAPTER 39

In 1917, the Attica brothers' business initially dealt with isolating chemical compounds from naturally occurring materials that, after rendering, were distributed as fragrances throughout the world of wholesale. Their business grew exponentially. By the time of their deaths within a month of each other in 1969, they had owned a multimillion-dollar pharmaceutical company traded on the New York Stock Exchange with the symbol AOP, i.e., Attica Ossining Pharmaceutical. In 1942, the brothers' preeminence was solidified by the procurement, then integration, of Ossining Chemical into the original company.

AOP outbid the competition and was the primary supplier of the new sulfa antibiotic, originally developed by Bayer in 1932, for use by the United States during World War II. This transaction realized extraordinary profits. A group of investment bankers purchased Attica Ossining Pharmaceutical Corporation for a sweet eighty million dollars from the brothers, David and Jacob, in 1960.

David told his lawyer, "For better or worse, our families will be rich forever." Jacob, recognizing the aggressiveness of the new owners, asked David, "What will become of our company?"

Under the bankers' direction, management underwent restructuring, and the bottom line now ruled in all company activities nationally and abroad. Newly minted MBAs applied their ruthless number-crunching, with the blessing of the recently hired and unbelievably over-compensated executives, to wring every dollar of profit possible out of the company's operations.

Changes imposed were streamlining the workforce, increasing the workload for those employees retained, and encouraging management to micromanage the workers at all levels of responsibility. With this shift in policy, the unit cohesiveness and pride of accomplishment that had resulted in the most exceptional quality control when the Attica brothers were in charge gradually eroded as each employee began to dread and fear the nit-picking atmosphere within which they labored. Soon the company culture allowed cutting corners in production to achieve imposed deadlines and production quotas.

An established shortcut was to alter the standard temperature used in a chemical reaction. This trick and other shady techniques accelerated the rate of a chemical reaction's completion. There resulted the creation of a higher yield in a shorter time therefore, increasing efficiency and profit. However, in employing these dubious industry practices, it was imperative to check the drug or other chemicals produced for contaminants for they could be toxic. AOP did not!

Since shortcuts were universally adopted within the company and consented to by the President, CEO, and most employees, they became the new accepted normal. As time passed, among the employees, there was also more frequent and less constrained discussion about their work conditions. Workers were demoralized and angry. Many were embarrassed by their work product. There was talk of unionizing.

However, the company and its executives did prosper. AOP's stock's dollar value became inflated to the collective appreciation of their investors. To display their status, AOP's corporate offices were moved to 6000 Avenue of the Americas in New York City.

No one foresaw that their aberrant but profitable policies instituted in 1962 would in 1988 destroy AOP's stock value and also influence the outcome of a presidential election.

CHAPTER 40

To gain background information, Matt did more research into Senator David Sokolov and the politics of an election year. The journalist's efforts were fruitful.

With dramatic fanfare, in mid-1986, Sokolov had announced his candidacy for the Democratic Presidential nomination. His campaign's primary thrust was to accumulate an enormous financial backing, allowing him to dominate all presidential candidates, Democratic and Republican.

"We've got this thing sewn up!" the Democratic National Chairman boasted to the senator's staff. It was January of 1988. By this time, the Democratic platform supported liberal issues; financial pledges were reaffirmed and endorsements solidified. Political action committees had aligned with their most appealing candidate and party. Occasionally, the PACs and individual donors covered their bases by supporting candidates from both major parties. Analysis of published poll numbers determined the best allocation of resources to obtain the most voter bang for the buck.

The chairman asked, "How many dollars and how many candidate visits to selected districts would be necessary to lock up a state's primary and its pledged delegates?" There was an effort by presidential candidates and their parties to achieve dominance in pledged delegate numbers as early in the year as possible. States jockeyed for positions of importance in the selection of the winner by initiating their primaries early in the year.

Attica Ossining Pharmaceutical was in the driver's seat. Their accepted principle was that money talks. Senator Sokolov's deviant advice encouraged AOP's disbursement of corrupting funds through its board of directors to those who would guarantee the ignoring of loose quality control for AOP's manufacture of drugs in the United States and offshore in China. This maneuver had resulted in decreased expenditures for internal oversight, which culminated in the accumulation of obscene profits. To ensure this state of affairs persisted, the company continued to donate profusely to the Democratic Party's war chest, and for good measure, supported some PACs that, in turn, gushed fealty to the senator and his political party.

Senator Sokolov encouraged his team, "Let's keep this express train rolling."

AOP had received national acclaim for its support of research in the field of infectious disease. The crown jewel was its generous support of Dr. Ryan Larkin's investigation into the KM disease. The NY Times, NBC, CBS, and other major news outlets were excessive in the extent to which APO was showered with praise. Its stock value continued to soar, and the board of directors, with little hesitation due to their euphoria of success, irresponsibly approved a concept for the company's expansion that invaded and almost emptied their liquid cash reserves. The prevailing attitude was not to worry; the depleted funds were not an issue due to AOP's sterling track record of profitability.

Senator Sokolov was riding a wave of popular endearment. He manipulated the press to receive accolades for aligning AOP with the funding of multiple research projects. Therefore, he was considered the ad hoc protector of the people. He reveled in his sarcasm, saying, "I'm their Russian white knight."

Not apparent to the nation was the looming danger of Sokolov's concession to Big Pharma's influence not to make decisions that were best for America, but for the pharmaceutical industry, due to his complete subjugation by AOP and the many other Big Pharma companies.

The Iowa Primary took place at the end of January. It was followed in February by those of New Hampshire, South Carolina, and Nevada. All these contests resulted in a landslide of pledged delegates toward the senator's achieving the Democratic Presidential nomination. Following Super Tuesday, at the end of February, Senator Sokolov prevailed with an overwhelming number of pledged delegates.

A reporter asked, "How do you think you are doing?"

"I can't wait to receive our party's nomination," he bragged to the press.

The Democratic National Convention took place in Chicago's United Center in mid-August 1988. The keynote address was delivered by a young black United States senator from that state, a retired Army Colonel, who bewitched the audience with carefully calculated dosages of eloquence, pride, and humanity. This gentleman, a decorated combat engineer who served in Vietnam, was immediately thrust into the limelight and was established as a future presidential candidate.

Optimistic and persuasive speeches by a variety of dignitaries illuminated the stage. Patriotic music blared. Thousands of placards, with a nominee's name, photo, and slogan, colorfully danced under the ceiling of red, white, and blue balloons contained in nets above the crowd. These were to be released upon choosing the Democratic Presidential candidate.

Sokolov celebrated in saying, "I can see all these balloons floating down around me."

Like a swarm of guppies in a fishbowl, the delegates' restless hovering occasionally dissolved into an erratic explosion of activity within their state's appointed position on the convention floor. There were frequent boisterous shouts in support of the California senator, followed by the intense applause of approbation.

To no one's surprise, Senator David Sokolov was selected by acclamation as the 1988 Democratic candidate for President of the United States. His acceptance speech was the standard fare of promises impossible to keep, assurances impossible to sustain, and foresightedness impossible to imagine. He then announced his Vice Presidential running mate. It was the honorable governor of New York State, a retired Air Force Vietnam veteran and attorney. AOP's President and Chairman of the Board, Jim Parry, had introduced

Senator Sokolov to the governor a month before at a Democratic fundraiser at the Waldorf Astoria on Park Avenue in New York City. The implied message from the board and delivered to their puppet politician was, "Here is your choice for VP."

The governor was a downstate politician who had loyally represented AOP's voting district in the New York State Senate for fifteen years. He was appointed New York State Attorney General and made national headlines with his prosecution of those trafficking kidnapped children. He then ran for and became governor three years earlier. AOP's board of directors also owned this governor.

There were now about seventy-five days remaining until the National Election. To reinforce his position, candidate Sokolov crisscrossed the country to rallies in states where he was the choice. He also visited those states wherein his approval was less reliable in an attempt to win over voters and perhaps win that state's electoral votes.

The Republican National Convention, a few weeks later in Milwaukee, proclaimed the Montana governor as their nominee. He was a true conservative who won a close race over his six primary opponents. He supported the death penalty, had served as a Marine in Vietnam, was an avid outdoorsman, advocated for the second amendment, and was a lifetime NRA member. The Montana governor pleaded for veteran rights, had been CEO of a multinational chemical company, was faithful to his wife of twenty-two years, and adored his three children. He was a popular public figure without detrimental baggage but lacked the national pedigree that Senator Sokolov had established. "Come on, guys, I need your help," he pleaded to his advisors. He would receive an overwhelming boost from a truly unexpected source.

CHAPTER 41

Interrupting his review of national politics, Matt was asked by his editor to represent the Milwaukee Inquirer in covering the Presidential debates. Maggie enjoyed politics and loved having him home. She knew the dirt on Senator David Sokolov from her discussions with her husband. She was looking forward to this political faceoff.

Matt continued his search and uncovered more about that year's obligatory presidential debates. The details involved in scheduling these spectacles resulted from negotiations among both nominees' representatives and the debate producers and moderators. It would take place at the CNN studios at the Omni Center in Atlanta, GA. CNN's studios in Washington, DC and Los Angeles would also have live feeds. The positioning of the podiums, the order of presentations, the time allotted to answer questions and to present rebuttals, lighting, audience participation, and a hundred other issues had to be successfully negotiated for the presidential debates to appear on national television.

CNN, the first all-news network, had been created by Ted Turner. An outspoken breed of news personalities generated the network's success; they also made great debate moderators.

The successful negotiations defined the dynamics of the debates; a decision did result in having co-moderators, one male and one female. This arrangement arose from the popularity of the CNN woman commentators and the prominent emerging role of women in the media. Debate questions would be developed by these professionals to be succinct, neutral in tone, and representative of the public's concerns.

Matt and Maggie's current dinner discussion was the election. She said to Matt, "I think Sokolov's a degenerate."

He replied, "I agree," and headed back to his desk at the Inquirer, after gulping down his dinner. She attended to the high-school-aged twins.

The paper had sent several reporters to interview the Democratic nominee in Chicago just prior to the debates.

The candidate was asked by an Inquirer reporter at his headquarters, "What do you think your chances are?" He answered, "I'm a shoo-in to win the Presidency of the United States. The pressure is off. The debates are just a formality."

Matt was hoping this prediction would not come to fruition.

Matt's editor praised him for the quality of the future Presidential Debate coverage. "Your writing is balanced and informative," he concluded. He then coached, "You better get back to your lethal white blood cell story."

"I know, boss, it's taking a while," Matt responded.

Just notified in a group email about Ryan's latest breakthrough, Matt said, "I'll return my attention to him and travel back to his lab and gather more of Ryan's story for my exposé."

He rushed home to Maggie and the kids and enjoyed the meatloaf, his favorite, she served. Her trick was to add beef bouillon and Italian seasoned bread crumbs.

Matt apologetically informed her, "I'm off to St. Louis in the morning to see Larkin."

She replied, "Not so soon, I'm accustomed to having you home."

Having traveled the same route so many times, it felt like he landed immediately after takeoff. In St. Louis, the George Washington University's architecture and campus still impressed him. He reprogrammed himself to be accommodating to the researcher's rapid-fire information sharing.

Sitting in his small but comfortable office, Ryan began his review for Matt. With the precise identification of the chemical composition and structure of the two elicited compounds, A and B, by Dr. Warren at Metropolitan Medical College, Ryan would now begin designing experiments to unravel the mysterious relationship between these chemical compounds.

He queried his lab, "How does the usually protective and life-supporting macrophage white blood cell become transformed into a vicious enemy of the body resulting in a potentially gruesome death?"

By mapping out its basic structure, contents, and determining each element's function within the cell, the necessary understanding of the macrophage emerged. "We desperately needed this information," Ryan reiterated.

He reviewed for Matt his lab's progress. Ryan's people successfully developed techniques utilizing the macrophage white blood cell subtype I to more precisely deliver drugs into targeted areas for the treatment of disease. In those studies, two subtypes of the macrophage white blood cell existed, i.e., I and II. The CDC had established that patients with macrophage white blood cell subtype II did receive protection against developing the KM disease from a mutated gene group in Chromosome 6 of subtype II's nuclear DNA. However, these macrophage white blood cells lacked the ability to deliver drugs to targeted areas of the body. Several experiments defined that mutation as the generator of the protection against the KM disease.

Macrophage white blood cell subtype I did not demonstrate the mutated gene group on Chromosome 6 in its nuclear DNA but excelled in drug delivery. Of significant concern, patients with subtype I showed susceptibility to the KM cell changes that lead to death.

Now Ryan reviewed how he would move forward. He proposed a sequence of investigative steps to define the development of lethal changes in macrophages of subtype I. All evidence and discussion considered compound B to be the initiating factor.

Next, it is imperative to delineate the journey of compound A, to follow A as it travels from where it is manufactured near the macrophage's nucleus, through the cell's body (cytoplasm), and into the vesicles. Finally, the researchers must commit to confirming how it enters the body's circulation and what it attacks down range to produce the KM patient deaths.

They refined the hypothesis to propose that compound B overwhelmed the normal state of affairs inside the cell, most probably within the energy-producing mitochondria that resided near the nucleus. Their function in producing ATP was necessary for each cell and therefore, the patient to survive. The theory continued that once inside the mitochondria, the B molecule then coerced the production of compound A.

Ryan envisaged to Matt, "Our lab proposed, would it not be great if we could prove that a specific metabolic function within the mitochondrion suffers derangement by compound B?"

Ryan now reviewed with Matt the solutions his lab pursued to answer these questions.

With a phosphorescent marker attached, compound B was spread over a Petri dish containing hundreds of cultured subtype I macrophages. The mixture was then warmed to body temperature in an incubator for twenty-four hours. Ryan described the anticipation within his lab as palpable when the allotted time for incubation had expired and the Petri dish was retrieved. A projection of ultraviolet light through an electron microscope bathed the surface of the manipulated macrophages. To everyone's delight, there appeared a dense concentration of compound B phosphorescence close to the nucleus of each subtype I macrophage white blood cell. A riotous cheer erupted that startled those passing in the hallway. Ryan was delighted. Increased magnification revealed their prize. It became evident that the cell's mitochondria near the nucleus had concentrated the B molecule.

He told Matt, "As theorized, B compound had found its way into the subtype I cells and appear to be inside the mitochondria. The experimental results were proof."

The most potent magnification tool, the electron microscope, disclosed the specific site of attachment within the mitochondrial. It turned out to be its inner wall.

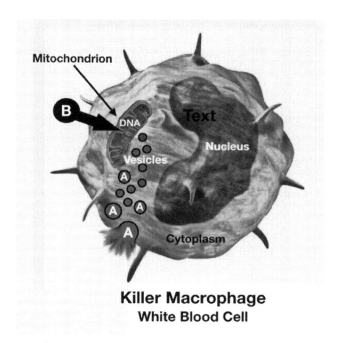

Killer Macrophage
White Blood Cell

Ryan had ascertained the proof that patients whose blood contained the susceptible subtype I macrophages were at risk of developing the KM disease.

Ryan was so excited as he raced through his current revelations while Matt was vigorously taking notes. Matt teased Ryan, "Good thing, I'm taping this conversation."

He replied, "Ok, ok," and continued, "But wait, there's much more!"

The researcher recounted that his group continued to brainstorm. "What was going on inside each mitochondrion?" was the united concern. Compound B did concentrate on the inner wall of the double-walled, infinitesimal life-supporting mitochondria. This same location was known to be the exact site where mitochondrial DNA resided.

"That DNA creates the table of contents of the book of life, so to speak," said Ryan.

Could compound B enter the macrophage's body through a pathway in the cell membrane that it chemically altered and hijacked? Probably so, since that process is known to occur in nature. Did compound B then assault the mitochondria by taking advantage of specialized channels in this tiny organelle's wall? Molecules needed to sustain life entered the mitochondria through the same channels.

The mitochondrion's responsibility was to join oxygen with other molecules to form ATP. This process supplies, through ATP, the necessary energy to drive all the body's processes for maintaining life. Multiple mitochondria in each of the body's diverse cells produce ATP that is programmed to accomplish a defined energy task for only its category of cells.

Ryan informed Matt, "The macrophage white blood cell nucleus contains the dominant DNA that supervises all the cell's functions. The nuclear DNA sends signals to the DNA that resides on the inner wall of the mitochondria to program it to complete its appointed mission."

Ryan said to Matt that they must considered the question, "Could the patients with macrophage subtype I, who are susceptible to the KM disease, suffer an alteration of their DNA within its nucleus by exposure to compound B?

"This was a good question. But, an *erroneous thesis*," Ryan said, "Because the tagged compound B was *not* found inside the macrophage subtype I cell nucleus but in the region of mitochondria."

He announced, "In the KM disease, the mitochondrial inner wall DNA erroneously directed the production of the lethal compound A under compound B's deleterious influence."

Ryan declared, "Compound B overrode the harmonious instructions that usually emanated from macrophage's nucleus DNA. That's where we found the compound B, inside the mitochondria."

CHAPTER 42

Matt frantically continued his rapid notations. Ryan was possessed with excitement and felt compelled to present his findings as quickly as possible. His untucked shirttail and frenetic gesturing were out of character.

Ryan continued. "I decided to reinvigorate my group's efforts." He proposed to his lab, "Perhaps we may appreciate more about this KM disease process by investigating its devastating results and working backward." He challenged his team with a new question, "Where do the devastating bacteria originate that causes the KM clinical picture of tissue infection and necrosis?"

Ryan arranged to meet with a professor of medicine and chairman of the infectious disease department at Washington University's Medical School. This physician and his researchers became aware that the intestine, also known as the gut or more specifically, the colon, harbored an extraordinary number of benign and life-threatening bacteria. The integrity of a layer of cells lining the intestinal wall prevents bacteria from invading our bodies.

The infectious disease physician told Ryan, "This effective barrier is called the mucosa." He added, "Our lives depend on it."

Ryan responded, "I had no idea!"

The expert continued that many colonic bacteria are beneficial to our health as long as they remain contained within the colon. He suggested, "They may even influence our genetic makeup." The researcher continued, "There are disease states wherein the violated integrity of this mucosal barrier allows the gut's bacteria to pass through the mucosa and invade the bloodstream thereupon infecting patients. The overwhelming growth of these organisms in the patient's blood, called sepsis, may lead to death."

Ryan queried, "What is the mechanism of this violation?"

The doctor offered, "We propose the production of a destructive enzyme antibody secondary to the immune system's response to an environmental threat to the body. Many believe this new protein antibody may break down the gut's mucosal barrier." He elaborated that the problem may be an autoimmune reaction wherein the body's immune system mistakenly sends the destructive enzyme antibody to attack itself in the gut.

The professor continued with Ryan, "Conclusive experiments exist that demonstrate destructive enzyme antibodies destroy the specialized proteins, called *tight junctions*, that weld together the colonic gut's mucosal barrier cells which form an impenetrable barrier due to these connections." The professor concluded that an attack by a destructive enzyme antibody which disrupts these protective connections will allow dangerous gut bacteria access into the patient's body.

Back in the lab, Ryan asked his research group, "Could it be compound B that disrupts the critical function of mitochondrial DNA in regulating and monitoring the production and release of the familiar enzyme antibody products?"

Looking at Matt, he said, "Could compound A be the renegade destructive enzyme antibody resulting from compound B's influence?"

To confirm this new theory, a review of the gastrointestinal texts revealed that tight junction proteins indeed do seal adjoining cells, therefore, guaranteeing the integrity of the mucosal cell barrier. This function is vital to prevent invasion by destructive bacteria from the large intestine into the bloodstream. Destructive enzyme antibodies are protein molecules that are capable of breaking down the tight junctions sealing adjoining mucosal cells.

Does compound B's activity alter the subtype I macrophage mitochondrial DNA signal, which results in the creation of modified destructive enzyme antibodies that act as a renegade weapon? The altered mistakenly

attaches to and destroys its incorrectly programmed target, the tight junction proteins. Could the KM disease be explained by proving compound B mutates macrophage inner wall mitochondrial DNA, resulting in the production of compound A, a renegade destructive enzyme antibody, that enters the bloodstream and compromises the gut's impenetrable tight junctions?

Bacteria could then enter the bloodstream by penetrating the mucosal barrier through the resulting intervals and multiply within the body. The resultant overwhelming numbers of bacteria would create sepsis, which causes, as seen in the KM disease, a fatal infection.

"Sounds like the KM disease to me!" was the lab's universal response.

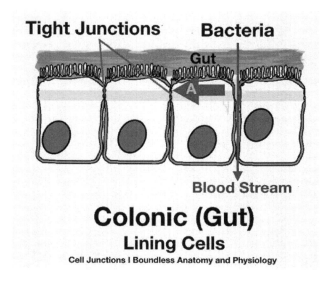

Colonic (Gut)
Lining Cells
Cell Junctions I Boundless Anatomy and Physiology

Matt had to keep up as Ryan skipped to another theory. The researcher added, "There must be more to the KM disease than just a bacterial invasion of issue." The infectious disease professor had told him that in a healthy individual, normally functioning macrophages engulf and destroy bacteria. Macrophages in KM patients were altered and became ineffectual and did not pursue, engulf, and destroy the invading bacteria.

KM patients presented evidence of being immune-compromised, i.e., they ineffectually fought the infection. A specific gamma-globulin protein antibody, which traditionally fought bacterial invasion and infection, was depressed in the KM disease. There was clumping and precipitation of these protective blood proteins and the disintegrated KM cells that occurred within the capillaries in the damaged skin of KM patients which obstructed the smaller blood vessels. Decreased blood flow hindered the delivery of oxygen, nutrients, and anti-bacterial proteins to the diseased tissue. These components were essential in fighting infection and retarding tissue destruction. Therefore, the gangrenous disease prospered.

Ryan again addressed Matt, "Why was the KM disease associated with injury to a patient's skin, whether it be either planned surgery or wounding?"

The unfortunate Claire Ferrier underwent a simple excision of a skin lesion in Cameroon just before her return to the States. Privates Borrows, Jamison, and Church suffered explosive wartime injuries. All four succumbed to the KM disease.

Ryan added, "The answer was probably related to the fact that injury or incision of the skin caused an inflammatory reaction that stimulated macrophage white blood cell production and activity. As less mature white blood cells they were thought to be more susceptible to the challenge of compound B."

Matt was exhausted, both physically and emotionally, and did not have the energy to pursue this question. He and Ryan ended their conversation with the promise to reconnect in three weeks. Matt had to return home to attend to family and newspaper matters. He was burning the candle at both ends. His stress level was still manageable, but he had decided to seek professional help in negotiating this journalistic odyssey he zealously pursued.

Matt created special times for Maggie and his twins. In the psychiatrist's office, he relished the comfort of being able to honestly and uninhibitedly discuss his Vietnam experience, the abnormal macrophages, his oppressive guilt, and his frantic quest for answers. He told his doctor, "I never anticipated how quickly the weight would disappear from my shoulders once I began to open up."

The doctor replied, "I'm pleased your load is becoming lighter."

Matt reconnected with Ryan after three weeks to continue his quest.

The researcher related to Matt that the rational next direction was, "Would we be capable of demonstrating, as theorized, if compound A is the specialized destructive enzyme antibody that allows the invasion of deadly bacteria by destroying colonic mucosal tight junctions?"

Multiple cultures from the wounds of the condemned KM patients over the years had isolated destructive pathogenic bacteria that were well known to the infectious disease specialists. There were probably a thousand or more organisms to consider. However, *Pseudomonas*, *E. Coli*, *Proteus*, *Bacteroides*, *Enterococcus faecalis*, and penicillin-resistant *Staphylococcus* were the usual culprits.

When in combination to infect a patient, these bacteria were associated with the well-defined, tissue-destroying disease syndrome of bacterial synergistic necrotizing gangrene. This flesh-eating infection appeared to result from an invasion of the same bacterial organisms that define the KM patients. If not the same disease, the KM and flesh-eating diseases were certainly closely related.

CHAPTER 43

It took some convincing for the Division I breaststroke swimmer, Summer, to cancel her daily morning practice, but she finally consented to be interviewed. Her coaches understood her crucial role in the KM saga.

Mike Clark told Matt, "How could she refuse me?" She agreed to meet with Matt for an in-depth interview.

After a few weeks at home, he flew to Los Angeles and found his way to the UCLA student union. Across the expansive room he observed a tall, determined appearing athlete. Her hair was dark, her face attractive, and her smile engaging as he approached and introduced himself. She was talking with teammates about an upcoming meet. With polite smiles, they departed.

She led him to a quiet table at the rear of the cafeteria by large windows overlooking the campus. They ordered lunch.

Matt complimented her, "I hope my girls turn out as well as you."

Summer replied, "Thank you," and continued to eat her salad.

After some small talk, she began her story which was recorded by Matt. He sensed that she had made an effort to refresh her mind for the pertinent facts from months ago.

Summer remembered slurring through the murky sedation of her preoperative medications.

She had said to her mom, "Wow, I'm finally here for my surgery; I'm getting my life back."

Her mouth was dry from the atropine; the Demerol dulled her senses; the Versed relaxed her, and would bless her with retrograde amnesia. When she awoke, she'd have no memory of these moments.

It was February 8, 1987, and a sedated Summer Anderson shifted her weight to gain a smidgen of comfort on the narrow, poorly cushioned gurney, with its wheels safely locked in the surgical waiting area. Her head was slightly elevated. Through her drug-induced fog, she saw a blur of activity consisting of scurrying nurses, OR techs, transport personnel, and physicians in blue scrubs all surrounded by white walls. Dangling and fixed bluish-white masks obscured identities. There were background noises of hospital paging, rolling carts, the beeps monitoring equipment and subdued voices.

After enduring multiple blood tests and smears, a salt-restricted diet, and even a hotly debated bone marrow biopsy, Summer was minutes away from entering the operating room to finally undergo the replacement of her extremely symptomatic leaking aortic valve.

She said to her dad, "I'm tired of being poked and prodded; I want to compete in the pool again."

"Today's the day!" her mother said.

Mike Clark had personally assumed the responsibility of monitoring and documenting all information on numerous flow charts pertinent to her experiencing a successful outcome. He had argued for the painful bone marrow biopsy to ensure the fact that Summer's white cell production from stem cells was back to normal.

Mike and Summer's parents were at her bedside, subdued by their thoughts. There was the lingering fear that, although an extremely remote possibility, the KM disease somehow would invade and destroy Summer, in spite of all the precautions.

Her mother's soft sobs reflected the fear, "Am I enabling the death of my child?"

"Of course not, but medically, there's no choice," reminded her father.

Mike had become close with her parents, virtually a member of the family. They worshiped him for having sounded the alarm before Summer's originally scheduled surgery when he observed the abnormal macrophage white blood cells in her blood smear report, thus, avoiding a disastrous outcome.

Summer's father had served in Vietnam as a military air traffic controller at the sprawling Cam Ranh Air Base between 1968 and 1969. There existed between the two men a strong bond of both having been there. He trusted Mike implicitly, and both parents were comforted by his presence.

Mike accompanied Summer into the operating room. He had previously related the following details to Matt which she could not remember due to Versed's retrograde amnesia.

Multiple comforting expressions and direct instructions were given to Summer as the professional cardiothoracic team prepared her for an aortic valve replacement. The head nurse confirmed her name, the procedure, the surgeon, her blood type, the type of prosthetic valve, administered meds, concurrent diseases. After anesthesia induction, her chest was prepared and draped, and the go-ahead given. Following incision of the skin, the surgeon split her sternum, cannulated her major vessels, and placed her on cardiopulmonary bypass. Her aortic valve was thickly calcified, and its leaflets (trap doors) shrunken.

Dr. Schlegeter addressed the chief resident who was assisting, "How the hell did she even get out of bed with her aortic valve leaking so badly?" After encountering some difficulty dissecting out the diseased valve, he inserted a mechanical prosthetic valve. She was taken off bypass without incident and brought to the Cardio-thoracic ICU.

"Thank God," Summer's mother whispered, releasing a flood of anxiety at 10:47 a.m. "She's out of the operating room!"

The patient was now conscious. Summer did remember being in the specialized cardiac ICU. She told Matt her chest wall hurt some, but it was more of a throbbing, intense ache. There was a tangled, confusing array of

tubes exiting and entering her body in a diverse spectrum of transparencies, colors, and sizes. Summer did remember being surrounded by a symphony conducted in a rainbow of sounds of alternating intensities and pitches from voices, blood pressure and oxygen monitors, nearby cycling respirators, and pagers. The accomplished practiced efficiency of world-class cardiac surgical nurses and technicians attended to her. She was comfortably sedated but sufficiently arousable to follow instructions. Once taken off the respirator, she was encouraged to breathe deeply with the breathing aid to avoid lung congestion, change positions in bed, sip clear liquids, and begin ambulation.

By post-op day three, with all tubes removed, her pain became a more tolerable ache, and she ambulated well enough to be discharged home on day five. Summer did well, for she was young and had exercised to maintain her incredible strength pre-operatively.

The wait was agonizing, but Summer carefully slid into the warm green-tinged water of her high school pool for the first time about four weeks after surgery. The thick black lines beneath the water shivered with the undulating wave motion of the pool's surface. The somewhat stifling, moist chlorine-scented air was comforting. First standing in the shallow end, she proceeded to bounce off the bottom into the deeper end, gradually began to tread water, and progressed to a few timid breaststrokes. Even at this level of minimal exertion, which would have been problematic pre-operatively, she experienced no shortness of breath.

She gushed to Matt, "This was the greatest gift. I'm back in the pool."

"I can understand," he said.

Eventually, with each interval of increased exertion monitored by her high school swim coach, she was relieved and grateful for the reprieve from exhaustion gained from the aortic valve replacement. She could once again breathe easily while vigorously competing. Gone was the worry and disappointment of her heart not cooperating to maintain her effort because of a leaking aortic valve. As with an athlete recovering from surgery for an orthopedic injury, she knew she had to compartmentalize her past weakness and swim more vigorously without a second thought. She entered the high school pool daily.

She confided to Matt, "I was so pleased and encouraged by my rapid progress."

After six weeks, Summer was two-thirds of the way back to competitive form. It was late fall, and tryouts for the swim team had begun at UCLA. Based on the scouting reports of her previous competitive accomplishments, she automatically made the swim team without trying out.

After consultation with her physicians, the UCLA swim coaches, and academic advisors, Summer and her parents agreed that she would enroll in the second semester of the 1987-1988 academic year. She would then begin her necessary academic studies and progressively pursue her competitive form under the tutelage of the UCLA coaches.

Due to her rehabilitation, her first year at UCLA would not be considered an official year of competition. She would be entitled to a full four years representing UCLA in the pool. Of great significance, she received a full academic and athletic scholarship.

Summer visited UCLA several times during the months preceding her becoming a full-time student. Her new teammates were welcoming, for they understood and shared her passion for competing. She and the UCLA swim staff designed a recuperative training schedule that she would follow at her home gym and pool. It would be continued at UCLA when attending full time.

Summer developed a keen interest in her medical experience, became fascinated by the mysteries of the human body, and began to entertain a career in medicine. Her parents were supportive and purchased a used Harrison's textbook of medicine from a local bookstore. She studied the anatomy of the heart, its blood supply, and physiology. She primarily studied the aortic valve and the function of the left side of the heart that propelled blood forward into all areas of the body. She was thrilled to understand, on a medical level, what had made her so short of breath. She learned due to her leaking aortic valve, the volume of blood that was pushed out by the left-sided ventricle of the heart into the aorta to the body, did not fully go forward. Her heart tired prematurely, dealing with an increasingly overloaded left ventricle. This situation led to an insufficient oxygen level to sustain her intensity of exercising. Her body reacted by initiating the sensation of shortness of breath and the increase in breathing and heart rates. This scenario was her body's attempt to compensate for the low oxygen level.

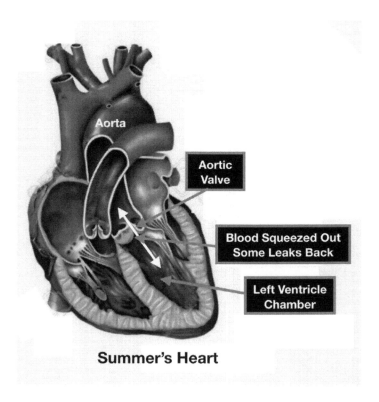

Summer's Heart

She shared with Matt, "Wow, this information is so interesting. I want to understand how my body functions."

It took several weeks at UCLA for Summer to ramp up her energy and organizational skills to accommodate succeeding in the pool and the classroom. She ate her meals at the swim team's training table. Her muscle mass became honed, her endurance increased, and her body fat decreased with exercise and ingesting the nutritional requirements of competitive swimming.

Weight gain began to appear on classmates she associated with on campus. Beer, shots, and pizza were the formula for the universally observed "freshman fifteen." Accepting walking to class as sufficient daily exercise, these ladies sought dietary supplements to fight the new bulging.

Summer was shocked to learn that a favorite compliment to the UCLA freshman weight loss regimen was T-Loss. It was the same Canadian Pharmacy acquired prescription drug which could have led to her death. She avoided possible demise when Mike Clark suggested postponing her first scheduled aortic valve surgery due to finding KM cells in her blood smear.

She became alarmed and informed her classmates of the drug's dangerous potential. Most were not impressed; a few did listen.

She implored her classmates, "This stuff almost killed me!"

Summer began to investigate. She asked her father to contact Mike Clark to obtain all his relevant information and warn him that T-Loss was still out there.

Reading Mike Clark's emailed summary had increased her anxiety level for the safety of all the women not only at UCLA but on other college campuses who may be utilizing this potentially hazardous drug. She asked to see the packaging for the T-Loss used by her friends.

There were many forms due to being repackaged several times to accommodate each distributing company's logo. A student from Quebec, Canada, who decided to stop taking this dietary supplement, supplied Summer with what appeared to be the original packaging and pills. The marketing name T-Loss was boldly displayed. In small print, she found the generic names of the active ingredients and the pharmaceutical company that manufactured the drug, Attica Ossining Pharmaceutical.

CHAPTER 44

Matt, back in Milwaukee, now talked with Ryan almost daily to keep current with the unveiling of compound B's identification. He emailed Michelle and Jon, Jesse, Duane, Declan, J. David, and Guy Marc the moment he received an update. Summer had immediately forwarded the packaged T-Loss dietary pills to Mike. He was delighted that Summer's recovery from her aortic valve replacement was just about complete. There were no complications, and her new valve was functioning with perfection in this elite athlete. Remembering Summer's warning, he became preoccupied with the pervasive use of T-Loss for weight control in college-age women.

"I'll let our group know and notify the FDA, CDC, and Department of Health and Human Services," he informed all his concerned friends by email.

Mike excitedly informed Ryan, "The T-Loss pills that Summer mailed me may be the key to uncovering the source of compound B."

All Ryan could say was, "You bet; I'm on it."

Mike jettisoned a bulk email to all those concerned, informing them about Summer's discovery and promised Ryan Larkin that he would overnight the renegade pills to his lab.

Sleep eluded both Mike and Ryan for most of the night; insomnia induced by sheer excitement.

"This could be the home stretch," Ryan told his lab.

Once Ryan received the delivery of the prized T-Loss pills, he engaged the group of original KM researchers who continued to work in his laboratory.

They understood the positive consequences of defining the chemical's origin that was the cause of the dreadful KM disease.

A longtime lead researcher was still there and ever the optimist. He predicted, "We're going to crush this!"

The first step was to transfer two of the suspect pills to J. David Warren's laboratory at Metropolitan Medical College on 69th Street just to the west, off York Avenue in New York City. He was engaged in this investigation, having derived several years ago the chemical composition and structure of both compounds A and B. "Will we find either one of these suspect compounds in the pills?" asked J. David of Ryan. "If we do, it's almost case closed."

The parameters of this new study were quite routine. The usual contribution of Dr. Warren's lab was to accomplish the tasks of not only identifying an unknown chemical's composition and structure but also synthesizing non-existent compounds from new designs to achieve the desired effect in treating disease. He was pleasantly surprised to identify that the majority of the T-Loss pill composition was two drugs in a 1:1 ratio. The first was an anti-parasitic drug routinely used for malaria prevention in countries where the disease was endemic. Indeed, it was the Attica Ossining Pharmaceutical proprietary drug Falciquin. The other was the psychotherapeutic drug, Relaxin, manufactured in the sprawling complex of buildings of the J. Meyer Pharmaceutical Company, in the beautiful countryside outside Hanover, Germany. This medication treated depression.

"This is a curious combination of pharmaceuticals," J. David remarked in an email to Ryan. He searched the appropriate pharmacologic literature and found a review article in the *Journal of Nutrition* in 1981, highlighting the positive effect in shedding pounds achieved when combining the two molecularly divergent drugs in a 1:1 ratio. Nowhere in the review of this subject could be found a scientific rationale for Falciquin/Relaxin efficacy but, so what. It worked, and it sold like hotcakes.

Because of its unanticipated benefit, AOP purchased the rights to utilize J. Meyer Pharmaceutical's Relaxin to be used in combination with its own Falciquin and marketed this new diet pill combination as T-Loss in the competitive and lucrative weight loss market. However, this new AOP diet pill soon developed the reputation of inducing severe nausea in too many patients, and its introduction as a significant weight loss drug failed. They discontinued production after a few years. The stockpiled medication found its way, at discounted prices, to less than reputable pharmacological companies that were now advertising it for sale.

In J. David's chemical analysis of T-Loss, there appeared an unanticipated trace chemical present at only five parts per billion. That would be equivalent to one drop of liquid in four million gallons of water. It was configured in a six-carbon atom benzene ring format. Because of its finite presence, isolating a sufficient amount of this mystery molecule for analysis required additional T-Loss pills. Several days passed, waiting for the other samples. During that interval, J. David had the feeling that he was familiar with this elusive molecule.

He questioned his longtime assistant, "I wonder if I encountered it previously?"

"We'll know soon enough," answered his friend.

Having followed the appropriate protocols, a useful amount of this elusive trace molecule was isolated. As he and his group utilized an army of analytical techniques, they gradually began to see the mystery molecule's composition and structure.

J. David exclaimed, "Yes, I most definitely have seen this molecule before."

Within the next hour, upon completing the final analytical maneuvers, the personnel of his lab were stunned into silence. There it was, compound B, the KM disease inciter.

"Holy shit" was exclaimed by a chorus of very refined individuals. The mystery of how compound B had entered Summer's body was solved. Dr. Warren then queried, "How did compound B come to be associated with T-Loss?"

"Was it from contamination during the manufacture of one of T-Loss's two ingredients or subsequently during the blending process in pill production?" he asked. J. David immediately informed Ryan Larkin that he had retrieved from T-Loss the same compound B that he had previously isolated a few years ago near the nucleus of the killer macrophage white blood cells. The deadly flesh-eating gangrenous infection that carried a 98% risk of a fatal outcome was closely associated with compound B.

Ryan, in his St. Louis lab, had proposed the thesis that the action of this six-carbon atom ringed compound B, within the macrophage's mitochondria, mutated its inner wall DNA. This change resulted in compound A production that lead to the distortion of the macrophage white blood cells and the KM disease.

Once the KM white blood cells had discharged compound A, they self-destructed and disappeared. They are not seen on blood smears once the KM disease is manifest. Moreover, the fragmented material from the cells' destruction added to the debris clogging smaller blood vessels in the area of injury, inhibiting blood flow and oxygen delivery.

"These two hypotheses were proven to be correct," Ryan exclaimed to Matt. "The flesh-eating gangrene KM disease results from the action of compound A, which is a destructive enzyme antibody that allows invasion from the colon of vicious bacteria."

Ryan's current question echoed that of J. David Warren, "What was the origin of this trace but deadly amount of compound B in T-Loss? Was Relaxin or Falciquin the culprit?"

Ryan told Matt of a scheduled Washington University break for the next two weeks.

He felt overwhelmed and was taking the time to rejuvenate on a hunt with Jesse.

He would summarize their hunting experience for Matt's exposé once he returned to his lab.

CHAPTER 45

The friendship of Jesse Holt and Ryan Larkin continued to flourish and open new horizons in their outdoor experiences. Both developed into excellent wing shooters and began to research hunting trips within the United States and abroad. Ryan needed this break. It was mid-August 1987.

He called Jesse, "It's that time of year again, goose season. We'd better do it now, for 1988 is an election year and you'll be busy with Sokolov."

The historic Mohawk River and farmlands in and around the Amsterdam, NY, area support an enormous population of the troublesome creatures. They fouled golf courses and front lawns. They infuriated farmers by plucking out the earliest slim, sweet green growth erupting from the corn seeds planted on thousands of acres. The deprivation was significant. There was little objection to harvesting pesky geese by any of the groups opposing gun ownership and hunting.

Jesse's wife, Kim, grew up in Amsterdam. She was a close friend of Michelle who was engaged to be married to the unfortunate KM cell Vietnam victim, Private Richard Burrows. Jesse enjoyed a relationship with the Burrows family, whom he met at his wedding. Each year he and Ryan were invited to goose hunt the farmland the Burrows leased.

Ryan planned to arrive from St. Louis two days before the season opener. He and Jesse met at Albany, NY Airport. This early arrival allowed them to rekindle friendships, do some scouting, plan blind placement, and seek out some skeet shooting and sporting clays to sharpen their skills.

The temperature on the morning of September 1st, opening day, was in the upper thirties and somewhat overcast, just right for the birds to fly in early and low. The wind direction was critical, for geese landed into the wind.

Expert goose calling by mimicking their vocalization lured the prey into shooting range.

At about 7:10 am, the birds began to appear. Most originated from their roost on the Mohawk River about a mile away. Over the next few hours, the lead birds, having not been shot at this season, willingly guided themselves and their flocks of varying numbers into the welcoming decoys.

Jesse, Ryan, and their companion sportsmen experienced a truly successful hunt. All harvested game underwent processing for human consumption. That evening, they enjoyed a dinner of smoked wild turkey breast, which had been harvested that spring by Richard's younger brother, John, and served with sweet potatoes, creamed onions, and red cabbage. After dinner, they enjoyed a twenty-five-year-old port in front of a blazing fireplace. Later that evening, Jesse brought Ryan up to speed on the senator's candidacy and his impressive poll numbers. Further hunting this season would be curtailed by the ramping up of Jesse's campaigning responsibilities for Senator Sokolov.

Ryan then related that the source of compound B in Summer Anderson's blood was from the dietary supplement T-Loss containing a 1:1 ratio of Falciquin and Relaxin. She had dodged a bullet due to Mike Clark's diligence. All other hypotheses they entertained in defining the KM disease lacked proof. He would face that challenge upon returning to his Washington University's St. Louis lab. Their flights home were trouble-free, and they returned to their professions a bit tired but feeling rejuvenated and inspired.

CHAPTER 46

By mid-September 1988, emails were flying among all those involved in the search for the truth about the KM disease. Matt received them all and noted their content.

Ryan queried each participant, "Do you accept these points as representing the direction of our problem-solving?"

1) *Compound B was the culprit* that, once inside the subtype I macrophage, attacked the mitochondrial DNA and altered its normal function producing a unique detrimental destructive enzyme antibody, compound A.

2) *Compound B was proven to be a contaminant of the T-Loss pill.* That was a drug with a 1:1 ratio of Falciquin and Relaxin, produced and distributed by Attica Ossining Pharmaceuticals.

3) *Falciquin* was marketed as an antimalarial drug, established in *malaria prophylaxis,* and prevented the disease in those individuals at risk who were exposed during the time spent in endemic subtropical and tropical regions.

4) There was a malaria connection for all KM patients, whether direct or indirect. More specifically, *they were all exposed to potential malarial infection.*

5) *Compound A* resided in the mitochondria and the cytoplasm of the KM cells and was collected by and reached a *dramatic concentration in the vesicles* of the abnormal macrophage white blood cells.

6) Macrophage *vesicles containing compound A* were known to affix to the cell membrane. After eroding and perforating the white cell's membrane wall, they *emptied their consignment into the body's interstitial fluid surrounding all cells.* It was assumed that compound A then migrated through a space in between the thin cells of the capillary wall into the body's circulatory system to be dispersed throughout the victim's body.

7) Life-threatening bacteria from within the gut were cultured in the necrotic wounds in all cases of KM infections. *Would compound A*, responsible for their invasion of the body, be *identified in a biopsy in the gut lining cells of the KM victim.*

8) *Patients* who reside in malarial at-risk areas, such as the tropical and subtropical climates of Vietnam, Cameroon, and others are *directed to take antimalarial drugs* to prevent that disease. The predominant medication was the Attica Ossining Pharmaceutical drug, *Falciquin.*

9) *Was compound B somehow introduced into the subtype I macrophage by the use of Falciquin?*

Ryan Larkin remained convinced that this antimalarial drug, Falciquin, was the culprit which had caused the KM disease since 1964. Two months after Ryan circulated his summary of the KM disease investigation, Jesse emailed Matt and Ryan with astounding information. The senator's campaign was in high gear, and Jesse became tasked to engage in-depth research to identify noteworthy achievements to bolster his candidate's reputation. In doing so, he had inadvertently uncovered sequestered documents that were not meant to be made public. They contained a dossier developed by Senator Sokolov's advisors on AOPs shady history and questionable activities to be used as protection against Big Pharma if their interests ever diverged, and they became adversaries.

Jesse learned that AOP's Falciquin appeared on the market in the early 1950s. It was utilized successfully by the military and governmental agencies during the Vietnam War Era and as part of most malaria preventive regimens recommended worldwide by the World Health Organization (WHO). The goal was to avoid the potentially deadly malaria parasite, *Plasmodium falciparum*, from establishing residency within the red cells of the victim after an Anopheles mosquito bite. This insect, referred to as a vector, distributed blood containing the parasite from an infected victim to a healthy individual when attempting to ingest human blood as a food source. Falciquin kills the injected *Plasmodium falciparum* parasite in the bloodstream before it invades the red cell, therefore, avoiding the clinical disease.

The chemical formulation of Falciquin never varied over its years of production. Initially, its production took place in the original New York State Attica Ossining facility just a few miles north of New York City in Westchester County. By 1961, the entire process was relocated offshore to Shanghai, China.

Due to successful political manipulations of Senator Sokolov from Oakland, California, at the behest of his Big Pharma puppeteers, there were few governmental pharmaceutical manufacturing guidelines for offshore companies. The only oversight of the manufacturing processes practiced by the drug industry in the developing nations, such as China, were voluntary.

"Are you kidding me!" was Ryan's email response to Jesse after having been informed of this dire threat to American public health.

Jesse then added, "There is also the danger from components necessary for a product's development obtained from unregulated local foreign distributors."

Matt said to both Jesse and Ryan, again by email, "I can't believe this recipe for disaster!"

Ryan suggested "This is too much information; let's switch to a conference call."

The other two responded with "Good idea."

Jesse continued sharing his information. In the early sixties, with a significant percentage of the six hundred million Chinese citizens clamoring to abandon communal farms, labor costs were negligible due to a take-it-or-leave-it hiring policy. Working conditions were deplorable, fire safety was non-existent, workman's compensation coverage was a fairytale, and there were no age limits when hiring children. As a result, AOP profits ballooned.

A substantial financial boost occurred in 1961 when they won the bid to the Departments of Defense and State to supply Falciquin for military and governmental distribution to employ malarial prevention in Southeast Asia and other subtropical and tropical countries. There was a sudden increase in demand for the drug required in protecting the growing number of military and civilian personnel involved in Southeast Asia. AOP now had to increase production to five million pills every six months. This quantity of Falciquin was two and a half times the amount currently being manufactured.

Jesse continued his revelation to his shocked associates. This production spurt, AOPs MBAs had stressed, must be accomplished with minimal increase in the company's expenditures so to maintain an increased profit margin and a stable stock price on the S&P 500.

Ryan inserted, "Whatever mechanism AOP applied to achieve the required increase in production may be central to our investigation." Ryan then had a lecture to give in a senior engineering course at the university and left the conversation.

Jesse told Matt, "Hang on for a minute. I've got good news for you." He said to the journalist, "The discussion of activity in China just reminded me that since things were moving fast, Ryan needed additional research money and sheepishly approached me." He added, "I'll condense the facts of our friend's appeal."

As is usually the case in academia, Ryan's investigative funds, when widening the scope of his research parameters, had dissipated at an accelerated rate. It was now May 1988, and additional financing was necessary to bring the KM project to fruition.

"We need a lot more funding, or else we're screwed," Ryan had pleaded.

Jesse continued, "My position in Senator Sokolov's presidential campaign's inner circle is strengthening daily." There was a multitude of cash advances by wealthy constituents seeking additional appropriations that could be generated by the Presidential candidate's influence when elected. Sufficient funds were available to be used on a discretionary basis.

Since all the previously laid out groundwork existed, and Ryan's research was exceeding expectations, not only did the senator come through but also Attica Ossining Pharmaceutical. AOP did not wish to lose out on renewing an enormous public relations opportunity. They matched the 1.8 million-dollar governmental research grants generated to support Ryan's quest by Presidential Candidate Sokolov.

Matt and Jesse understood that both the candidate and AOP were now inescapably padlocked to the KM research results.

CHAPTER 47

Matt and Maggie were enjoying an after-dinner vintage sherry as he began to share his thoughts. She was his sounding board and his strength.

"My efforts and sacrifices will be worth it. We are close to a KM solution," he blurted out. "It's been a long haul. I especially feel guilty for the pain I caused you, Maggie. The separation, lack of support with the twins, and my mood swings when at home." He admitted that he struggled to mentally dismiss the recurring doubt of the group's being successful in its quest.

Maggie, "I love you and will always stand by you."

Matt's mood suddenly became celebratory after reading the most recent email he received from Ryan containing vital information Declan had uncovered. Late in June 1988, Declan learned a critical fact from a talkative hernia patient who worked at the Department of Defense in a section that monitored drugs being utilized by the military and their side effects. He revealed that every six months, since the mid-1950s, the Food and Drug Administration collected and cataloged samples of all the drugs being purchased and utilized by every United States government department and agency. To confirm drug potency, efficacy, and demonstrable purity of these items, the FDA employed random testing. The hernia patient also informed Declan that the CDC stored blood from patients who suffered from disease outbreaks wherein its cause was unknown at the time of the agency's investigation. In later years, when the CDC identified a new disease-causing agent, and individuals have symptoms similar to those in previously unsolved outbreaks, that stored blood undergoes testing to see if the new agent was indeed the cause of the prior illness.

"Matt, Falciquin pills have been in a federal storage facility all this time. Blood samples from KM patients may exist in storage, cataloged by the CDC," stated Ryan's email.

"Currently, in 1988, this procedure continued for handling undiagnosed disease, etc.,"

This repository of samples for all the relevant years of Falciquin production between 1951 and 1988 would be available for our experimentation.

Matt could not contain himself, "Oh my God, this windfall is our Holy Grail," he replied to the email.

Matt immediately called Ryan, "I can't believe our luck. What do you plan next?"

Both decided it was getting late, and the conversation would continue by landline the following morning.

At 8:30 am, Ryan greeted Matt good morning and promptly continued where they left off the evening before. He told Matt that he had a choice of approaches in the investigation of the government's collection of biannual Falciquin samples for compound B content analysis.

Should he design experiments to determine if the application of a Falciquin solution onto healthy but susceptible subtype I macrophages will create the well-documented KM white blood cell abnormalities?

Or, should he engage J. David to search every FDA sample for the B compound? This same six-carbon atom ringed molecule had been identified by him several years ago in related experiments and in the T-Loss samples.

If indeed he should confirm the presence of compound B in a number of the samples, they would then apply this newly recovered B chemical to healthy subtype I macrophage white blood cells and establish whether the dreaded KM change occurs.

Ryan decided, "I'll open door number one. Option two would impose an enormous amount of work on J. David's facility."

"I'll give you a heads-up when I have viable results," Ryan told Matt.

After two weeks, Ryan called Matt with a progress report. Matt then shared all the information with all members of their investigative group. Larkin did not know the concentration of compound B circulating in a patient's blood that was required to instigate the macrophage white blood cellular alterations described in the KM disease.

"I could not use human subjects. That's a no-brainer," Ryan said. He asked his researchers, "How do we derive the level of the compound B molecule, equivalent to that amount contained in a patient's blood when they took Falciquin orally as an antimalarial drug on a daily basis? The plasma concentration is critical."

Ryan continued, "I must replicate this human Falciquin plasma concentration when bathing the healthy subtype I macrophage cells in a Petri culture dish with compound B to confirm if compound A, the destructive enzyme antigen, is produced."

To overcome this impediment, Ryan said that he decided to dilute Falciquin in the experimental human plasma Petri dish bathe to a concentration equivalent to that found in the circulating blood of a 160-pound chimpanzee. Over the preceding week it would be fed the dosage of Falciquin directed by the WHO for a 160-pound human.

Ryan continued to relate that the usually relaxed atmosphere in his lab became tense as each step of the complex processes of investigation proceeded. The isolated subtype I macrophages were confirmed to be healthy by determining the pH of their Petri dish bath solution. The annually stored Falciquin pills obtained from the FDA were dissolved in individual human plasma solutions that would mimic the concentration that occurred in humans. The samples, carefully labeled with that day's date and time and the place and date of its manufacture, were then secured in cold storage to be used at a later date. There were now eighty samples for the period from 1951 to the present, 1988.

Ryan reassured Matt that he did notify the CDC of his probable isolation of the agent, i.e., compound B, responsible for the KM disease. He suggested that they send the blood samples of patients whose blood that agency had preserved with the KM disease symptoms to Dr. J. David Warren's lab at Metropolitan University Medical College for analysis.

The CDC responded that because of the KM disease's rapid onset, its symptomatology was not well defined, and few patients received that diagnosis. Also, almost universally, patient deaths occurred soon after the onset of symptoms. Due to these two factors, the efficient gathering of blood samples for storage was all but impossible. However, there were only eight suspicious specimens they would submit to him for analysis. Sadly, J David's lab did not isolate either compound A or B in the stored material received from the CDC. Ryan told Matt that it would take a month to six weeks to complete this branch of the investigation.

Ryan then switched gears with Matt saying, "I need your advice. I may be losing it."

In addition to his teaching responsibilities, he was juggling two major projects involving the infection-fighting subtype I macrophage white blood cell: the drug delivery system utilizing macrophages and the quest of the KM disease investigation. At times, he felt the weight of the world on his shoulders. Ryan admitted to Matt that the rigors of the years of intense discipline to achieve correctness in solving the KM mystery began to take their toll. Of his numerous KM colleges, only the veterans had an informed understanding. Matt, as a Vietnam veteran, fully understood and was reassuring. He knew well that a portion of what had been one's previous self was lost forever in a war zone when exposed to its significant stressors. A warrior is forever changed. Part of him remains there.

On the surface, Ryan kept appearances appropriate for whatever social situation he entered. However, he began to experience symptoms of epinephrine release daily. They were the familiar racing/pounding heart, hypervigilance, sleeplessness, and other signs of PTSD that he first suffered in Vietnam during a Viet Cong rocket attack on the 95th Evacuation Hospital at Da Nang in 1972. He was capable of rationalizing and compartmentalizing his PTSD after leaving Vietnam with his comrades at Fort Carson, Colorado within a few months before discharge and the start of his PhD studies at Washington University in St. Louis. Small resurgences had occurred over the years that were successfully self-managed, but this was different.

CHAPTER 48

Matt, who himself had similar symptoms intermittently, realized it was time to increase his understanding of the details of PTS, where symptoms are not debilitating, and PTSD, the clinically diagnosed debilitating disorder. Beginning with the first troops returning from Vietnam in the early 1960s, there began to be observed by family, friends, and healthcare professionals, a definite change in the veteran's personality when compared to their pre-deployment self and those who did not serve. It was called delayed stress.

Matt knew that war is and always has been a brutally powerful insult to one who grew up in a peaceful, secure society. A young citizen must discard his peacetime morality, wherein killing is prohibited. They are inducted into the foreign environment of the military culture, stigmatization, and basic training wherein killing is not only sanctioned but also encouraged at a moment's notice. The new inductees, who at an average age of twenty-two years and still mentally processing with the volatility of a poorly disciplined adolescent brain, are caught in between the moral codes of peace and war. They exist within a moral limbo, never entirely governed by either moral code but trapped within a complex hybrid of both moral extremes.

Delayed Stress, now in 1988, had an officially recognized diagnostic designation, Post-Traumatic Stress Disorder. The Veterans Administration was finally offering disability compensation for that diagnosis.

Upon discharge, a majority of veterans never again spoke of the Vietnam they experienced. Some coped with the lingering horrors by storytelling. Others continued their self-medicating substance abuse habits they had embraced in Vietnam to thwart their psychological pain. Alcohol, marijuana, and heroin were the favorite escapes.

By the mid-1980s, a Vietnam veteran's capacity to sustain the internalizing of their traumatic military experiences began to erode, and the incidence of PTSD in these veterans became an epidemic. Many died prematurely from violent causes related to alcohol and substance abuse, suicide, reckless behavior and driving, and other risk-taking.

Veterans sought relief from the panic, rage, violence, racing heart, sweating, feeling cold and clammy, insomnia, desperation, feelings of helplessness, and depression experienced in the throes of PTSD. If increased substance abuse with alcohol, marijuana, and opioids fails, suicide presents as the only effective choice to finally escape from their malignant demons.

Few clinicians responsible for these active warriors' and veterans' welfare realized that PTSD was an expected and physiologically normal response to entering the stressful military environment. By no means is it an indication of weakness. Medivac personnel, corpsmen, nurses, and doctors involved in treating the consequences of combat, the mutilated, profusely bleeding, and dying warriors, were acutely prone to PTSD. They engaged with youthful gruesomely wounded patients almost daily. They were intimate with war's consequences.

Dr. Declan Burke had informed Matt that he, as all Vietnam veterans, experienced being in a war zone one minute and within a few days, thrust back into peaceful society and expected to act appropriately. He, as all returning veterans, suffered to some degree from PTSD. Declan also struggled with demons. Initially, while still on active duty, he self-medicated with excessive drinking and pot consumption. To his advantage, he was assigned for his second year in the Army to Fort Campbell, Kentucky, where just about all doctors in the medical and surgical departments had experienced Vietnam. They were reticent to share feelings with others revealing their emotional challenges and joined the group in self-medicating: drinking and pot-induced mellowness. All were heading for medical and surgical practices at major universities, in large cities or small towns. There was no way they wished to leave the service as damaged goods.

All had experienced the same horrible Vietnam environment. Now when together, their self-imposed boundaries of isolation were allowed to recede, and they began to share their traumatic stories, guilt, regrets, losses, feelings of medical and psychological inadequacy, and nightmares.

They weaned themselves off alcohol and pot coincident with the shared expelling of their demons. Most were mentally stable at discharge from active duty but well aware there was still work that was required to prevent the demons from resurrecting.

Once out of the Army, to deal with his PTSD, Declan chose the path of storytelling wherein he routinely dissipated negative energy. He became a veteran advocate. Lecturing in a variety of venues, he told his story and educated the non-veteran about serving in Vietnam. He understood the warrior's mentality and offered his services on the local psych ward to inform the staff, physicians, and support personnel in how to communicate with a veteran hospitalized with PTSD.

However, Declan was now thoroughly engaged in the pursuit of defining the origin of the KM disease. This quest also consumed Ryan Larkin, Mike Clark, Duane Wall and Matt. They were bound together as brothers after eighteen years in the effort of saving lives. The veterans had met and bonded with non-veterans consumed with solving the KM disease tragedy. There was Jesse Holt and his wife, Kim; Claire's husband, Guy Marc; KM's first victim, Private Burrows' fiancée, Michelle; and Jon, her computer savvy husband. These six had not been in Vietnam but were indelibly affected by that war's virulent legacy. This group of people shared a commitment to resolving the KM disease mystery.

CHAPTER 49

In about a month, during a landline call with Matt, Ryan Larkin updated his research pathway to define the KM disease. They were both relaxed in the evening at home. Family time and dinner had gone smoothly, and the kids were in their rooms. Both wives were reading their latest book while sipping a favorite Sauvignon Blanc.

Each of the eighty FDA anti-malaria drug specimens and their controls, which spanned the years from 1951 to 1988, were diluted in human plasma to the chimpanzee-derived critical human concentration. Each of the eighty specimens were applied to the surface of healthy subtype I macrophages in a Petri dish bath and incubated for seventy-two hours at body temperature. Electron microscopy was employed to examine each of the eighty specimen dishes and controls for the presence and concentration of the killer macrophage (KM) white blood cells. Photographic documentation recorded the results. All the cell cultures would be frozen in liquid nitrogen to preserve for future investigation.

With eighty specimens and controls, the samples were kept sequentially by year. Meticulous record-keeping was of paramount importance to ensure accuracy. An army of statisticians was engaged from an accounting giant to guarantee flawless documentation of the experiment's results. Completion of the experimentation and recording the results required four weeks. By mid-October 1988, the documented results were viewed by the team members. Yes, indeed! The application of Falciquin, assumed to be contaminated with compound B, was verified to induce the KM changes in healthy subtype I macrophages. However, only in the Falciquin samples from 1964 to 1972.

"This finding is unexpected," Ryan told Matt.

Samples from the years from 1951 to 1963 and 1973 to 1988 did not induce the abnormal KM morphology in healthy subtype I macrophages. Ryan added that almost simultaneously, J. David Warren's Metropolitan University analytical lab documented that during that same 1964 to 1972 time interval, there was contamination of the antimalarial drug Falciquin with compound B.

His analysis of samples from 1951 to 1963 and 1973 to 1988 did not reveal compound B contamination. Did this explain the curious finding of KM changes being found only in subtype I macrophage white blood cells when applying Falciquin manufactured between 1964 and 1972?

Ryan rejoiced to Matt. "After all this time and effort, we're almost there!"

Matt added, "This heavy monkey will soon be off our back," and sighed deeply while sipping his favorite brandy.

After successfully analyzing the Falciquin samples sequestered by the FDA for the Department of Defense and State, Ryan introduced indisputable scientific evidence that Falciquin, manufactured by AOP in the years 1964 to 1972, was harboring compound B which caused the KM disease. His researchers had theorized that compound B initiated the KM disease by corrupting the subtype I macrophage's inner wall mitochondrial DNA, which led to the release of the potentially lethal compound A that was a destructive enzyme antibody.

Falciquin pills from that same AOP production line, 1964 to 1972, were prescribed as a preventive measure to all our military, civilian contractors, and governmental appointees assigned to Vietnam. Mandated by the WHO and CDC, Falciquin was swallowed by the world's susceptible population that either resided in, visited, or traveled through tropical and subtropical regions of the globe to prevent them from being infected by the malarial parasite. All who swallowed this pill were at risk of dying from the KM disease. Jon's computer program demonstrated that about thirty-two hundred innocents worldwide had perished due to the ingestion of Falciquin manufactured during that time!

Ryan continued, "The tragic truth was that the peak global incidence and mortality of the KM disease occurred during the late 60s and early to mid-70s.

Matt finished the thought with, "That is during the time frame that Falciquin contaminated with compound B was being manufactured and dispensed as malaria prevention to unsuspecting victims. Avoidance of potentially lethal malaria did succeed, but many deaths still occurred during that time frame by inadvertently switching one disease for another."

Ryan finally challenged, "How and where did compound A, the destructive enzyme antibody, cause the KM disease? We theorized the gut, but this hypothesis must be proven."

CHAPTER 50

Declan assumed the responsibility of detailing the compound A effect and emailed Matt and their group what he uncovered. He learned that several groups of researchers around the world were also pursuing the details of identical abnormal KM white cells and published their findings.

All KM involved researchers agreed that the deadly KM disease, which closely resembled the synergistic gangrene flesh-eating infection, was now thought to be a result of compound A activity. This chemical is a destructive enzyme antibody mistakenly produced by the subtype I white cell mitochondria under the influence of the contaminating compound B.

1) *It was proven,* with reproducible culture results, that in KM patients, there was an invasion into the bloodstream and diseased soft tissue by bacteria usually confined to the gut.

2) *Compound A was retrievable* from the damaged mucosa of the colon (gut) in KM patients. Electron microscopy identified the compound A molecule adherent to the disrupted tight junctions. These areas should have held adjacently bound mucosal cells solidly. Their disruption destroyed the integrity of the colonic mucosal barrier against invasion by deadly colonic (gut) bacteria.

3) The *deposition of compound A was found in tissues* directly adjacent to the initial rash and near the gangrenous tissue changes which implied additional cell barrier disruption in the tissue which allowed the deadly bacteria to invade, colonize, and inflict potentially lethal damage.

The experimental data derived at George Washington University in St. Louis by Ryan Larkin was reviewed and re-reviewed by critical lab personnel, accountants, and other interested researchers. The data and derived impressions were proven to be rock solid.

CHAPTER 51

"But, how did it occur that Falciquin only in the years from 1964 to 1972 was contaminated?" Ryan implored his lab personnel.

Attica Ossining Pharmaceuticals had shifted its Falciquin manufacturing to Shanghai, China, in 1961. If that move was the genesis of compound B contamination, this vile chemical should have been detected by J. David Warren in the Falciquin pill samples from 1961 through 1963, but it was not.

Ryan asked his lab, "What occurred in 1964 to open the door for compound B to find its way into AOP's prized and lucrative anti-malaria pill, Falciquin?" He added, "Where was this product most utilized during those years?"

All associated with this investigative odyssey knew the answer: Vietnam.

Beginning in 1964, the troop levels in Vietnam were escalating. President Lyndon Johnson had acquiesced under the influence exerted by Secretary of State, Dean Rusk, and Secretary of Defense, Robert McNamara. Both fool-heartedly, beginning in 1964, spearheaded the idea that a massive buildup of American fighting forces in Vietnam would turn the tide in our favor; all these decisions based on artificial intelligence from gung-ho, self-serving career diplomats and military commanders.

Then there was Tet 1968.

In response to this embarrassing development, President Johnson refused to accommodate General Westmorland's request for additional troops. After much discussion with his advisors he halted the bombing of

North Vietnam and set the stage to begin decreasing troop levels dramatically at the end of 1968 and early1969.

The Tet Offensive, initiated in January 1968, was a coordinated and aggressive military campaign throughout all of South Vietnam by the North Vietnamese Army and the Viet Cong. They planned to attack and overrun most American-held cities and bases to demonstrate their unconquerable strength, thus encouraging southern military personnel and citizens to defect to Ho Chi Minh's communist cause. Their effort failed. Bloody confrontations killed and maimed large numbers of soldiers on both sides. However, the fact that this massive coordinated attack occurred in the first place demonstrated that all the United States government's public hype professing our winning the war was a nonsensical lie. Johnson subsequently relinquished the aspiration for another presidential term, anti-war demonstrations erupted, Vietnam veterans were vilified, and our country's military was ordered to draw down until all fighting forces were gone by 1973.

In recent months, group emails kept Matt and the others up to date. The one from Jesse on a quiet Wednesday evening in mid-October 1988 changed everything. Jesse excitedly announced to Ryan and the group that he had an explanation for the 1964 to 1973 timeline.

Jesse had recently uncovered an addendum to Senator Sokolov's original dossier on AOP, which he had previously unearthed, documenting incriminating evidence of wrongdoing by AOP.

"Now this information will connect the dots," Jesse announced to all enthusiastically.

He reiterated that during the entire course of the war, all troops sent to Vietnam followed orders to ingest malarial prophylaxis to kill the parasite if it was injected into one's body by the Anopheles mosquito. This directive enacted by the Departments of State and Defense remained based on the World Health Organization's (WHO) thoroughly accurate researched conclusions.

For many Vietnam soldiers, contractors, and numerous civilians serving in-country, this order became potentially deadly.

AOP, through the influence of Senator David Sokolov, had won from the Departments of Defense and State in 1961 the lucrative contract to supply Falciquin to all those who would be stationed in Southeast Asia and exposed to malaria. That group included soldiers, pilots, sailors, Marines, contract workers, and civilian government personnel. The escalation of troop levels in 1964 resulted in a massive surge in demand for AOP's Falciquin, as directed by the WHO, to protect these men and women sent to Vietnam from developing malaria. AOP's executives were well aware that there was insufficient time to adapt the manufacturing facilities in Shanghai to accommodate the heightened demand for this preventive medication. Shamefully, there was no inquiry by AOP as to whether there could be a risk of adverse results when the plant manager proposed a shortcut to increase the rate of Falciquin production. All AOP executives had turned a blind eye to the consideration of negative consequences.

Given this obsequious go-ahead, the plant manager who supervised the Falciquin production in Shanghai ordered the chemical reaction for this drug's manufacture to be run at a temperature of *one degree* Celsius higher than originally programmed. This order exceeded the temperature accepted as the safety standard. There were no apparent strains on the equipment and because of the elevated temperature, the rate of the chemical reaction accelerated and the Falciquin production rate increased twelve and a half percent faster than before the change.

This innovation did sustain a supply of Falciquin equivalent to that required by its new demand.

The plant manager received a promotion.

Without knowledge of AOP's increased temperature in Falciquin production and the unintended creation of compound B, the World Health Organization and CDC continued to encourage those in subtropical and tropical environments to utilize this anti-malaria drug, Falciquin, to prevent the potentially fatal parasitic disease, malaria.

The one-degree change condoned by AOP was a potentially deadly decision.

CHAPTER 52

Having been informed by Jesse of the increased Falciquin production temperature, Ryan knew he must prove that lethal KM outcomes were the result of AOP's actions to increase production.

Ryan again engaged J. David's lab to replicate Attica Ossining's Shanghai operational decision to expedite the production of Falciquin; that is, to run the original chemical reaction that produces this drug at the *one-degree* Celsius temperature elevation.

A few weeks later, J. David confirmed that running the production of Falciquin using AOP's accelerated specifications at the higher temperature did indeed result in the appearance of compound B. The contaminant appeared in the same concentration found in the 1964 to 1972 Falciquin samples sequestered by the FDA. There began a flurry of emails among those engaged.

Matt quickly inquired, "Were all foreigners who resided in Vietnam at risk of developing the KM disease during that time?"

Ryan declared, "No." He and the others had proposed there were several critical reasons:

1) The *side effects* of antimalarial meds could be so sickening that a significant number of those in-country just gambled against the mosquitoes and refused to take their medication.

2) Those with *subtype II* macrophages were inherently protected.

3) *Nuances* of an individual's area of operation, genetics, and unknown alterations in cellular and organ chemistry may very well have provided protection, the *unknown factor*.

Ryan then questioned, "Why did victims continue to suffer from the contaminated Falciquin long after its accelerated production terminated in 1972?"

Claire Ferrier, MD, suffered an excruciating death in 1985 from the KM disease. By then, Falciquin's production was pure as demonstrated by J. David Warren. Jesse responded that his continued investigation into AOP's business plan had revealed that residual compound B contaminated Falciquin, produced between 1964 and 1972, was stored in warehouses in Patterson, New Jersey, and Shanghai, China. These two global sites then replenished AOP pharmaceutical supplies to regional international repositories, which in turn distributed them to pharmacies within that region's geographic area.

For many years, even after discontinuing the potentially lethal production process of Falciquin utilizing a *one-degree* Celsius elevation in temperature, local pharmacies continued to be supplied with and dispense compound B contaminated Falciquin. These dangerous pills from accelerated production during the interval from 1964 to 1972 were stockpiled for distribution until their expiration dates prompted disposal. Therefore, the fatal KM threat continued for those visiting tropical and subtropical climates for well into the late 1980s and early 1990s. There was no indication to change the anti-malarial drug regimen endorsed by the WHO and CDC due to overwhelming medical evidence of the efficacy of Falciquin in performing malaria prophylaxis.

Since AOP stockpiled excess uncontaminated Falciquin in the same facilities, which pills the patient received, contaminated or not, was an existential game of Russian roulette.

Ironically, due to this global WHO policy, Claire Ferrier, MD, accepted the established medical practice and ingested the tainted Falciquin, causing her death. She lost her life having no clue she had unknowingly participated in a game of Russian roulette created by corruption and promoted by an accepted WHO guideline!

CHAPTER 53

Matt was relieved to know he was entering the home stretch. He told Maggie, "The other shoe is about to drop." He would organize his notes, edit his exposé, and submit it for publication after the election. The readership was currently addicted to the elections and few sought out other news. The fourth and final Presidential Debate on CNN was scheduled for nine in the evening, Tuesday, October 28, 1988.

The Democratic candidate, Senator David Sokolov, had a commanding lead in the polls.

The Republican candidate, the Governor of Montana, was a virtual unknown at the start of the race but had gained momentum and was closing the void by a few percentage points each day. However, time was running out, and only a miracle would secure him the electoral votes required from traditionally blue states to claim the Presidency.

A concerned Ryan contacted Jesse and asked him to return his call on a secure landline.

By this time, as the senator's speechwriter and member of the inner circle of advisors, Jesse had invested an incredible amount of time and effort into Sokolov's success. However, as he became more familiar with the senator and his advisors, he realized that those around his boss with the most influence were the most significant contributors, mostly Big Pharma represented by Attica Ossining Pharmaceutical.

Jesse had accumulated a strong resume during his tenure in Washington and could quickly secure just about any position he felt qualified to pursue. He had internalized the moral and ethical compass of Ryan, Declan, and all the Vietnam veterans with whom he had become associated. He understood their victimization and was impressed with their resiliency and lack of the need to seek retribution. They just wanted to be treated fairly.

Jesse would undoubtedly receive a position in the new administration of President Sokolov. He doubted he could survive in that intense and public lifestyle. He also realized that, with his current time commitments, he was losing touch with his family. In the White House setting, there would be a more significant demand on him.

Jesse returned Ryan's call, "What's up?"

The researcher explained to him all the discoveries and ramifications of the collective body of information now available on Falciquin. It was this drug which was criminally contaminated with compound B, that over decades, Ryan said, "Had caused so much misery."

As documented in Senator Sokolov's dossier, AOP executives demonstrated a total disregard for public safety. An example was their claiming ignorance of the source of Falciquin's lethal contamination. Ryan implored Jesse's understanding, "They ignored their analyses of this pill that disclosed an unidentified ringed compound not present before increasing Falciquin's *one degree* Celsius production temperature." APO should have ceased its production and investigated the pill's contaminant. They did not and sanctioned the lethal shortcut to increase product output for corporate profit. This mindset dominated, in spite of a growing number of reports of deaths in patients taking Falciquin.

Ryan then revealed to Jesse the information he had received from a reporter friend at the Washington Post who was following the Falciquin story. This fellow detailed the senator's conspiracy, several decades ago, wherein Sokolov had paved the way for offshore manufacturing in China by US companies, especially Big Pharma. Safeguards for the public were non-existent since production quality was monitored exclusively with in-house oversight, not an outside agency with the power to regulate.

Additionally, duplicitous AOP financial maneuvers involving Sokolov that were uncovered by the same reporter confirmed that Attica Ossining controlled the senator's every decision. Jesse's intuitive suspicions of AOPs immorality, conspiracy, and deceit were now supported and became a reality.

Ryan felt uncomfortable to do so but suggested to Jesse, "You should publicly sever, as completely as possible, all major ties with the candidate," for this same reporter contact had revealed this information to one of the CNN Presidential Debate moderators. At the next Presidential Debate on October 28, this moderator intended to challenge Sokolov concerning all the information they had just discussed.

Jesse responded, "Will do. I'm out! Thank you."

They agreed that within a few days, candidate Sokolov's campaign and aspirations would be history. The profound irony was that both the senator and Attica Ossining Pharmaceuticals had boisterously funded Ryan's research efforts. Both were seeking approbation for their generosity in the guise of benefiting humanity. Ryan's completed research disclosed their dirty secrets. There was now indisputable proof that, without a doubt, each was culpable in the devastation wrought by Falciquin, contaminated by compound B, upon humanity by the KM white blood cell fatal disease. They had set up the CDC and World Health Organization to dispense a deadly guideline.

About halfway through the fourth Presidential Debate on October 28, 1988, the statesman-like CNN moderator sprang the accusation, in the form of a question, that indicted the senator and his Big Pharma cronies for being responsible for the international deadly KM tragedy.

The CNN host had waited for that moment when candidate Sokolov had demonstrated the most obnoxious and arrogant attitude toward his underdog opponent. Initially, Sokolov lost his cool and his face turned gray. Anger then flashed across his pampered face, now drenched in sweat. His head then became a deep red-purple color. His eyes glassed over and squeezed shut as he accepted his annihilation. His jaw then dropped, exposing perfect teeth and the shadowed depths of a speechless dry mouth. His hands shook uncontrollably from his body's panic response, and his mind raced furtively to form what he knew already would be a useless, weak rebuttal.

His final response was to walk off the platform consumed with rage. He challenged a frightened advisor, "How the hell did this happen? How did you guys not know?"

The impact of this nationally and internationally televised revelation immediately spelled disaster for Senator Sokolov and his presidential aspirations. Sokolov dejectedly said to his closest advisors, "I've just lost all that I have achieved."

Behind his back, two of them privately shared, "He's fucked."

"Oh yeah, we are too!" echoed a Big Pharma executive already planning his exit strategy.

The older of the two advisors added," You better sell your AOP stock first thing tomorrow morning."

NOVEMBER 4, 1988

The Governor of Montana won the Presidency in a landslide with a generous contribution of electoral votes from many, usually Democratic blue states.

NOVEMBER 22, 1988

The result of blending J. David's and Ryan's findings with Jesse's incriminating research on Senator Sokolov and AOP launched Matt's exposé in the Milwaukee Inquirer as national front-page news. An intense debate erupted following Ryan's published discovery of why compound B was found only in the Falciquin manufactured between 1964 and 1972.

"Are our politicians and industrial leaders that corrupt?" asked a TV personality of his audience. It became a universal public concern.

"Where was the FDA?" asked a reader in the comment section.

Matt replied to her, "A good question."

Another asked in reply, "Were they part of the scheme?"

Matt's explosive revelations were picked up by the state, national print, audio, and visual media, and soon disseminated globally. Over the next month, talking heads on the major TV networks, CNN, Fox, CNBC, etc., could not get enough of him. Once the media circus died down, Matt's recurring nighttime headaches all but disappeared. His appetite returned, and he put on a few pounds. His stress level was now manageable. He had free time. Maggie enjoyed having her husband at home. His twins felt the same. No longer having his mind at bedtime being stimulated by his quest's unfinished business, Matt could now fall into an undisturbed deep sleep.

"My demons and PTSD are under control. It was not my failure that resulted in the KM disaster," he declared to Maggie. He had no control over the motives and actions of Attica Ossining Pharmaceutical, its executives, and Senator David Sokolov. Most importantly, his work was the impetus for increased oversight of Big Pharma. He educated the global medical community as to the cause of the KM disease.

"I have absolved myself of the obsessive guilt from my abandonment of pursuing this KM cell observation at Walter Reed Army Medical Center so many years ago. I could not have done differently; that's all we knew at the time. We were not capable of visualizing the future. I feel so much better!"

She replied, "Thank God I finally have the Matt I married back."

He answered, "I thank God that this fourteen-year odyssey of guilt and remorse is no longer poisoning my relationship with you, the kids, and my life. Thank you for standing by me," he whispered in her ear. Then he added, "I love you."

Maggie responded, "Me too."

EPILOGUE

Dr. Declan Burke, at age sixty in the year 2000, had had enough of the elite academic life. He was finished with invitations to guest lecture at medical conferences around the world, directing the George Washington University surgical residency training program, and supervising cutting-edge research in the metabolic response to trauma. He became a professor emeritus, retired from all professional pursuits, and followed his dream of breeding racehorses. He and his wife partnered with several like-minded physicians at George Washington University in DC, and purchased a three-thousand-acre horse farm near Charlottesville, Virginia. He decided to reside on the property and manage the operation. Declan had grown up on a farm in rural West Virginia and relished returning to his roots and working with his hands in the welcoming fertile Virginia soil. He continued educating the public, the military, and the medical profession on the etiology of PTSD and its prevention by interventions before discharge.

Jesse Holt and Ryan Larkin eventually partnered in a start-up company that became a successful international consultant in refining biochemical/biomedical procedures to eliminate contaminating substances.

Jesse continued to develop his political contacts and negotiating skills. He maintained his primary office space at Donoghue, Casano, Rapello, where he was now managing partner. There had been no blowback by the senior partners from his association with Senator

Sokolov, for he had cautioned them to dissociate themselves from him well before the disastrous 1988 CNN Presidential Debate.

Ryan became a celebrity following the disclosure of his role in determining the etiology of the KM disease travesty. He was awarded full professorship with tenure in the Department of Biomedical Engineering at Washington University in St Louis. Ryan was considered a world expert in the mysteries of biological contamination. He enjoyed his opportunities as a visiting professor to engage an unending supply of younger vibrant minds. He and Jesse continued to share hunting experiences and had expanded their horizons to include dove and duck hunting in Mexico, driven pheasants in England, and partridge in Patagonia, Argentina.

Jesse's wife **Kim** thrived in the conference planning industry with her primary account, representing Jesse and Ryan's interests worldwide. She relished her role as the quintessential loving grandmother to both her children's offspring, visiting them in Boston and New York.

J. David Warren, PhD, soon after publishing his investigative findings concerning Falciquin with Ryan Larkin, was offered a coveted appointment at Colorado University in Denver. He became a fully tenured professor and Chairman of its Medical Biochemical Department, with primarily the same responsibilities he had at Metropolitan Medical College. J. David loved being back in the environment of the Rockies with hunting, camping, and hiking. He and his family flourished.

Michelle graduated law school. She is a full partner with the Alexandria, Virginia based firm of Wilson, Morini, Lentini, Fontana, and Peterson, and represents those perceived to have been wronged by the self-serving centric attitudes of large industries which impact the health of susceptible Americans. She has specialized in those companies which contract with the military. It's been several years since she has visited Private Richard Burrows at the Vietnam Veteran Memorial in DC, but she thinks of him often as she pursues identifying miscreant activity. Her husband, **Jon**, is an adjunct professor of computer engineering at American University in Washington, DC, and continues to thrive at a newly formed, hugely successful company, Volcano.

Mike Clark published a textbook defining the steps to religiously follow when hospitals wish to initiate a cardiothoracic surgery department. Its appendix referenced a lifetime of flow charts, patient reviews, outcomes, and detailed how-to diagrams. He's retired from the University of Wisconsin Hospital. Mike enjoys his motorcycle and travels worldwide to lecture and consult on his favorite subject.

Duane Wall, for his life-long efforts at George Washington University Hospitals, received a seat on its Board of Directors. Renamed in his honor, the massive lab complex advertises its title as the Duane J. Wall Wing. He retired to Napa Valley and joined his brother in the wine industry. He has cultivated a unique strain of a varietal Cabernet that he grows, harvests, and supplies to his favorite vintner for wine production. He also oversees a cooperage that produces quality wine barrels from oak wood that is derived worldwide. Each variety of charred oak infuses distinctive characteristics into the wine it ages. He treats the 85th Evacuation Hospital Reunion attendees with a generous supply of wines to sample.

Summer Anderson succeeded in becoming an All American in her junior and senior years at UCLA in the breaststroke. She graduated Phi Beta Kappa as a biomedical engineer and is currently a third-year general surgical resident at Massachusetts General in Boston. She plans to pursue cardiothoracic surgery at Cedar Sinai in Los Angeles. Her mechanical aortic valve is functioning beautifully. She and **Mike** communicate frequently.

Attica Ossining Pharmaceutical, following the CNN revelations, suffered financial ruin. Condemned by its industry and being used as a scape goat, AOP was absorbed by a Chinese pharmaceutical company for pennies on the dollar and parasitized of its components. The statute of limitations on manslaughter is infinite. District Attorneys and plaintiff attorneys of all stripes were scrambling to either indict before grand juries or bring civil suits against those considered to be this tragedy's responsible individuals. The problem is, all its wealth suddenly evaporated and the responsible executives are dying off.

Senator David Sokolov became the poster boy for political greed, deceit, influence peddling, ineptitude, and dishonesty in government. Not convicted of fraud or RICO violations, he remained a free man. The value of his AOP stock plummeted. But he did have sufficient assets to live, albeit a much more conservative lifestyle. The public haunted him to the extent wherein he and his wife fled and relocated permanently to their less than elegant Shanghai condominium situated for safety in a guarded and gated community. He had purchased and utilized this property when traveling on business to Asia. There were unsubstantiated rumors that disgruntled AOP Shanghai employees who lost their lucrative jobs and upper-middle-class status were still planning revenge.

Matt Rogowicz entitled his Pulitzer prize-winning Washington Post manuscript *One Degree* and concluded this exposé with these descriptive words:

A gentle light snow fell, dusting her hat and shoulders.

Michelle's reddened eyes were wet, issuing forth a steady soft flow of warm salty tears that cooled and wetted her winter breeze-flushed cheeks.

A scarf that Richard had given her for Christmas so many years ago protected her neck from the cold December breeze.

Her plaintive sobs were partially muted by a raised gloved hand and the heavy air.

She was alone at the Wall, viewing, above her head, his snow-encrusted name chiseled into the reflective black granite on this familiar panel, Private First Class Richard P. Burrows.

Her head remained bent in supplication.

"Now, I will say goodbye. Now, I know that you did not leave me; Vietnam took you from me." "I'll always love you. I will do my best to replace my anger with only thoughts of our happiness."

Michelle now knew the whole story.

She would be forever indebted to Declan Burke, Ryan Larkin, Mike Clark, Duane Wall, Jesse Holt, J. David Warren, and all who pursued the science and the truth.

So would the rest of the world!

SUBSTANCE AND VALIDITY

I enjoyed creating *One Degree* as a work of blended fact and fiction.

The named characters in this discourse are men and women I've encountered in my lifetime. They include the dedicated physicians, nurses, and corpsmen with whom I was privileged to serve at the 85th Evacuation Hospital in Vietnam. Two Vietnam Dust Off pilots that flew crazy missions to the 85th Evac and survived their tour. The Pulitzer prize-winning exposé author's character, Matt Rogowicz, who produced the award-winning Albany, NY, area PBS Vietnam War documentary, *The Wounds We Feel at Home* (www.wmht.org/woundswefeelathome/).

Ryan Francis Larkin, a decorated Navy Seal, who succumbed to his demons and was lost to suicide in 2017. His father, Frank, a former Navy Seal and Secret Service Agent, is an honored friend.

Vietnam combat and wounding, evacuation, medical resuscitation, and surgical treatment are factual. I served in Vietnam as a trauma surgeon.

The Vietnam Veteran Memorial in Washington, DC, the Wall, should be visited by all Americans to grasp the magnitude of that war's impact upon us as a nation.

The fabric of the Army in Vietnam did fray and fall apart after Tet '68.

Veterans of the 85th Evacuation Hospital '70-'71 do indeed gather every two years.

You may relax. Falciquin, Relaxin, T-Loss, compounds A and B and KM white cells do not exist. As far as I know, the Departments of Defense and State do not collect and store drugs supplied to their personnel. However, the CDC, NIH, and USAMRIID do store patient's blood from outbreaks whose cause remain unknown at the time of their investigation.

The Atticowski brothers, Attica Ossining Pharmaceutical, Senator David Sokolov, Summer Anderson, Privates Burrows, Jamison, and Church, and Claire Ferrier, MD, were conceptualized to fit the storyline, are fictional, and do not infer a subliminal message.

The concept of influence peddling began with Adam and Eve.

Research techniques described are a blend of late 1980s reality and my imagination.

The Chavez brothers, Frank and Matt, at *New Mexico Trophy Hunters* are professionals and create world-class elk hunts.

The infection-fighting macrophages, the double-walled mitochondria and its DNA and also ATP, destructive enzymes, tight junctions, sepsis, bacterial invasion from the gut, and flesh-eating synergistic gangrene do exist.

I have no idea, and I'm too tired to check if there are macrophage subtypes I and II, but it sounded good and helped develop the plot.

I referenced the historical segments of the Vietnam war and Korean War and US involvement in both countries to the best of my ability.

The Presidential electoral process was marginally changed.

I elucidated my concerns from having served in Vietnam and during my participation as a veteran advocate for almost fifty years: Agent Orange, the Veteran Administration's history of intransigence in awarding disability payments, and the travesty of active duty military and Veteran Post-Traumatic Stress Disorder, substance abuse, and suicide. Please visit the *Welcome Home From Vietnam, Finally, A Vietnam Trauma Surgeon's Memoir* web site for additional information on these topics of concern to active duty personnel and veterans.

Thank you to retired Colonel Patti Hendrix, RN, with whom I served in Vietnam, for the most detailed and time consuming initial review of my manuscript.

And, thank you to my wife of fifty-seven years, Robin, for her diligence in reviewing ONE DEGREE's manuscript to insure it was readable. I have a tendency to over use medical and technical terms.